WAKE, SIREN

ALSO BY NINA MACLAUGHLIN

Hammer Head: The Making of a Carpenter

WAKE, SIREN

OVID RESUNG

NINA MACLAUGHLIN

FSG ORIGINALS ⟫ FARRAR, STRAUS AND GIROUX   NEW YORK

FSG Originals
Farrar, Straus and Giroux
120 Broadway, New York 10271

Library of Congress Cataloging-in-Publication Data
Names: MacLaughlin, Nina, author. | Ovid, 43 B.C.–17 A.D.
   or 18 A.D. Metamorphoses.
Title: Wake, siren : Ovid resung / Nina MacLaughlin.
Description: First edition. | New York : Farrar, Straus and Giroux, 2019.
Identifiers: LCCN 2019020215 | ISBN 9780374538583 (pbk.)
Classification: LCC PS3613.A27358 A6 2019 | DDC 813/.6—dc23
LC record available at https://lccn.loc.gov/2019020215

Designed by Abby Kagan

Our books may be purchased in bulk for promotional, educational, or
business use. Please contact your local bookseller or the Macmillan
Corporate and Premium Sales Department at 1-800-221-7945, extension
5442, or by e-mail at MacmillanSpecialMarkets@macmillan.com.

www.fsgoriginals.com • www.fsgbooks.com
Follow us on Twitter, Facebook, and Instagram at @fsgoriginals

10 9 8 7 6 5 4 3 2 1

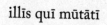
illīs quī mūtātī

By birth we mean beginning to re-form,
A thing's becoming other than it was

—OVID

Turn and face the strange

—DAVID BOWIE

CONTENTS

WAKE, SIREN

DAPHNE

Open the cabinet. Move the cinnamon. Move the nutmeg. Move the coriander, the cardamom pods, the cumin, the cloves. Move the small dark bottle of vanilla extract and the oregano and the garam masala you've only used twice. There, the small jar with whole leaves the length of your pinky. Those are me, mine. I was the first of all the laurel trees, and my bay leaves still season your sauces and stews. Dried, I smell of tea and salt and thin-sliced meat and your grandmother's pantry, with lemon at the edges; it's something like the way a museum sometimes smells, all those perfect things preserved. But the way you know me now, I wasn't always this way. When I was young and in a different form than this, I kept what I understood quiet, but I understood so much.

For one: I knew when they wanted me. Some people can't tell. Some people are blind to this. Not me. That heat behind the eyes. I could see it. Heat and hunger. That was always part of it. Eyes that lingered even when I wasn't the one talking. That crackle in the air, that elevated energy of desire as though the particles around us were speeded up. I could smell the friction. I could feel it behind my ribs. They'd lean in, wanting us to share our smells, or lean back, wanting to show their shoulders. It was so plain. Most of all, the biggest tell: the weakness. The way we are when we're at the mercy of our want. It's hard not to feel a little tender at that point, but this was also when things could get bad. They'd feel that weakness, some of them, and not know that's what they felt, but they wouldn't want to feel it, feared it—how frightening desire can be, how scary want, we're rendered raw and open to wound like a just-hatched bird with all those veins. To want something is to enter into the risk that you might not get it. They wouldn't know it was fear they were feeling, but they wouldn't like what they felt and they'd want to make themselves feel brave and strong. They were overbold to hide it, to try to prove—mostly to their own selves—how tough they were, how courageous, how *dominant*. Hey, pretty girl. You busy tonight? Is your father immortal? Is your mama from Mount Olympus? I'd like a taste of that. I'd like to fuck that.

I always knew.

No chance. I wanted the woods. I wanted the weight of game on my shoulders. I didn't brush my hair. I wore a simple white band to keep it out of my eyes. Do you understand?

"You owe me a son-in-law," my father, Peneus, a river god, said. He thought I was in his debt, maybe the way some parents think that about their kids, that they're owed something for giving them life. "You owe me grandsons," he said.

I owe you nothing, I thought. You think this is the achievement of a life, a woman's only purpose? Wrong. Marriage is bondage. A crime. Can't you see how free I am? But I was soft-spoken and kind when I told him, Dad, listen, I'm sorry, please understand who I am, that the woods are my home, I'm devoted to Diana, what I need is the air and the hunt and the hills. I can't be someone's bride, shackled to the stove, shoving babies out. I know I disappoint you, but I hope your love for me allows you to hear what I'm saying. He got tears. We both felt weird. He looked me up and down and said quietly, "The way you look is going to make what you want impossible." I ignored it. I dodged one bullet, but was hit by another.

When men are weak and they're scared, they'll try to prove themselves, which is how Apollo came to insult Cupid and Cupid came to seek revenge. Apollo had just killed a massive python, shot it with an arrow, and, feeling all puffed up and powerful, he happened upon Cupid. And to feel even bigger, it helped him to make someone else feel smaller, the true sign of the weakest sort of man. He started bragging to Cupid about his kill using words like "infinite shafts" and "swollen snake," and you didn't need much imagination to know what he was getting at. He told Cupid that the bow he was holding was way too big for him. "You can't handle it, man," he told him. "You'd need shoulders like mine to use it," and he grabbed the beef of his own shoulders and laughed. "You even work out? Don't try to compete with me, boy," he warned, suspicious (fearful!) of this small god. He had to make him know, I'm bigger, stronger, better.

"Your arrows slay, mine transfix," Cupid said. "Think you're such a big man. You're no match for me."

So, a pissing match. Whose is bigger? Whip it out. Show me.

Both small.

Cupid, stung by Apollo's insults, made two arrows. One tipped with lead, that would render its target disgusted by love, and the other tipped with gold, which would make someone love to the point of madness. Apollo got gold. Guess who got lead. My interest in men had been none before; it was rendered even less so now. The arrow hit me in the thigh, a dull poing and then a hotter pain as the rounded tip split my skin and touched my blood.

He couldn't help himself, that's what people told me afterward. And my father's words, the ones I'd ignored, about my looks preventing my freedom, had their ring of truth.

First thing Apollo said to me, "Do you know how beautiful you'd be if you brushed your hair?" A burn disguised as a compliment. Some might've heard just *how beautiful* and none of the *if you did this thing that adheres to what I find beautiful.* Some might've felt flattered, noticed. Not me. I heard it for what it was and his eyes moved like hands all over my body. My neck, my wrists, my bare arms, and I could see him imagining what he couldn't see below my clothes. A tightness took hold in my body, all the alarms rang at once, and my muscles were flooded with the juice that says run.

So I did. And he followed.

"You're like a lamb running from a wolf," he said, and I could hear the smile in his voice. "You're like a deer running from a lion. You're like a dove flying away from an eagle. You don't get it! That's not what this is about! Just slow down! I'm not going to hurt you, baby. I promise I won't ever hurt you."

I kept running.

"You're going to scratch your legs," he yelled from behind me. "There are all these brambles! You're off the path. I don't want you to fall. Hold up! You're going to get hurt!"

I knew the pathless places and I didn't care if thorns tore the skin of my calves.

I kept running.

"I'm not some scraggly goatherd," he said. "I'm not some dirty bearded farmer who lives on a mountain and only bathes twice a year. Don't you know who I am?"

And this is when I knew I was fucked.

The smile went away from his voice—he was getting frustrated, mad that I wouldn't stop. It was making him feel small, and when men feel small they are dangerous. I could hear him closer behind me.

"You're running because you don't know who I am. Don't you know that? You into music? It exists because of me. What music are you into?" He was trying to sound nice, but there was something frantic and cruel now in his voice. "Hey, hey, I invented medicine, honey, but there's no herb I know that's gonna cure the fever I caught for you."

I kept running.

"MY SHAFT IS SURE IN FLIGHT!" he yelled and I could hear the twigs cracking beneath his feet right behind me. "STOP RUNNING."

I kept running.

I was fast, but the gods are tireless and Apollo was fueled by Cupid's spell. I could feel him right behind me. I could feel him at my shoulders. And he laughed, a short laugh that came from deep in his guts because he knew he'd caught me. I could feel his breath through my hair on my neck. His fingertips brushed my arm, then my hips. From somewhere I didn't know existed in me, some well that holds fear, my body gave me more speed. I pulled ahead for another moment. He kept coming.

Fire in my lungs. Fire in the muscles above my knees. The only thing I wanted was to disappear. To evaporate into the air, to dissolve into a mist and settle on the moss and the leaves. I just wanted to be gone. To explode into vapor. To turn and shove him so hard he'd fly halfway around the world.

"I've got you," he said.

We were reaching the shores of my father's stream. I cried out to my father. "Change me. Take away this shape. Please! Now!" He did what he could to help—those who love us can never protect us all the way, but they will try and try. As soon as I said the words I was stilled. All of my muscles stopped moving and all feeling drained out like sap and seeped into the earth. My arms flung above my head and grew and grew. Out of my fingers, twigs began to grow, my arms thick branches that rose toward the sky. Every sensation exited through my feet, which were suddenly descending into the dirt, deeper, deeper, penetrating into the warm, wet soil. My legs, which moments before had burned in flight, fused together. My hips narrowed. Over all of my skin a surface of papery bark. I could feel my chest rise and fall from the chase, and from the deepest relief. But my lungs were quick to press against a new sort of casing. Pressed on all sides.

I laughed to myself. I'd won. Stick your dick in this and you'll get splinters.

It didn't stop Apollo, though. He rubbed up against me, his hands explored me up and down, his fingers in every notch, his palms in each crotch between branches. He licked me where my armpit would be and I felt his hard dick against me. He reached around me, gripped me, and pulled me into him. I edged away as best I could. I disappeared myself into this new form. I'm not here, I thought. I've gone. He can't hurt me. He kept rubbing me, pressing and grinding himself into me. I'm not here. You're too late.

As he thrust and ran his hands up and down the length of me he whispered to me. "You're not going to be my wife, but you're never going to forget this. Do you know what that means? It means you're always going to be my tree." He squeezed a burl and bent one of my branches until it almost snapped. He groaned as he released it and it went snapping back against the others. His breath was hot and smelled like dandelions and earthworms from licking me. "I'm going to wear your leaves in my hair," he whispered, his lips against my bark. "I'm going to have you on me all the time. And you're never, never going to lose those leaves. You get it? They're going to stay through every season like that unbrushed hair of yours. You understand?"

And I shook my leaves. I shook them and all of them rustled. My whole crown. These leaves would wreathe the heads of the victorious. Because I was victorious. I'd won. I shook and shook. As if I were nodding. As if I were telling him yes.

ARACHNE

Growing up, cousin Phip sold puppies from the alley by the deli there. He leaned out from the alleyway and said, "Doggies have 'em have 'em" quietly as people walked past so it sounded less like someone wanting to sell you something and more like the idea of it came from inside your very own head. This was smart selling. You never knew what sort of puppy you were getting. Sometimes it's foxes, sometimes it's dog, sometimes it's wolfies, sometimes something in between. He got out of poor, did Phip. But then he became not rich, not poor, just nothing, because they sent him to jail. They didn't like him selling the breeds on the street. Another cousin, Ruby, she had her business. She used the bed in my dad's room for her business. She went in, came out, and flashed a palmful of cash. "So easy," she'd say. Lie.

My dad worked dyeing fabric and purple stained his fingertips. The skin on the tips and the skin below his nails. Like all the blood was gone to all his fingertips in the moment when they're purple before they turn white and fall off. The way cousin Phip did with the dog tails sometimes. Elastic banded them. Red purple white, flimp, off they fell. Tails on the ground. My dad, though, bent over barrels of purple and breathed in the purple particulars—I think that's what they're called— all day. He had purple specks around his mouth when he came home, and purple specks on his neck. My dad had purple freckles. He leaned over a barrel all day with cloth in his hands and he leaned over the sink soon as he was home. Some of the purples washed off him down the drain. Some stayed on his skin. Always on his fingertips. And purple in his lungs, inhaling it that way. The particulars float up. Just because you can't see a thing doesn't mean it isn't there. Back bent, fingers stained, lungs stained, and my dad was good at the work and proud of the work and he'd come home and tell me some piece of cloth he'd dyed had sold for a bag full of cash to some rich-bitch princess wanting deep color for a cape—except he never called her a rich-bitch princess, that's what I'm calling her. He showed nothing but respect, and I always wanted to ask, if they buy it for so much, how come you make so little. But I never asked it.

He brought home scraps and he showed me sewing. He showed me how to weave. He told me, "Not like Phip, not like Ruby. You don't sell dogs on the street. You don't wear lipstick if you don't want. You find your way." He said those words a lot. You find your way. They're words that don't make a lot of sense even if you think hard about them, that only come to make sense out of a long time and thinking about it, but not in a direct way, like letting it sort of linger at the side of your brain instead of it occupying the center of it. You find your way. It was always there in my brain and I didn't know what it meant, but then I did.

I liked the loom from when I was small. I learned early and it's most of what I did. I got taught the basics, then I taught myself more and I just kept doing and doing and I impressed my own self. I'd finish up a tapestry and I'd lay it down on the floor. I'd stand above and think, Goddamn. It wasn't there, now it is. Every time it felt like a miracle. I'd look at the skeins in a heap by the loom, all their separate threads, and I'd think, Goddamn, first strands one by one, then this all together. This thing whole. Something out of something else. I made this transformation. The act of art is metamorphosis. It's where I found my pride.

And it turned out I wasn't the only one impressed. Neighbors on the block, when they stopped in, maybe to bring a casserole, maybe to bring some pastry, maybe to just see by me to make sure I was okay (no mom, good-but-gone-a-lot dad, people's concerns), they saw, too. And they said, "Oh oh ooooooh. Look at you. Look at what you've done." And first I thought, this is just nice people being nice. But nice isn't telling others and having others tell others about how wowed they were. That's when you can start to believe it might be good.

So people started coming. They came to look and I'd sit there and take their praise. Oh the colors oh the way they bleed one to the next oh the detail oh the scene it's like a painting it's like it's real, you got a gift, you were touched by the gods, you own skills like no one's ever seen. One thread on top of the next, one hour on top of the next, I just kept bettering. You find your way. This was my way. I was young but my name was known, and not just on my block and not just in my village, but in places miles away. People heard some things about me. They heard I was good.

They heard I was the best.

Rich people, besides money, got options. They've got options so much they don't even realize the options they've got. Poor, less options, sometimes none. I think people forget that it's not just money. So my dad sells a purple robe to some fancy dan, and this fancy dan sees the color's special and he's feeling all puffed up for having good taste enough to find my dad. He thinks the difference is that he can afford to buy this robe, and my dad can't. That's a difference, but that's not the difference. Fancy dan has time to figure out what his path is. He has time to wonder: What do I want? How do I get it? Poor, harder to think about what you want. Less time wondering, more time worrying. More time making sure enough purple cloth is made so there's money enough for food and roof. Plus, you think too much about what you want, you're swallowed whole. Rich, you've got to worry less about having to sell puppies from a box by the alley and whether they'll take your body into jail for it. Rich, you've got to worry less about being bent over a barrel so your back's curving even when you're not bent over the barrel. Rich, you've got to worry less about questions of roofs, questions of sweaters, questions of bread.

I paid attention, I stayed awake, I knew about options, what it was to have them, what it was to not, and I knew I wanted some. One way to options is being fine at something, being finest best of all. So each day I sat at my loom and sometimes it's the last place I ever wanted to be, but I sat there for knowing it was the one way to get better, to keep doing and doing.

I watched the people I knew reach the limits of their options. Again and again. It was as though the kids I grew up with, my pals on the block, from the village, it was like all of a sudden there were these walls erected, these tall, smooth white walls, and they'd be walking along, living their lives, and then, slam, straight into this wall. And there was no going over and no going around, just dead-ended a hundred percent. Eagle, Ben-Ben, Paulo, they went to prison. Kevin, he got killed by the police. Spice Rack, Henrietta, they got killed that way, too. Alma went wrong in her head because she kept drinking from this one well we knew had the poisons, but she drank anyway because that's the way she always did it and there was nothing that would change her mind. Gloria got sick and the doctors said, We'll cure you, but you need this much. She didn't have that much. She died. Sylvia talked so much about being tired. "It's tiring being poor," she said, and then one day she gave herself permanent rest. Sometimes when things go so bad, when there's no hope of bettering, that's where you get led. Maybe where my mom got led. Or where she led herself. To her own end, that is.

I tried to keep that big white wall from arriving in my life. And what I learned is that it's not just about being finest at something, not just about being the very best. It's about speaking it that way, too, about knowing it and owning it and saying it. I knew it. I knew I was the finest. And I said it. I had pride.

"This is the most amazing weave work I've ever seen," people said.

"Thank you. I haven't seen work that's finer myself," I'd say. Grateful, yes, and also knowing. Say what you know.

Once a person whispered: "You must have learned from Minerva."

Wrong. I learned from my dad and I learned from myself. And the fact of it was, I was better than Minerva.

And then I wondered why I wasn't saying that out loud. You don't get to be big in this world if you don't know how to own your skill. You don't get over that smooth wall if you don't go after the thing you're good at with everything you've got. And even then, other walls might rise.

So I started saying it out loud. "I taught myself, and I'm better than that weaving goddess. Any single day of the week I could outweave Minerva. She should come and try me." I liked the way it sounded. "Get yourself down here and we'll see who's best," I dared her. They've got a lot of power, but we've got power, too. More than they want us to think.

An elder lady with a gray knot of hair and cheeks that dangled off her face like thin-sliced meat had the nerve to tell me to take it easy. "It's enough to be the best in the world that you know," she said. "You don't have to outdo the gods." She said something against outgrowing my britches, that I should think about taking back what I'd said about outweaving Minerva. That I should think about apologizing.

Old ladies think they know. She comes into my place to watch me weave and look at what I've made and thinks she can tell me a thing? No. She's lucky I didn't smash her face, because that's what I wanted to do. All people do is tell you why you can't or won't or never will or shouldn't try. These scared old ladies. "You're old," I told her. "You're old and the years got you dim. I never asked once for your advice. I advise myself. I'm sure of myself, and it's hard for you to hear. And I'll keep standing by what I said. Minerva should come and try me."

"So be it," the old lady said, and she showed herself to be Minerva in disguise. The other folks in the room bowed and gasped and clutched their hearts. Not me. I stood with my shoulders back and my eyes front. I hold my own is why. The blood that rose to my cheeks in blush, it was surprise, and it was pleasure. I was getting what I wanted.

That's a chance.

I sat at my loom. She had hers. We started. My blood moved faster. I raced the shuttle back and forth across the warp, the strands collecting. It's what I'd spent most of my eyes-open hours doing. The weight of the shuttle in my hand, the speed of the slip through the wool, the treadles up and down, the squeaking, I knew this all, like it was my own body, as familiar as the inside of my mouth, as familiar as the weight of my leg, the sighs from my belly after a meal. I was motion and color and threads combining and I could tell, in a blurred way, that I was doing the finest I'd ever done. The patterns and shapes kept coming and awareness as to how it happened left me, like I had disintegrated into just the making, gone from myself, and just aiming energy toward the wool. The best of all feelings. And never more so than in this session at the loom.

At some long periphery, like she was in another galaxy, Minerva worked with fury. Now and then I heard her breath and heard her swish the shuttle across the wool. The sweat slid down my back, my shoulders ached. I didn't care what she was doing. I barely knew what I was doing, only that I was doing it, it was happening, and it was fine.

Minerva finished first. She spread the tapestry and all I saw from the side of my eye was a weave of olive branches around the edges. Peace offering. It made me work harder and faster and bolder. She wanted peace because she knew I was going to win. There'd be no peace.

I near collapsed off my stool when I finished and a woman nearby had to hold me up. I couldn't believe it when I saw what I'd done. I'd painted with wool.

I painted my whole poor world versus all the deathless gods who live guiltless. Who live guiltless and without consequences. All we know is consequences. We've got mountains of consequences on top of us that press us and bury us and keep us down.

That's the bull raping Europa, and the waves looked so real you'd think your hand would come away wet if you touched it.

That's the eagle before he violates Asterie, carrying her off in his talons.

That's Leda, getting herself crushed underneath the swan.

That's Jove disguised as a satyr giving Antiope twins inside her.

That's Jove turned into gold spray and entering Danae unconsenting.

That's Jove in the form of fire, tricking Aegina.

That's Jove playing a shepherd, fucking Mnemosyne nine nights in a row.

And Neptune, as a bull, Neptune as a ram, a stallion, a bird, a dolphin, tricking us on earth. All the lies. All the power over people. Power born of layers and layers of lies. And Phoebus as a hawk, a lion, a shepherd, lying, tricking, fucking. And all those gods, all those deathless ones. They never met regret. They don't fear mistakes because they don't know consequences. Never guilty, never punished. I showed you all, showed each crime, showed all you criminals. And yet we're the ones to pay. How's it work? You murder. You rape. You violate. And it's us who fall. Why am I the only one to say it?

I say the names of all the fallen.

Europa, Asterie, Leda, Antiope, Alcmena, Danae, Aegina, Mnemosyne, Proserpina, Bilsaltes's daughter, Aeolus's daughter, Medusa, Melantho, Erigone, and so many more. Taken down in innocence. I showed the truth.

And was it an accident that I showed this guardian of virginity as many sexual violations as I could fit on a tapestry? Nope, it sure wasn't. And of course she didn't like being bested, and of course she didn't like the feeling one bit that some poor mortal could outdo her. But I'll go ahead and bet that her reaction came from this mirror held up to her and her world, seeing the twisted immoral forms "love" could take, knowing she'd done nothing to guard in them what was sacred in her.

So what did she do? She acted like a brat child. She grabbed what I'd just made. And she started tearing. She shredded it. This god, this deathless one. All those scenes. All that color. All those crimes made clear for all eyes to see. Too much. She tore it apart. I stood. I watched. Finest thing I'd ever made, truest tales told, in tatters. Something drained out of me, seeing that work a wreck. Some force I had just seemed to slide right out of me and a tired landed on me like it had never landed before.

But tearing it apart wasn't enough for her. She needed me to know better what was what so she took my box-wood shuttle in her hand, whose weight I knew like it was my own bones and blood. She grabbed it and she hit me. I have been in fights. I know how it feels to be in danger that way. When there you are maybe yelling some, maybe fighting, and you're on your two legs and then your arms get grabbed and you get thrown and you fly through the air into a bureau or a wall, tossed like a sack of laundry. It hurts but it doesn't hurt because you know how to leave yourself. It hurts but it doesn't hurt because all your thoughts are on exits.

But all the fight was out of me. All the energy was out of me. It had left me when I saw what I'd made in shreds on the floor. Like I could do the very finest thing of all, and still, instead of praise, I get punished. You do wrong. You get punished. You eat Skittles. You get punished. You stand in the wrong place. You get punished. What drained the energies right out of me is that you do right, you do finest, you do the best undeniable, you still get punished. That big white wall I'd been trying to avoid, it rose up in the moment where all the walls should have come right down. I got tired the way Sylvia got tired. Minerva hit me once, twice, three times. I took it. Four, five, six. Across the forehead. I felt the blood slide down and in toward my eye. Seven and that's when I knew enough. And I took what energies I had and I grabbed a rope and I noosed the loop and quick I strung it over my head to end it. There was no going any further.

Oh, but then Minerva takes pity. She says, "You're deserving not to die, but you're still deserving punishment." You know what's next? I live, but I live eight-legged. An angry little spider. Weaving webs, and they're as fine as you've seen. I still go. I find my way. She thinks:

harmless spider. She thinks: she doesn't do harm and her webs can be invisible except in the dew, and they're weak enough to get swatted through with a broom, and people won't come to look and sigh and wow. And if they do, the next thing they'll do is wipe the web away because folks don't want spiders all around. Let her think it. Let her think how harmless. Let her think she did a good job punishing. But I learned about consequences. I learned how certain choices echo back and pin you.

Besides being turned into a spider, I heard Minerva say another thing. So it wasn't just the finest thing I'd made, and it wasn't just the beating, and it wasn't just the being turned into a spider. "This is how you're going to live. And this is how all who descend from you will live." If I had babies, they'd be spider babies, is what she was saying. She went on. "Understand what it means? You fear the future."

Didn't she know? I guess she didn't. You live the way I live, you grow up the way I grew up, you watch what happens to the people it happens to, all you do is fear the future. There's no other choice. You're rich, you're guiltless, you're deathless, the future's something to fill with boats, ambrosia, giant pets, afternoons that last forever, every sunset seeming like it's there for you. It just becomes a question of what to do with the fear. Same way I had my dad's words and I found my way before at the loom, I find my way now. I fear the future, so you know what I do?

I have babies. I have babies and babies and babies.

And they live for a bit and then what happens, my babies have babies. Each of my babies has babies. There are already babies beyond you can count. Picture as many of us as you can. And then more because it keeps going. And how many babies will my babies' babies have, and how many babies will my babies' babies' babies have? Oh, more than you can count. We will be so many. And we will keep coming. More and more together. We find our way. We're doing it right now. Do you know? Who should fear the future? You.

CALLISTO

I am a bear.

I live in the sky.

When I was young and I wasn't a bear, there were always leaves in my hair and dirt under my nails and when I found pine needles in my pockets I would break them in half and smell them. I wore the clothes I wore because they were right for the life I lived. They let me move the way I wanted to move, and I moved well. Strong, fast, I had long legs and my lungs took in so much air. I traveled the forest with my quiver and bow. Other women bent over sewing at home. Other women bore babies. Not me. Not then. I was out in the world, in the woods, on my own, and I knew I was lucky to know what I wanted and be good at it, too.

Diana, virgin goddess of the hunt, saw how good I was and she prized me. It's hard to think about those days in the forest now—sometimes I'll be up here and I'll think about the trees towering, the birch and oak and aspen, the leaves making lace against the sky and the light falling through it. I'll think about the ferns and the moss—the glowing green of the moss!—and the twisting roots that swell out of the ground. I'll think about the small creatures and the large ones, the brooks and springs. The hollows, the ditches, the mushrooms the color of bone that rose at the bases of the dogwood trees after a rain, the maiden grasses with their silvery sprays that swayed in the meadows, and the secret groves that only I knew. I can't think too long because every time I do I end up returning to that afternoon in my mind and my memories of the wood turn stinking and hot. And once I'm there I can't go back and I burn with the memory of it. And now I'm burning again so I'll tell the story I retell myself all the time.

It was one of those days that burns from the start. I'd been hunting all morning. The small flowers were my friends, white and purple, and the small birds who darted branch to branch, and the summer soaked into my bones. My body was damp with sweat and I went to a place I often went to rest, a circle of birches and juniper trees, all ancient, in a corner of the forest where no tree had heard the sound of an ax thudding through the trunk of one of its brothers or sisters. The ground was soft, bedded with needles, and the shade felt especially sweet and it was private. I hung my bow on a bough and took my quiver off my back and laid it on the ground near the base of the biggest juniper. I stretched my body out on the ground and rested my head on my quiver. It felt so good to surrender my weight to the earth and the air was thick with heat and the smell of the juniper. The needles and the berries, blue-gray like the sky at the end of a rainstorm, began to blur above me as I let myself drift toward sleep. Birds chittered around me and the summer bugs sang their lulling buzz. My sweat dried on my skin, tightening the way it does after you've been in the ocean. I fell asleep, not that long, the sun hadn't moved an hour's worth across the sky. Something stirred me awake and there at the edge of the circle of trees was Diana, staring at me and smiling between two birches.

I leaped up and rushed to embrace her.

"Where've you been hunting today?" she asked.

I spoke fast, words tumbling out like a brook, and gestured to the east, my hands flying in excitement. Diana interrupted my talk and pulled me toward her with another hug.

I've thought on it now for centuries. Somewhere, I knew. In the dark place we forget to trust. And I ask myself over and over: Why didn't you run? Her voice was Diana's voice, her face was Diana's face, but there was something not right—how to explain it? When she wrapped her arms around me I remember thinking, *This is not her smell, not the smell I know of hers, of woods and blood and wildflowers.* That day it was something hungry, of onions and skunks and the pissy tang of the fox den. She held me differently, lower on my back, with greater strength. She kissed my cheek and I kissed hers and right then I felt something strange, and all at once it was as though I was watching from outside. She kissed my cheek again and her lips lingered. And then she kissed my mouth and I could smell her and she didn't smell like herself and that's when the kiss changed.

Her tongue in my mouth, filling my mouth. No one's tongue but mine in my mouth before that. And her hands reached up under my cloak and I don't know if I'd had my eyes closed before but they were open now and I saw that it wasn't Diana at all. It was Jove disguised and something pressed against my leg and the one thing he said was *Don't you scream*. And he pulled off my clothes and swept my feet from beneath me and I felt the full weight of the god on my body and I thrashed and I kicked and I bucked my hips as hard as I could, not in pleasure but defense, and I used my teeth and my nails the way the animals do when they're angry and scared. And he pressed himself into me and there was a tearing and a bright hot pain and a liquid heat that I felt on my thighs and I knew there'd be blood. But I did not scream. I did not cry out. I fought and fought and there was dirt in my mouth and tears all in my eyes and the birch and the juniper blurred and his skin under my fingernails, the onion stink of his skin.

He huffed and bashed himself into me, again again. He took my breast in his hand and used his tongue on my nipple and kept huffing and panting and I elbowed his head. His thighs were thick as the oak trees, but I did not stop thrashing. His wide, flat tongue all over my neck, and above me the sky through the leaves. Finally it was done and he was gone and I lay in a heap on the needles and leaves and felt slick all between my legs, but I couldn't look down. There was a scent I'd never known from myself, like the white-petaled Callery pear that blooms in the spring, that acrid musk, that honeyed floral tang with something unwashed below it, something of flesh, from a place deep in the body. Rotten, what he spilled in me. My whole body shook. Why didn't I run? Slowly I gathered myself. I brushed leaves from my hair and pulled twigs from my back that were pressed deep into my flesh. A mud puddle nearby from a recent rain, and I washed myself with the mudwater and I looked around and I hated every tree. I hated every root and rock. I hated the paths and the shadows and the light. I hated the smells. I hated the smell of the forest. I hated that grove of trees. I hated it all with everything in me. I put clothes over my body and began a slow walk away from the grove. The birds screamed. I don't know how long I walked and I don't know what direction I went. I heard rustling in the brush, twigs snapping, soft voices, and there through the trees I saw Diana again, and my heart flew like a rabbit's heart flies, red wet heart flying inside me, because I thought it was Jove again, disguised and back to take my body as his own. But then I saw other nymphs and they were smiling and laughing, game on their shoulders. Diana called out to me and I approached slowly, dripping with shame. I could not meet their eyes, though they embraced me and showed me their kill. I stayed silent and my face was flushed, my cheeks burning. *They all must know that I am ruined*, I thought. *They see it. They know.* I kept my eyes on the ground and held a small stone in my hand and clutched it. But they didn't know. None of them knew. None of them knew because none had been touched the way I was touched and none had been wrecked the way I was wrecked and what was torn in me would never be torn in them and I was alone in my knowing and this was not a relief.

The moon slimmed and swelled nine times and still they knew nothing. Until another warm afternoon when all of us gathered around Diana and she was happy and weary from a hunt and said, "Let's bathe in this spring! Cool off! Rest!" And everyone removed their clothes, all these lean, strong nymphs whose bodies were their own. "Callisto, come on," they said, but I lingered to the side. "Come on, get in!" One started to tug at my clothes and I flinched from her touch. But they'd come to know one way or the other. So I pulled my cloak off and the forest went silent and they knew then what was true. Diana, who'd favored me more than all the others, spit on the ground. "You defile this place. Your body is not your own. Get away from me." My shame seeped out from me, like the blood from that tear, and I wept as I wandered away, punished for being victim, outcast as though it was my fault. Would Diana have felt different if she'd seen how hard I fought?

Diana wasn't the only one who'd been disgusted.

Juno, Jove's wife, waited for the birth of my son to dole out her punishment, enflamed that Jove's seed had taken root in me. I birthed a son I did not want. Arcas was his name. Juno arrived as I walked with him up a hill toward the cliffs. She grabbed me by the hair and yanked and slammed me down to the ground. I did not fight this time. I lay facedown and I felt her on top of me and all I said was please please please. If only she'd seen me fighting her husband. And I smelled the grass and the dirt and a shining black beetle headed away from my face and Juno's knee pressed into my back, *You think you're so beautiful, you whore, tempt my husband*, she said. Please, please, please. She was wrong. I never thought I was so beautiful. I was strong and fast and I loved the forest until her husband, in his violation, stripped the place of all its pleasures.

I tried to beg, but my voice started to change and dark stubbly hair grew from my arms and my arms got thicker and my hands swelled and fingers fused together and thick claws grew from the tips with leathery pads below and my jaw widened and inside my mouth, which had been so familiar, my tongue slimmed and lengthened and the teeth inside were sharp. My back rounded and my legs shortened and widened and claws grew, too, from my toes. And a growl came out of me, deep like the sound of falling rocks, something dangerous and angry and scared. I bounded off, four-legged, unable ever to speak. And though I could see my strong claws and could wrap my tongue over my dark brown nose, my mind was my mind. And I did not let myself rest in the forest because I knew what could happen if you surrendered yourself to sleep, even for a moment. I wandered in shadows, exhausted, and when I saw other bears I forgot I was a bear and I feared them. Dogs chased me. I was hunted as I used to hunt. All the time I was scared.

Even when, sixteen years later, I came upon my son in the forest, Arcas with bow and arrow, on a hunt with his friends, he who had been just a tiny baby when Juno ripped me to the ground and changed me, he with no knowledge of my fate or the violence of which he was the outcome. Our eyes locked and with a mother's love I tried to tell him it was me, don't be afraid, and I took slow steps toward him. But he didn't recognize me. Of course he didn't, this bristled beast in front of him. And he raised his arrow toward me and I thought, *Yes, now, please, this is how I want to die, end the fear,* and I raised myself on my hind legs and spread my arms apart to widen his target. My heart, my heart. And I hoped he had my gift of aim. I lifted my head and I smelled the smells of the forest, the sun on the leaves, the leaves on the ground, two rabbits nearby, a hawk swirled above us. I waited for the arrow to plunge into my flesh and stop my heart and end my fear and I roared once, the loudest roar, a roar so loud the rabbits fled and the birds fled and the earth shook. But Jove wouldn't let it happen. Oh, no, for him, this crime was too much, a son killing his mother. Jove, perpetrator of violence, did he think he was correcting the wrong? That this balanced the scales? No, I bet not. I bet he did not give so much thought to it, that this, too, was simply a way of affirming his own power.

He swept us up into the sky, where we are, now, even now, still now, a series of stars, big bear and little bear. I stay and burn and will stay and burn and my fire roars, but no one can hear it. I'm one of the luckier ones though, because I see the children on earth pointing up at me. Look, look, they say, the big dipper. It's part of me, the lights in the sky that the children learn first. And I think: *I wish I could scoop you up, young ones. I wish I could ladle you up into me and keep you safe for all time.* I see them down there, pointing and smiling. I am not invisible. But I don't want them to know that when I seem especially bright, when I blaze in the sky, it's because I'm remembering that afternoon when my body was no longer my own.

There are so many other stars, all of us burning. And I see all the stars around me, and I wonder, Are you the same as me? Is this what we all are? Fires fueled by fury, burning through the nights? Is that why you're up here, and you, and you? No place on earth for a fury so hot and bright? For a roar so loud? I wonder this. I see some blazing brighter and I think: What are you remembering?

AGAVE

Help yourself to whatever. There's some beer in the
fridge. Wine's on the counter by the cutting board. Is it
too early for that? I don't know—the kettle is probably
still warm if you want tea. There's like twenty different
kinds in the pantry. I had some turmeric ginger earlier.
Lemon, honey. Honestly, I can barely move. Is it Sun-
day? I literally have no idea what day it is. I can hear the
mourning doves though. So it must still be pretty early.
Did you hear them on your walk over? Sorry, you must
be able to smell the wine evaporating out of my pores. I'm
still scraping ox flesh out from under my nails. I haven't
showered yet, no. And no, no, none of that's my blood.
Ox probably. But, well. Yeah, most likely ox. And sorry,
I know these cut-offs are short, but I want the least

amount of cloth touching my skin right now. Like no chance I'm putting on a bra today.

You've met Karen, yeah? My snake? Come here. Here, my legless one. You don't have to hang out under the couch. She's the only thing I can bear touching me right now. I love feeling her muscles move as she coils up my leg. I used to wear an anklet that had tiny bells that jangled when I stepped. Karen is much better. Sometimes she's a belt, a garter, an arm band, a necklace. Around my neck like now. Last night I was wearing a necklace that had field mice strung through their eyeballs. When I woke up this morning she had five lumps, and I had no necklace. Anyway. This is Karen.

But yeah, so things got a little debauched these last few days. A little frenzied. I think I've slept like a total of three and a half hours over the past four nights. I woke up today with the morning sun in one eye and felt like I was waking up for the first time in my life. Smeared in blood and dirt and fur, my hair snarled, grit embedded in my scalp. And in that half-awake state with my eyes closed against the sun, I started seeing fragments of what had happened. First, a swirl of color, all the garments open and swishing in the wind and swishing as we danced, as though we all had these satiny licks of flame of color surrounding us, coming out of us. Then a maenad friend of mine, she's amazing, so strong, really thick-armed, in a dress the color of dawn, she's holding a deer over her shoulders. I'm sure at some point she ripped its limbs off, but I don't remember that part. I remember passing a vessel back and forth with one of the older maenads, and we gulp and gulp and it's streaming down our necks and we're laughing like fucking maniacs, who knows about what, and then she throws the vessel against a tree and the pieces weep down to the ground and we grab each other and spin. The drumbeat throb is getting louder, louder, louder, all of us moving in the rhythm of it, thumping, spinning, screaming in the pure and total joy of it. We thrust and flail. It's starting to be just noise, just color, chaos, all the women's bodies becoming just one body. It's dark and the drums get deeper deeper louder and the lanterns blur and the light swirls as we move, as we're swirling faster and faster, and smoke rises into the night. All these women swirling. And the drums are going going going, and the boundaries are starting to dissolve. And then it's just abandon, everyone undone, everyone in this state of boundarylessness, and there's no sense of yesterday or tomorrow, of where I end and you begin, this ecstatic union with each other, all of us swallowed up in it, rising up in it, with the drumbeat throb, with the dissolving outward into everything. Time becomes no time, no past no future, we're flung into infinity. And one of the last things I remember is seeing a maenad lying on her back and her dress is open and her hair is all pooling out on the earth and crows start coming out of her nipples, like hatched from there full-size and they keep coming and coming, crow after crow out of her breasts, beaks and wings and glittering dark eyes. And her eyes are wide like she's never seen anything so beautiful, and the crows helix up into the sky, flying in spirals. And I remembering thinking, *Oh, I'm watching a poem. I'm watching a poem made of crows. I'm watching a poem of no words.* And that's when things really shift, and I'm edging up against infinity, which means I'm as close as I'm ever going to be to death until I'm in it. Thereness and goneness. Total propulsion. And this is when sight doesn't matter. And this is when language doesn't matter. Oh god, this is especially when language doesn't matter *at all.* Like maybe that's one of the main parts about it. There's no language. No words. And there's no language to describe it. No words right now. I mean, these words aren't even close. In these nights, I'm telling you, it's unreal, like—an end to the limits of the self. And then you emerge. Having touched something very very big. I come out of it something else. I come out New.

I remember you talking about that time in the mountains, when you woke up in the middle of the night having to piss and you went outside and looked up and it was stars everywhere. And you felt like you were swept up into the endlessness of it, that you were both dissolved and wholly there, and nothing mattered, that you could be blown off into the sky and that was okay. How it was the realest thing, edging into infinity, because that's edging into death. And you said something about being the farthest away from everyone you loved, but feeling more a part of the world than you'd ever felt? Am I remembering that right? But so you understand. You understand about the ecstasy of it. Some people get it watching the gladiators. Or in sex. I've heard.

Sometimes if you run for a long time. Music. Wine. Plants and herbs that bring you visions. Anything that changes time, dissolves the boundaries, makes you lose yourself, creates this swirling union with the All. But fuck, listen to me. Sorry. I get like this after these festivals. My brain is cooked. At some point after the crows I must've collapsed, depleted, unconscious, fully spent. I woke up, limbs draped over other limbs. Sticky, thirsty. I'm going to have some kombucha, do you want some? It's fermented. A little hair of the dong.

Dog.

Better. Sorry. I got babbling there, and that's not even what I wanted to tell you. I'm still blown away and some of it is still a blur. Like I have this *sense* of things happening but like all blurred edges, the way you remember dreams. I'm sure more will come back to me. But so anyway I hobbled home with another maenad friend and she was like, Did you see it? And I was like, See what? And she was like, Hang on, have you even heard? Heard what? About Pentheus? And I was like, Fuck that guy. And she was like Totally, but listen to this. So that's why I called you over because I had to tell you this story.

You know about Pentheus, yeah? Total prick. He's this asshole jock, this clean-cut rapey beef-brained fucklet. He's got that hair that's way short on the sides and all slicked back at the top and he spends like sixty hours a week at the gym and is one of those way over-chiseled dudes who you know spends like twenty minutes a day flexing at himself in the mirror. Like we all know that six-pack is to distract against your grubworm of a wienie, Pentheus. And he's known for being gross about basically everyone who isn't a white dude, like he's 100 percent convinced that people who don't look like him are going to topple civilization as he knows it (the civilization he's been rewarded by under the system that's stood for however long history has lasted). Just like a classic grade-A-sirloin angry asshole. And the dangerous kind, too insecure to let people live and let live and too dumb to know that insecurity is his problem.

But so it turns out Bacchus is his cousin, which basically freaks him the fuck out. And Bacchus arrives on the scene—and you know Bacchus. He's draped in purple robes, looking like the man version of an orchid, and he's flaunting and partying and has ribbons blowing off him and garlands in his hair, and maenads and nymphs draped all over him, and he's carousing and drinking and leaving grapevines in his wake, and people are going nuts, just, like, losing their minds for him. Like screaming and fainting for him. And Pentheus bugs out because Bacchus doesn't fit into his idea of what a god should be. Like, this isn't Mars, stomping around with trumpets of war blasting around him, all muscled and armored. And this isn't Jove blasting thunderbolts and screwing any nymph he sees. Like just because Bacchus doesn't conform to Pentheus's narrow sense of manly-man godly-god, it means he's a fake.

And so Pentheus starts saying to anyone who'll listen that Bacchus isn't a real god, and everyone's being tricked, and what's wrong with you guys. And he sounds like this spoiled little child. Like, "Look at me, look at me, I have big muscles." I heard him yelling at a group of people, "You guys are idiots if you believe this prancing queen is a god. This gaywad, this faggot, this she-man. This is no god, can't you see that? He's barely a *man*."

Put a sock in it, dick cheese. The good thing was that no one paid attention to him. Everyone was totally dismissive, like, Get a clue, dude, Bacchus is a god. Get on board. You'll be happier. Because obviously. I mean, Tiresias forecast all of this, telling him, "You're gonna regret being on the wrong side here. Like, you're not going to believe in Bacchus's god state, and you'll live to wish you did." And instead of actually *listening*, I heard he spit on Tiresias, asked where the other two blind mice were, and kicked him out of the kingdom.

So no one's listening to him trying to argue that Bacchus is fake and they're all idiots for losing their shit over him, and so he orders some of his guys to go get Bacchus and bring him back to him. And like, are you joking? So his men try to do as they're told, but obviously you don't just walk up to a god just like, Yeah okay cool, here we are and we're just going to tie your hands up with ropes and now you'll be doing our bidding, you know? Like, Oh, I'm sorry, I'm actually immortal? And I can turn your ropes to fog or turn you into a marshmallow? So maybe back the fuck off? I feel bad for those guys. Talk about mission: impossible.

But so they bring back one of Bacchus's priests instead. And the guys present him to Pentheus and Pentheus is pissed, but he asks the priest why he's into Bacchus. And then the priest gives this long-ass story about being a farmer and an orphan and having nothing then becoming a sailor and a ship captain and being on some island, and seeing Bacchus as a young boy and knowing for sure that this boy was a god, and the rest of his crew was like, Um, no, dude, that's a hot young boy, and we can get a shit ton of money for him if we sell him. And priest man is like, You can't sell a god! And they're like, He's a hot young runaway twink and of course we can sell him. And the kid asks the priest man to take him on a boat to Thebes and he agrees because he's able to see the immortal shine in his eyes. But then there's mutiny and instead of veering east toward Thebes the crew steers west, disobeying the captain, and ignoring the wishes of the smooth-skinned curly-haired love muffin they've got leaning over the taffrail looking out to the horizon.

And I guess this is when Bacchus decides to reveal himself, which I get. It's like, Oh, you think I'm some child to be sold as a slave? You think I'm powerless? Let me show you something. It's like, I know for me it's those moments when people think I don't know something, or I'm not strong enough to open a jar or that I wouldn't be able to understand how to fix the axle on my cart, or can't string my own bow, or it seems like they think they know more about this or that, I feel this sort of wrath come over me, and this really almost frightening sort of sense of power, like, Don't you know I could destroy you right now? Don't you understand I could talk circles around you and make your head spin and make you feel like nothing? Worse than you just did me? Like, You're going to condescend to me? It makes me feel like I grow to like seven feet high and there are all these dark-furred, shadowy clawed creatures in my belly trying to get out to eat the face off whoever just felt like they knew more than me or can interrupt me or that their thoughts are more important than mine. I don't want to generalize, but, I mean, typically, this is usually men over the age of fifty. And sometimes younger. But anyway, sorry, again, sidetracked. All to say, I get why Bacchus would've been pissed, being so totally *underestimated*.

And you know, he can be destructive as fuck. Like, yeah, party and debauch and booze and whatever, but also, like, he's a destroyer. And so they're all on the boat, moving along, rising and falling on the waves, heading the opposite direction than what Bacchus wants, and the sun is shining and there are seagulls here and there, and then all at once, the boat stops. The waves haven't stopped. The wind hasn't stopped. It's as though the boat dropped thirty anchors at once and they all hit sand simultaneously. It just simply stops moving. Right in the middle of the sea. And dudes are like, Oh fuck, shit ain't right. Can you imagine how fucking terrifying that would be? Like, there you are, rolling along on the waves, carried by the wind and the current and suddenly, splash, you come to a complete stop. Man, it gives me goosebumps just thinking about it. So the boat stops and they're all like, Shit, sensing that things are *not good*. And then, one by one, they're ripped off the boat, their bodies are twisted, they grow fins, scales cover their bodies, and they're dropped into the ocean as fishes. See ya.

So Pentheus listens to this tale, which I hope I got right, and was like, "Well, that's the longest, boringest story I've ever heard and you're a fool and you're going to jail." This fucking idiot, man, I'm telling you. So his guys take the priest down into a cell, but then the word is, his chains broke off and the lock came unlocked, but Pentheus has no idea about this, and he decides he's gonna go see Bacchus for himself.

So he makes the journey to Cithaeron and he arrives on the shore where we were all starting to party and celebrate and get ritual some nights ago. And this shit's secret, you know? And this shit is most definitely not for men. And so apparently he's creeping around, can hear all the pounding and wailing and chanting and howling, and he gets spotted by one of the revelers, who, in her state of frenzy and wildness, sees him as a boar. And fuck me, get this, it's his fucking *mom*, Agave. So Agave spots him, and is like, Sisters, sisters, let's get this bristled beast, let's get this boar. And can you imagine a more perfect animal for him to be? And so he senses he's in trouble, like the energy shifts in the air, and in an animal way he knows that things are about to be bad. His very own aunt comes up to him first, stalks up to him, and she fucking rips off his right arm. And then his other aunt comes up to him, and she rips off his left arm. And he's standing there, screaming, begging, waving his stumps—I guess that makes three now, heh—and then his mom comes over. And you've seen Agave, she's tall, broad shoulders, long wavy dark hair, looks kind of like Anjelica Huston. Like, formidable. And she looks at him with disgust, and she grabs his jaw with both hands and she rips his fucking head off. Spine, tendons, skull, throat, veins, ripped, smashed. Blood spurting, he slumps, feet twitching at the ankle. Agave screaming. And then the other maenads fall in and tear him to fucking pieces. Like, they turn him to fucking pulp.

Can you fucking believe this?

And like, I don't know, I have this weird sense, now that I'm saying it, it's like, was I there? Did I see this? Like all of a sudden I feel like I can remember tearing at something, and the feel of hot blood, and like this spread of body parts, and did I hold an organ in my hand? Some slick liver? Laughing? Laughing? Like, I can hear laughter. I can hear laughter in my mind. All the women laughing. Just like the most righteous, untamed, victorious laughter.

TIRESIAS

Two things about the blindness. One: it's a blindness with the sight of dreams. I cannot see how many fingers you hold up, but I can see the whirlpool spin of time, the then-this that follows the if-this. I know the specific ends as much as we all know that anyone who lives will die. I was blindsighted.

Two: blindness now and then allows me to feel like a traveler in a foreign country, the way walking down a street in a city where you don't speak the language allows you to dissolve. You become a shimmer of senses. You forget your self. You forget what you understand yourself to be and what other people understand you to be. A feeling of extraordinary freedom, to be lifted temporarily from the encumbrance of self-consciousness! You are gone and there is only the dark rich scent of coffee from the café, the flap of a light blue curtain blown from a window left open on the fourth floor, the sweet singe of exhaust from the scooters, syllables tumbling from mouths like pure music—instrumental, the stray dog by the curb covered in sores snapping weakly at flies, the nervous flutter of clucking from chickens in pens, the man with the cart on the corner with his warm chestnuts which smell like biscuits with butter and honey, the dark eyebrows on that woman, the small boy holding a tattered stuffed animal pig, the gold-and-blue tile on the wall, like colors you've never seen before, somehow deeper and richer than the ones you know from home, the barges sliding down the river leaving slicks of oil in their wake, the clatter, blang, and pulse of traffic, something warm from the oven, golden loaves, that nourishing yeasty smell, and a woman emerging from the bakery in a stylish red coat with bread in her bag, two teenagers with backpacks shoving each other and by accident bumping a man in fancy shoes who looks startled then smiles, a child screaming at his brother and kicking the air. You're gone except for what washes over you, and you are wholly there and not there at all. No one can see you! You don't exist in this place! It's uncomfortable in some ways—the experience of your own absence—and it's exhilarating because you are unburdened of the weight of people's wondering about you and you wondering about yourself.

Sometimes I feel that. And sometimes the blindness is a wearisome blank, not white or black, but gray-gold like the dawn. I wrap a tattered bandage around my eyes. Sight then sightlessness then an in-between, a see-ing without seeing, the same color as my sex. Male then female then male again, and now a shambling rover with bandaged eyes who can never say it all. The things I say are true. I cannot—I did not? I would not?—say all the things that are true.

There are things I wish I said.

I have not always been a man. And I have not always been blind.

Juno is a woman of passion, appetite, and force. One late afternoon, violet light approaching, she lay in bed with her husband, and it's safe to guess that each was in that softened place that comes after knowing another's body, when still-damp limbs are strewn, when muscles moments ago tensed and clenched, release and dissolve, minds washed in postcoital ease, nursing tenderness and intimacy. They were in the state of closeness born out of the feeling—rare, fleeting—of being known, of grant-ing entry, of gaining entry. (How easy to mistake these feelings for love.) Voices get softer, touches gentle and no slave to pace, a gratitude, a relief (I am not alone, I am for a brief time joined). A collapse of the hard edges that divide us most of the time.

Side note: you know as well as I do, this does not happen with everyone, and it does not happen every time. Sometimes you feel so separate you exit your body and it's as though you're watching as it performs its fleshy, earthy acts. And sometimes it can make you the most aware of where you end and the other person begins. And in that separation is one of the deepest sorts of loneliness.

But Juno and Jove had delighted in each other in their wide bed as light faded on Mount Olympus and they sprawled languid and grateful. And maybe Juno said something about how amazing it was, how she felt her orgasm in her shoulders, how she turned into electricity itself, which is, as she's told Jove before, the strongest kind of coming. And maybe that prompted Jove to describe his own experience of climax, and then, perhaps with her fingers running through his curls, he mused—such is the intimate, idle chatter in this state of closeness and glow—who do you think enjoys it more, men or women?

In their carnality, the gods are not so far removed from human states. Their lusts and longings, the wide spectrum of their proclivities. They take interest in mortal acts of love and they descend to our bodies and our beds to taste what we taste, trying to understand their own pleasure better. I cannot say for sure—I am not a god—but I'd wager mortal pleasure outdoes the pleasure of the gods. Our pleasure is not an option for eternity, and sweeter for it, I suspect.

"What do you think, Juno? Women or men?" And after Jove posed the question, maybe Juno removed her hand from caressing his head and looked a thousand miles into the distance.

"Men," she said. Of this there is no doubt.

And maybe Jove laughed. "My moon, you're wrong. It is women for sure."

And maybe Juno was silent. And maybe Jove didn't register her hand out of his hair, or the tension stiffening her body. "Let's ask Tiresias," perhaps he said. Such are the whims of a god. "He'll know."

And perhaps Juno said, "Woman or man, he has only ever been human."

I lived seven years of my life as a woman. I'd been walking through the woods on a warm afternoon and came upon two snakes mating on the path in the sun. I don't like snakes and I didn't want there to be more of them, so I rustled them apart with my staff and they slithered away. But I'd disrupted something I shouldn't have, a pairing natural as flushed cheeks after wine, and I went all at once from man to woman, a transformation total and abrupt.

A body doesn't have an opposite. Black and white, colors both. Dog and cat, creatures both. Man and woman, people both. A destabilizing transformation nonetheless, not just new form but new ways of moving through the world. But the mind adapts to all but agony, and it did not take long to feel at home in this new shape. I spent seven years in dresses, with breasts. I spent seven years coming to know an experience similar to mine as a man before, and wholly different. In the eighth year, I came upon two large snakes, tan with red diamonds, twisting again around each other obscenely, and I reasoned, if splitting the snakes changed me once, perhaps it will change me again. I ran one hand over my left breast, and inserted my stick between the two huge snakes, and back to man I went.

Was it punishment, being turned into a woman? I don't know. Is it punishing to be a woman? It is. It will continue to be.

My experience living as a woman and a man was known, storied, and meant I was summoned up to Mount Olympus to settle their question. Still upon their bed, their hair wild, Jove smiling broadly and Juno sitting up, rigid, her eyes aimed at an absence. My heart thudded in my old chest and wings flew against the walls of my belly. I looked all around their chamber, saw the tangled sheets, massive mirror, curtains woven from morning light and strands from the tail and mane of Pegasus, a green violet spray of peacock feathers fanning out from a vase on a bureau, a bowl of acorns atop a dresser, and hung from the ceiling, a mobile in the form of an eagle made with feather and wire, a six-foot wingspan, glittering eyes, pushed by the caresses of a gentle breeze and moving in slow, slow circles above the bed. *What now*, I wondered. *What am I in for now?* I listened as Jove explained. "So," he said, "who takes more pleasure in sex? Women or men?" He laughed as he said it and looked at Juno with a smile on his face. She met his eyes, but her smile back was forced and cold.

My mind moved fast. I thought of being a boy and going to the shoe store with my mother and the woman who worked there kneeled at my feet and her shirt fell away from her chest and I couldn't see much, but I could see a little, all that promised volume. I hardened as she slipped a shoe on my foot, for the first time that I can remember. I hardened that night again as I lay in my bed in the dark remembering, imagining, nothing so specific as an actual body, but swells, flesh swells and a pressing. The other boys had talked about it, about the stiffening and the pulling and what comes out. I touched myself tentatively and appreciated the firmness, the smoothness, its rise, and I gripped myself the way I'd seen the boys gesture in the grove of trees behind the butcher in town. I closed my fist tight then moved it up and down—and then the spasm and the spurting and I was afraid for a moment but the boys had told me and one had even done it in front of us, tugged, grunted, spurted, white stuff on the ground, so I knew what to expect. I touched it with my fingers and I smelled it (I would taste it someday, too, but not that time). It felt like snot, like melted wax. The smell was sharp and clean. So simple. An image, a hardening, a tug tug tug.

And I remembered being a woman. The memories came fast, moving too quick to hold one. A slideshow of pressings and penetrations. It wasn't the same. For one thing, there was no group of girls behind the butcher. No whispered laughing discussions between friends in bedrooms with closed doors. No one grabbed my hand and pressed their fingers into my palm and said *Like this*. The women friends I had weren't saying, I use these fingers, I move my hand this way, I touch there, I press there, I put this much inside, I move this fast, this slow, backforthupdownroundroundround. Not even jokey gestures in the alleys to align ourselves in the pleasure of the act. Not a secret, exactly, but not discussed. No one leaned her back against a tree, put her hand between her legs and moved her hand against herself until her cheeks pinked and she flexed her quadriceps and ticked her hips just so, up, up, and made a small tight noise that came from the back of her throat that maybe would've been louder if she hadn't had an audience. No woman ever, ever said to me, *And then I got so wet.*

We didn't talk about it. And at first I thought that I'd missed the clutchy gatherings with girls where they said, *This is how I do it and this is how it feels,* having landed as a woman full-fleshed and -fledged. But as I spoke with them, many women revealed there had been no such conversation. Private touchings, no discussion. Orgasms were not a given. If I were still a woman, I would say to the girls, *Learn your body, know your pleasure, talk about it. It is not a shame. Wanting and enjoying does not make you dangerous and it does not make you bad.* I wish I had said it then. Such a message can't be heard coming from a hunched old man with bandaged eyes.

As a woman, it took a man taking three fingers to me and rubbing until I squirmed and kicked to know, if he can do this to me, I can do it to myself. And so began my own exploring and I touched myself in all the ways I could, told the people who shared my bed how to touch me there, firmer, left, like that, perfect, yes. And I came to know well how I worked, and I was taken by the variety. Sometimes, a dense and concentrated heating. Sometimes, a flex and purr, or a round bursting throb. Sometimes, a crack against a wall of ocean, cracking, cracking, and the sudden break. Sometimes, a total everywhere whiteness.

As boys, we went to the bathhouse and knew the notch in the wall that allowed us to see all the women naked. We took turns peeping through the hole, all of us pressing against our pants. It was an understanding. Nothing like this as a woman. And why? I bow my head in shame to know I am in part to blame.

I stood in front of Jove and Juno and my mind raced. What did I know? What is absolute about bodies? A mental scan through my memories of life as a man showed so many satisfying thrust-and-grunts, atop, below, penetrated, penetrator, lost, ecstatic, joined, separate, exhilarated, jackrabbiting or slow and easy. Always the baseline animal pleasure. Then through my woman memories, much the same: the exhilaration, the dissolving, the blurred-vision frenzy, the back-forth give-take of feeling my own strength and muscle in tension with someone else's, the wishing sometimes it was over for discomfort or for boredom or both, the hair-grabbing, the back-arched pant and press, teeth against a shoulder. The outer electricity and the tight heat of the inside accessed. It is the same and different.

I am only one man. I was only one woman. How can I speak for all? And even within my hybrid existence, every kind of pleasure has not been revealed to me; I have not tried everything there is to try; I have, like everyone, been limited by fear and propelled toward certain pleasures, away from others. Have I missed the ultimate? Might one man or woman know a profounder pleasure than I myself have had? Of course, of course.

I looked at the rug—magenta, lapis, gold—beneath

my feet. They wanted an answer. They did not want to hear that it was an impossible question.

Who likes it more?

I thought of the transcendent times. The handful of mind-destroying fucks. I remembered the moments of the purest abandon and wildest pleasure, where it almost, almost felt out of control, where I slipped into ecstasy, became a field of sparks, and was also still real and true and whole. The greatest pleasure is loss—self, control—an act of surrender. As a woman, reaching that state of surrender surpassed the experiences I'd had as a man, a fuller and more total pleasure, a dissolving more complete. When I lost myself, I lost myself more fully, a wild charged electric thing, a cloud of pure color, fervent, breathless, wowed. When it was right, it surpassed the pleasure I'd had as a man ten to one.

When it was right. Standing at the foot of Jove and Juno's bed, rattled by the summoning, my mind failed me. *When it was right.* It was right so much less often for me as a woman. The surrender was greater, the release more powerful, in part exactly because it was harder won. When it came to women sharing their lives or bed or both with a man, there were steeper repercussions, graver consequences. There were things I learned as a woman that I had not known as a man. Use your second smallest finger to apply salve below your eyes—the skin is most delicate there, and that is the weakest finger. Don't fight in the kitchen because of the knives. The times you most want to press against another person are the times when your womb invites into its home the

possibility of a guest who'll stay nine months. If it's with
a man you share your bed, be careful then. As a woman,
I only shared my bed with another woman a time or
two. Again, my experience is limited; I am only one. But
some of these kernels of knowledge, the things I came
to know as a woman that I had no sense of as a man,
all the risks and troubles, tip the pleasure scales toward
men, who can enjoy themselves in a way unencumbered
by some of the large and lasting consequences that can
come from ten minutes tangled in a half-light trance.
Unencumbered like a person in a foreign city. Unencumbered like the blind old man with bandaged eyes.

The gods wanted an answer. Well, Jove wanted an
answer. "Men or women?" he said, head cocked. I looked
at Juno. Her expression telegraphed a searching skepti-
cism, a disdain, and maybe fear, too, at my answer? Is
that what I saw in the set of her jaw, in the upward tilt
of her eyebrows? Did she foresee what I would say and
know what it would mean? What I should've seen was
her openness to a more blurred truth, her certainty that
there was no way to make an answer to this question.
But what punishment would've befallen me if I'd said to
Jove, *There is no answer to what you ask*? No answer was
the answer; Juno knew that to be true. But my answer
was given shape by fear. I tell the truth. I can't tell all
the truth. It's true I was afraid.

Another question blazed across my brain: Would
I have been invited up to settle their debate if I were
still living as a woman? Would they have rated my
perspective? Would I have been believed? And, the

question pounds, unanswerable, would my answer have been the same?

I cannot say.

The last bit of late afternoon light entered the window and the massive mirror flung it onto the ceiling in a bolt of white. The mirror was framed with crude scenes carved into the gilt, a man and a horse, a woman on her knees, dozens of lean little Cupids with menacing grins. On the wall on Juno's side of the bed, one of her moon-phase paintings. Against the indigo, the crescents and swells had a white-gold radiance. The paints of a goddess glow. In a heap on the floor, Jove's robe. Juno had kicked her sandals off as she'd walked in the bedroom door. These immortals, these two who will not know end, what do they know of pleasure?

For us, earthbound, finite, for we who will die, to dissolve with another body is to brush against immortality, it is to be absorbed into an endlessness. We pursue these moments with so much of ourselves. Joined with another body, in whole surrender, in total pleasure, we transcend temporarily our own eventual ends, we enter a place unbound by future or past, we enter into oblivion. We enter the infinity that death is, and we are alive to know it and exist within it for moments. One could argue, and perhaps I would, as a human on this earth, it is the profoundest of experiences offered up to us, woman or man or both or neither.

The gods chase this same oblivion, but what breaks over us as a vast rush of eternity, they experience as the closest thing they can to knowing what it is to die. It is the moment they come closest to mortality. And it explains their fascination with our mortal desire. They taste our ends; we taste their endlessness. In that, we are offered more. Our pleasure harder won, we pay for it with our lives. In all our bodies, in all our states of being, we seek what does and does not bend to time.

If only they'd asked me instead: who takes more pleasure, humans or gods. That I could have answered.

But this was not the question posed to me. What I could not realize quickly enough as I stood in their bedroom is that their question was not trivial at all, that the asking and its answer would yield ramifications. Though I could not know it then, I know it now: the question and its answer are about the order of things, the way power propels itself across people and time. Between chaos and order lies a porous border, patrolled by grasping, flawed, and fragile guards loath to hand over what they have. Jove, all-mightiest, wanted his sense of things confirmed, wanted his understanding of order to be underlined. He said louder and with more force, "Which is it already?"

I squirmed and bluffed. "It's an honor to be before you. But I wonder, with all the respect that's due, why concern yourself with the pleasures of us lowly human forms—we can't compare to you in any sphere."

"Of course you can't," Jove said, "but what exists in your world is echo and shadow of what exists up here. Dimmer, fainter, but no less true."

"It's a stupid question," Juno said.

"Juno, sweets, you, a beautiful female form, goddess

beyond compare, you have no idea what a man feels like, and I have no idea what a woman feels like. Don't you want to know?"

"That's not what this is about and you know it. You just want Tiresias to tell you that all the nymphs you fuck like it more than you do."

"What's that?"

"You're afraid."

"Tell me what you said."

"It doesn't matter."

It did though. I let the pair continue their squabble. Jove looked at me again.

"Men or women?"

"I would be so curious to know what pleasure is like for the gods," I said.

"There aren't words for that," said Juno. "Just answer. We both know what you'll say."

I looked again at the floor.

"At its best, at its rightest and fullest and most powerful, the answer is women. Women take more pleasure than men." So I said.

The last thing I remember seeing is a storm in Juno's eyes and two feathers drifting toward the floor as she pressed herself up from her pillow. In her disappointment, in her understanding of the limits of my answer, she stripped me of my sight. She punished my male-mindedness with blindness. She punished my dismissal of the complexity, the discomfort, the fear. She was right. In the simplicity of my answer, I confirmed the perception of the most powerful god, his worldview and his wishful thinking. What I said without saying: women with their ten-times-better pleasure, how can they resist, they'll open themselves to any option, they need to be controlled because they cannot control themselves. And so goes a man's thinking: women love sex so much, take more pleasure than I can imagine, and so, it stands to reason, of course she wants me, she can't resist me—and how puffed it makes him, how proud and worthy-feeling. But then comes the question: but does that also mean that there's *no* man she can resist? Is she being driven by her desire, galloping away from me? The thought terrifies, makes him fear what he might lose, and possessiveness takes hold, a need to exercise his power. The worst of our behavior rises out of the snarled nest of our fear.

I wish I'd said: Juno, Jove, almighties, not only am I not equipped, the question has no answer. Pleasure is as individual as our fingerprints, for every person on this earth. Desire, fear, and need press up against our chests, between our legs, in ways that shift through all our lives.

I did not say that. And for what I said, I lost my sight, a punishment I've come to know that I deserved. In a new state of gold-gray midnight, trying to blink sight back into my eyes, I heard Jove say, "My moon, relax. We were joking around. You didn't need to blind the man." Once done, no god can undo what another god has done. Jove could not restore my sight, but he pitied me. "Tiresias, I'm sorry. My wife has gone too far. She has taken your sight, but I will grant you a different sort of seeing." And so Jove gave me the power of prophecy.

And such is how I wander the cracked and snake-strewn paths, burdened my whole life—first second sexed then second sighted—by knowing more than most. I could never say it all. The things I said were true. I could not say all the things that are true.

There are things I wish I'd said.

SYRINX

We're her sisters. You help your sisters. You see one of your sisters on the street in some trouble, you cross the street and say, "Everything cool, sis?" And if everything isn't cool, you do the thing you can to help. There's trouble in this world, and lucky you if you haven't found any.

So we helped Syrinx back then and we're helping her now because she'd rather have us speak than her because she hates the way her voice sounds, the breathy foghorn ache of it. You know the sound. You've seen the dude in the wool tunic in the square leaning up against a building blowing into those pan pipes with a hat at his feet with some coins. Those pan pipes, their proper name is Syrinx.

We river nymphs have each other's backs and we say what's real and we keep watch. We'd seen the way Pan was in the woods. Two-horned god of the pastures and flocks, of the goatherds, of all the lonely wilds, he spent his time lusting after nymphs. Squalid god. Waist-up manhood, pumpkin-colored curls and his bushy beard, who knows what all lived in there, orange eyes, and his waist-down goathood with thick furred legs, leaving hoofprints on the forest floor, his fat animal hard-on leading the way.

He caught sight of Syrinx, total virgin who planned on staying so, and that's her choice. She devoted herself to Diana, also her choice. She got mistook for Diana all the time, as a matter of fact. Main difference between them was the bow—Diana's gold, Syrinx's wood—but you know you're gorgeous when you get second-glanced as a goddess.

So Pan sees her and goes nuts and follows her through the woods saying the nasty shit he says and she ignores him and keeps walking, pretending she's deaf the way we all have even though we hear it, and then hear it that night when we're trying to fall asleep, and then hear it a week later when we're angry at our socks being hard to put on or at the weather that day, like it's a complete mind-boggle, a guy sitting on some steps can say, *Better bundle up tonight, it's gonna get cold*, and somehow it makes you wonder if you're going to make it safely to wherever it is you're going. Like somehow, *wear an extra sweater* is all menace. Like you can't take a walk without some guy *inserting* himself into your day. Into your mindspace or your spacespace. Like it's theirs to own. And some days the deaf ears work, some days that *smile for me, sugar* can just dissolve into the static of the afternoon, along with the sound of a goat getting slaughtered or the chatter in the marketplace. But some days it doesn't. Some days it's not just noise and it sticks and echoes in the cave of your mind with all the other comments and gestures and moments, this wretched chorus of unwanted noise, that have made you wonder in a very real way: Am I about to be killed? Is this where my life ends? Sex and dread and threat. Fuck. It's all too much sometimes. That's why it's good to have sisters. That's why it's good to have a team.

Anyway, Pan is trying to get Syrinx's attention and she doesn't want to hear it, but she feels him getting closer and she knows what's what and she knows when her body's talking to her and what to do if her body says, Okay, splitting time.

So she bolts and of course Pan follows her. He doesn't know when to leave well enough alone. Wouldn't be able to take a hint if it was a garden snake slapped across his face. He goes from the usual disrespect, telling her where he's going to put his dick, how he wants to feel her inside, how he wants to sink into that strong ass of hers, to the straight-up perverse, talking about how he wants to watch her lick a sheep's balls, and how he wants to rope her to a honey locust tree and put his horn in every one of her holes and feed her all the flowers, how he wants to whip her flesh with nettles and when her skin is raised and red and peckled with bumps, he wants to jizz all over her and use it like massage oil, then lick it off her body. This fucking faun.

She's sprinting and crying and she starts screaming. And she arrives at a river she can't cross, and that's
where we are, and we're nymphs of the river and she's a
nymph of the woods, and we're her sisters and we heard
her and we know what's up with Pan, and it was just
like, We've got you, sis. We've got your back. And we
think fast because once the change is made there's no re-
versing it, so we do the calculating quick as we can, and
we know the fate that she'd prefer. And like that, we
turn her into reeds, just as Pan reaches out to grab her.
And instead of grabbing hold of Syrinx, he wraps his
arms around the reeds. She's all just hollow stalks by the
river's edge. And he's all friggin' woebegone because he
missed his chance, and he starts sighing, making a real
show of it, and his hot breath, which smells like sheep
pussy, passes over the hollows of the reeds and makes
this sound of foggy lament, and Pan loves the sound,
even in his sadness over not getting a chance to bone
Syrinx. He blows and blows and his cheeks puff out and
his face turns all red and he's sweating and wild-eyed,
tooting and wailing on the reeds. "Oh baby, this is how
I'll talk to you," he says. "I'll put my lips to you and blow
and you'll answer."

And we know we saved our sister, we know we did
right by her, and that given the choice between being
reeds and being forced to have Pan on top of her stripping her virginity from her, well, we know what she'd
choose. But we think about it. Sometimes we wonder.
Because the fact is, Pan still hooves around the forest
and still gets handsy, or worse, with the nymphs and

is drunk a lot of the time and his beard is longer and dirtier, disgusting old satyr. He hangs around doing what he does and Syrinx isn't ever going to string her bow again. And the thing is, he loved the sound of her so much, he snipped reeds to different lengths—and we know Syrinx can't feel it but we're still like, shit, seeing our girl get cut like that—and he attaches them together with string and hot wax and there's low notes and high, and we hear her voice, and that's how the pan pipe came about, sounding like if sad ghosts had voices, which is maybe just exactly what it is.

ECHO

I *know* my power. I *know* the way I shift the energy of any room I enter. The heat and light that comes off of me. I *know* it. Look at me. The command of my height, the spread of my shoulders, I stand with *strength*. I am *immortal*. See the swell and lift of my breasts, nipples that press against the saffron robe that drapes my body like it was painted on my flesh. Do you see? Not just beautiful. *Powerful*. The sweeping rise of my throat, the warmth and ferocity of my mouth, the wide bones of my skull, the swell and lift of my cheeks, skin the color of coconut flesh. Blond-white hair that sweeps like a cresting wave above my forehead, my cheeks flushed, and my eyes hold every moonrise and the spark and current of every ounce of menstrual blood released from all the women who bleed.

I am *for* the women. Don't you see?

But there are so many and they are so new and they are so tempting for my Jove, my beloved, who cannot resist young women, who cannot resist the nymphs. Like Semele, a child really, with her black hair that fell straight around her jaw, her big young sad-dumb eyes, her open trusting smile. She had no idea the bad-news situation she'd found herself in. And if it had just been some simple one-time lay, fine, forgive, forget, but she got pregnant, he made her pregnant, and to see her aglow, belly swelling, his immortal seed growing inside her mortal body, I could not have it. Her? Not me? Why? The answers my brain offers are a catalogue of my own failings. Have I gone stale? Is he no longer attracted to my body, tall and lean? Has familiarity fogged his ability to see me—am I invisible to him, across the breakfast table, in our shared bed? Have I disappeared? Am I not funny? Am I *too* powerful? Is my hair too blond? Too short? Would it be better if I had longer hair? Has the shared bone that is the marriage bond grown brittle over this long spread of time? Am I too much a given? What is wrong with me?

So, I disguised myself as Semele's old nurse and we chatted about this and that, and I slipped in, "My dear, so young, perhaps you do not know the ways of men— so many of them deceive you! If you want to know if the man who visits your bed is Jove himself, you've got to ask him to prove it to you. Ask him to show himself to you the way he shows himself to Juno. It's the only way you'll know."

One cannot see the true face of a god and live. I knew this meant her death. And so it did. Is it fair that she's a heap of ash, gritty with bits of her bones? Of course it's not. But what am I supposed to do with the anger? I share my *life* with him. Are these women to blame? It's not a question I can spend my time answering. Punishing them, watching them die, it's one way to let out the anger. But it brings me no relief. One gone, he finds another. And it happens again, again, again. These poor women. But this poor me. Someone has to pay. I watched Semele burn. It brought me no relief.

And Echo, too, you have to understand, one cannot deceive a goddess and expect life to go on as normal. I'd know Jove was down carousing, getting handsy with the nymphs, and I couldn't help but follow, even though I knew I was following a path that led directly toward more pain. And Echo, who never lay with Jove, who had curly hair and a funny laugh, would come and talk with me. I admit: I enjoyed her conversation. She'd tell me about the gossip of the woods, the mischief of the satyrs, the parties, and she'd laugh her funny laugh and look around, and I thought maybe it was nerves, from talking to me. But it was not that.

She was playing me for a fool, talking in my ear not because she liked me but so her nymphette friends would have time enough to scatter, to not get caught with my Jove's wide palm groping at their breasts.

There is no one on my team.

So I took away her talk. All she can do is repeat the words that others say. And when I watched her fall for

Narcissus, that self-loving twit, drowning in the depths of his own empty reflection, it did not make me happy. It brought me no relief. I watched her chase him, throw her voice his way every time he spoke. I watched her life force drain out of her as she retreated to a cave, rejected, alone, from body to bone to stone at the floor of a cave and her sad voice bouncing off the hills. This is one form the crushing of love can take. Mine takes another. I take revenge the way I can. I could no more murder my immortal husband than carve a hole into the sky. And I *understand* him. He cannot resist fresh adoration, needs attention. I *know* he is weak and his weakness makes me tender and it makes me so angry I can barely see.

My Jove. My love, my husband, my brother, my king, my thunderer, oh my lightning bolt, my wild mighty god, you own me, I am yours, my golden-shafted swan, my wooly bull, my broad-backed lamb (you know you are), I take your eagle in my mouth, I know you like it, oh my animal, you who share my blood, my bed, my life, eternally. Give me your thunderbolt, all of it, into every part of me, my Jove, my love, my horny fucking husband, my hungerer, my betrayer, my endless source of sorrow and rage, my bottomless well of pain, my pathetic useless liar.

MYRRHA

—This is really hard for me to talk about.

—We can go as slowly as you want.

—Really hard.

—You can say as much or as little as you feel comfortable with.

—Where do you want me to start?

—Where would you like to start?

—I don't want to.

—What brought you here today?

—I can't have all of this in my brain.

—Have you ever been in analysis before?

—No.

—I'm really glad you're here.

—It was something about the grip.

—The grip.

—The hold. My hold. It's been feeling like my hold on what's real is—*tenuous*. There's a clockface, and I'm the second hand and I'm spinning too fast, and the feeling is any second I might snap off from the rest of the clockface and go spinning out into—

—Into where?

—Chaos. Darkness. Someplace really bad. Broke off. Gone.

—Mmmmm.

—A bad clock. Unbound from reality. That feels like a possibility.

—That sounds like a frightening place to be.

—Part of me is nervous that if I say some of this out loud that's what will happen.

—Are there other times you can think of that when you said something out loud your grip loosened? You were flung into chaos?

—No.

—Mmmm.

—I'm not sure.

—Okay. You don't have to be sure. We can come back to that. I hear you talking about reality and what's real. What does that mean for you?

—Reality. This understandable world. Here I am, this is my arm, these are the boundaries of my body. I am a human being named Myrrha. I am not a toaster. You are not a rosemary bush. There's breakfast and gravity and the order of words makes sense and certain people you hate and certain people you love and there are dads and skies and beds and your skin holds your organs in.

—This is all real.

—This is all real.

—What's nonreal, besides darkness and chaos? What would it mean to find yourself there?

—Mmmmm.

—I'm thinking.

—Mmm.

—The understandable things become non-understandable there. You get snagged from the fabric of normal life. So I might not be sure about plants, and maybe I wonder if they can talk after all. And maybe it's a question mark as to whether if you hold your hand over a candle for four minutes, what would happen. And maybe your brother is your son, or your sister is your mom. And maybe the things you're supposed to think and feel you end up thinking and feeling the opposite, for example maybe you want to lovemake with a tulip tree.

—Make love?

—Be intimate. Grind against, maybe naked.

—Yes. Go on.

—The rules are different.

—The rules.

—Grammar. The order of words. Those things dissolve. Who you're supposed to kiss with your tongue. Calling your parents by their first names instead of Ma Mama Mom Pa Papa Dad Father Daddy. Not squatting on the steps of the YMCA on Putnam Ave. and taking a wet dump. Not walking up to some woman in a fur coat on the street and nuzzling against her and asking, Can you be my mom please.

—Is that something you've wanted to do?

—I have nuzzled up against a woman in a fur coat. It looked so soft. I was probably five. I can still remember how soft it was. I didn't ask her to be my mom.

—Can you tell me a little bit about your family?

—My dad's father was a sculptor. His hands were always dry and he smelled sour, like yogurt, rancid yogurt. My main memory of him was him telling me—I was probably six years old—him putting me on his lap and saying, "I hope you don't grow up to be one of those disgusting women."

—Do you know what he meant by that?

—Well, I got the sense that he didn't really like women that much, right? My dad's mom was a statue.

—She was cold? Your grandmother?

—She was funny. I think she hated my grandfather. She called him Pyggy.

—Piggy.

—My dad didn't talk much about what it was like growing up with them. Asking about it was against the rules.

—Were there a lot of rules?

—I didn't know at that point that nuzzling up against a soft fur coat was against the rules. I learned it. Some things you know go against the rules without being told.

—What sort of rules are those?

—Probably you know.

—I'm curious to hear your thoughts.

—Like it doesn't have to be said out loud that you are not a toaster. And it doesn't need to be said out loud that trees are not for lovemaking.

—I hear you mentioning plants a few times.

—So what.

—Have you ever wanted to be intimate with a plant?

—No.

—Mmmm.

—Of course not.

—Okay.

—Things like that can make you feel like something's wrong with you.

—Things like what?

—I had some dreams. It started with some dreams.

—Yes. Can you tell me about these dreams?

—You're going to feel weird.

—I really applaud your willingness to be vulnerable with me.

—When I was younger, maybe thirteen, fourteen, I started having these dreams.

—Mmm.

—And in terms of what we were just saying about plants, and being intimate with them, it was more, these dreams, or one dream really, again and again, it wasn't a plant.

—Mmmm.

—We were on the beach, in the dream, and we went swimming together and he was holding me and I had my legs wrapped around him the way you do in the ocean.

—He.

—My father.

—Your father in the dream.

—Yes, and in the dream he's holding on to my bottom and I like the way it feels, but at the same time I don't like that I like the way it feels.

—Mmm.

—I start kissing his neck. I hate saying this.

—I'm right here with you and we can take a break whenever feels right. Can you go on?

—I start kissing his neck. This is my dad. It's his shoulders and his hairy chest and scratchy, bearded face. I'm kissing him. Not in a daughtery way. Okay? Not in a way that daughters are supposed to kiss their dads. That's a rule you don't have to learn, it should just be in you from the start. You don't kiss your father slowly. And in the dream it feels good and bad at the same time. Does that make sense?

—It does. These sorts of dreams are very common.

—What?

—Yes.

—Other people have these dreams?

—It's our mind's way of working out some of our desires. Working out things we might want, or feel mixed up about, but that our brain won't let us acknowledge consciously. So it comes up in dreams. And they can be really troubling. But it doesn't mean that there's anything wrong with you.

—And then I start kissing his mouth.

—Mmmm.

—And he kisses me. And holds my bottom tighter. And I don't like it. It feels all wrong. It's horrible. Horrible.

—Mmm. Yes.

—And I look out into the ocean and the waves are getting much bigger and the sense is, you know when you sort of know in dreams what's going to happen? The sense is that these waves are coming for us.

—As punishment.

—As punishment? No. The sense wasn't punishment. Just these high gray waves moving toward us.

—How does the dream end?

—He's holding me tighter and the waves are coming and coming and they're white now, stronger, faster, and I wake myself up yelling before the biggest wave washes over me.

—You cry out.

—Horrible. What is my brain doing to me putting these sick dreams in my head? And I was afraid people knew. That they could see into my brain and knew that I was so sick.

—You felt ashamed.

—But see—god—have you ever had it where you dream something and then it alters the way you see someone the next day? I had a dream I got into this huge fight with my friend Cassandra, and the next day I felt mad at her. I felt really mad. I couldn't look at her. The dream jostled reality. I was mad. From the dream. Not from real life. Does that ever happen to you?

—I understand the experience you're describing.

—I had this dream and I hated the way it felt. But also, too—I hate saying this, this is really—I saw my dad the next day and I was trying to be normal and praying he couldn't see into my brain, and I could remember what it felt like to have my legs around him and what his chest hair felt like in my hands. And it was sick, a thing you really do not want to feel. And at the same time it shifted the way I saw him. If that makes sense.

—It does.

—It shifted it.

—How did it shift it?

—Have you ever dreamed of someone, I don't know what sort of person you might have crushes on, but has there ever been a person in a dream who all of a sudden you have a crush on who you've never had a crush on in normal life and then you see them in awake life and something's different, as if the dream delivered a crush to you? Do you know about this? Has this happened to you?

—I understand the experience you're describing.

—I hate saying this.

—Mmm.

—That's what it did with my dad. It altered the way—I mean, I didn't want to think about kissing my dad like that. But also—

—Mmmm.

—I started to like to.

—I see.

—Think about it.

—I see.

—Or maybe not that I liked to but that I couldn't stop.

—Thinking about kissing him.

—Yes.

—When you let yourself think about this, how did it feel?

—Mmmm.

—I'm thinking.

—Take your time.

—Like hunger.

—I see.

—But there are two kinds of hunger. There's the hunger where there's a void that can be filled, and that feels good. Sometimes I come home from school and I'm starving and it's so nice knowing I can eat an apple and some parmesan and some olives. And that hunger's really nice because you know it's going to stop.

—Is the other hunger less nice?

—It's the same hunger except instead of being hungry for an apple and some cheese you want to eat your mattress or your belt.

—Something felt—

—Unnatural.

—Against nature.

—But in nature, with animals, it happens.

—What happens?

—A stallion mounts his foal. Goats. Certain birds. I was jealous.

—Of the animals.

—Of law forbidding what nature allows.

—Law.

—Human law. Human rules. I understand it. I understand about civilization and order and how we have to separate ourselves from animals. I couldn't stop thinking how if I were a stranger I could be with him the way I wanted to, but because we shared blood, I couldn't. I would try and try and try to steer my thoughts away from it, and try to convince myself that I didn't feel what I felt.

—How did that work?

—It never worked. I wanted him to feel the same thing I did.

—Do you think he did?

—In the evenings, after dinner, I'd sit with him on the couch. And I was still young enough, fifteen, sixteen at this point, that we could cuddle up and there could still be an innocence to it. Except it wasn't innocent for me. I stopped—

—It's all right.

—I would take off my panties. At dinner I would slip them off. And then when we were on the couch together I hoped—

—Mmmm.

—I hoped that he would smell me.

—I see.

—And that if he did, something would shift in him. And I always prayed his hand around my back would drop lower, and if his elbow brushed my breast I'd think about it for days.

—Mmmm.

—I couldn't handle it.

—What couldn't you handle?

—Wanting something so much that I shouldn't want. Being too weak to stop myself from it. That's when I—

—What happened then?

—I couldn't handle it, and I didn't think I deserved to be alive.

—Did you try to harm yourself?

—It's okay. Take your time.

—I wanted to die.

—Can you tell me what happened?

—I tried to hang myself.

—But it didn't work.

—But I was too slow, and my nurse heard the rustling and I guess I was sort of crying and talking out loud and she came in and wrapped her arms around me and said, "No no no no you won't not tonight you won't."

—Were you glad to see her? Were you relieved?

—No. No. I wanted to die. I wanted to be done.

—Mmmm.

—She kept asking, "What's wrong, what's wrong, what's going on, why would you want to do this, you're young and beautiful and you have parents that love you and you have this good life." And I just cried and cried and couldn't say anything. It was too horrible. All I could say was I don't deserve to be alive. I kept repeating that. She held me and rocked me in her arms and she promised that whatever was wrong we could figure it out, that no matter how horrible it felt right now, it wouldn't always feel this way. And she promised not to tell anyone, and she promised to help me in whatever way she could.

—Did you trust her?

—I trusted her.

—Did you tell her?

—She said, "Maybe you're in love?" And I said, It's my crime.

—Your crime.

—And she said, "I promise I'll help you. Whatever it is. I promise I won't tell your father." And my whole body tensed. And then she knew. I spoke to her through my body. And she knew. And her body went tense against mine. And she finally said, "It's okay, it's okay, it's okay."

—What was it for you to know that someone else knew?

—It was a relief. Like oh finally maybe someone else can carry a little bit of this. And when she said it's okay, it's okay, I just wanted to believe her. But also, it made everything feel realer and so much worse. Before it had just been me and this horrible wrong part of me, inside my own private place of my skull, but now it was released, it was spoken.

—What does that horrible wrong part of you look like?

—I said it was released. It was spoken. Do you not think there is something disgusting going on here?

—What makes you ask that?

—You understand what I'm telling you, right?

—I understand.

—And so you just sit there and you don't react?

—Tell me about what that wrong part of you looks like.

—I'm thinking.

—Sometimes it's helpful to close your eyes. Try closing your eyes. Yes.

—A crater. Or more, a volcano. A dark rising that is hardened all over, dark, and if you fell down it, it would rip your skin. And at the top is this gaping crater, this opening. And there are creatures around.

—Creatures.

—Shadows. They're shadows. They've got big eyes and long claws and lots of small sharp teeth, and I can't see what color they are because they're shadows. And they move around, they slither around. Mostly they hide.

—What happens when you see them? What happens when they come out of hiding?

—I don't want to see them. I don't want to be near them.

—If you were to talk with them, what would you say?

—To these creatures?

—To these creatures.

—This feels weird.

—Try to imagine them sitting beside you. You can keep your eyes closed. They're sitting beside you. What do you want to say to them?

—I'm not bad. I'm not. You guys are there. You live inside me. But you don't own all of it. I'm not bad. I'm not bad. I took off my panties because something is mixed up. You can live in me. I can take care of you. You can come be on my lap. You don't have to hide. You don't have to be afraid of me. You don't have to be afraid. I'm not bad. I'm not. I'm not. I am not. Just come out. Let me see you. They're taking me to the opening.

—Mmmm.

—I'm walking up this steep hill and the surface is porous and so rough. And they're leading me to the top, they're this small army of shadows, maybe ten or eleven of them, slithering up the side of this crater space. Volcano.

—What do you see?

—At the rim. We're at the rim. It's red around the lip. A deep pink red. The creatures are circling it and they're lit up by the light coming from inside. Red glow. They're dancing around the rim, the shadows.

—Are you dancing?

—I'm too scared to dance. But I want to look in. I want to look into the opening.

—Can you look into the opening?

—I look in. I look in. I lean over and I look in.

—There is no bottom. There is only more dark. And there are thousands and thousands and thousands of the creatures lining the walls, slithering.

—Mmmm.

—I want to go in. It feels irresistible. Like there's something down there I should know. Something true. All the creatures are slithering all the way down. It's uninhabitable. And I know. I know from looking. I know from looking in that if you go down you do not come back, or you do not come back the same. I don't want to be there anymore.

—All right. Open your eyes. Here we are. How are you?

—Tired.

—Mmm.

—That felt strange. Did my voice sound different?

—How do you mean?

—Did it sound different?

—Did it sound different to you?

—I couldn't tell. I was talking.

—Does your voice sound different now?

—It sounds like the voice I know.

—You were talking about saying this out loud, about your feelings for your father, and that it was a relief and also frightening.

—She promised she would help.

—Did she help?

—I guess in some ways.

—How did she help?

—She arranged it.

—Mmmm.

—It was during a festival week when the women are away. My mother was gone. I knew my dad had mistresses sometimes. That was part of their situation.

—Did you meet these mistresses?

—Sometimes.

—Were you jealous of them?

—In some ways. In some ways I wanted to be them. I wanted my dad to look at me the way he did at them.

—How was that?

—More light. Different light.

—Mmmm.

—But also I wasn't jealous. I'd see them and think, You have him one way, but his blood is in my body and my blood is in his body. We share blood and you'll never get as close to him as that.

—And that was a comfort.

—Sort of.

—What did your nurse help arrange?

—You sort of look like him. I'm just noticing. Something in your eyebrows. And your beard.

—I look like him.

—A little bit.

—Does that feel complicated to you?

—Not complicated. But—

—It's okay.

—Curious.

—Mmmm. There are some very specific boundaries in the relationship between analyst and analysand and sometimes things can feel blurry. Intimate things get—

—I'm sorry.

—You were talking about your nurse helping you.

—Thank you. She told my father that a girl loved him. She asked if he wanted to meet her. He asked how old she was. She said, "Myrrha's age." He told her to send her to him that night.

—How did you feel about that?

—Terrified? Excited? That night started clear. Tons of stars, a good swollen moon. And as I made my way toward his room, the skies got dark. The stars went away, the moon went away. Dark low clouds. It was so dark. And I tripped. I stumbled a few times. My legs were shaking I was so nervous.

—Did you think about turning back?

—I almost did. I stood outside his door and I almost turned back. There was this awful bird cry in the night and I told myself to run. To leave that place.

—But you didn't.

—I opened the door.

—Mmmm.

—He was in bed. It was so dark. I walked across the

room. There's a different smell people give off when they sleep.

—He was sleeping.

—I climbed onto the bed. I put my body against his back. He rolled toward me. And then I was gone.

—You were gone.

—I left myself. I was there, but I was not there. My father had his hands on me. In the same way I'd imagined so many times. And I didn't know what to do, but I did. And he lay on his back and the hair on his chest was so thick. And he kept whispering. "So young, so young. It's okay, my girl. It's okay." He could sense that I hadn't done this before. "Don't be scared," he said. "Just like this."

—Did you want him to know it was you?

—No. No.

—Mmmm.

—Yes.

—Mmm.

—He placed me on top of him. I straddled over him and he was so gentle. And he kept whispering.

—What did he say?

—He kept saying, "So tight. You're so tight. My girl, you're so tight. You can feel me." And he got a little less gentle. He said, "It's yours, do you feel me, it's yours." And he started moving faster and I cried out, and then I was afraid he'd know my voice but he didn't. And he sat up so my legs were wrapped around his back and he held my bottom.

—Like your dream.

—Just like my dream. And it felt like this ring, that this is the way that blood should flow, that we were sharing each other the way that was meant. So tight, so tight. And I felt so proud. That I was making him feel so good. And that I felt so good. He held my bottom and rocked me on himself. I was proud.

—How did you feel afterward?

—I had more than his blood inside me. And I knew it was right.

—Did it happen again?

—Yes. I returned to his bed again the next night. He was so happy to see me. He said, "You remind me of my daughter." And my heart turned into a firework when he said that. It made me think that he *did* have the same feelings I had. And so I knew it was just a matter of time until this wouldn't have to be a secret anymore.

—What did the thought of it not being a secret feel like?

—It's what I wanted, for it to be real, for it to be un-hidden. And it was also scary.

—What was scary?

—How much I wanted it.

—Mmmm.

—He held me when it was over. He rubbed my breasts. I would wait until he fell asleep, then I would go back to my room.

—And it happened again after that.

—He had this way of pressing his hand against my chest, over my heart. And he'd stay really quiet and he'd say, "I feel you beating." And I'd place my hand over his heart but it was hard to feel it because of how thick the hair was. And he'd say, "Can you feel me beating? Can you feel me? Feel me."

—This felt good.

—I felt him. We were so close.

—And it happened again.

—You still have no reaction?

—Should I be reacting?

—I mean, if you're a human being probably you're having a reaction.

—Would it be useful for you for me to have a reaction?

—I mean sometimes it's good to have someone acknowledge that there is actually something wrong.

—Do you feel like there's something wrong?

—I know there's something wrong. You know it, too. You know. I don't understand why you're not telling me.

—You want me to tell you there's something wrong?

—I want to know that I'm not fucking crazy for thinking I'm crazy.

—You have a lot you're holding on to all at once. A lot of rich, complicated experiences and feelings.

—No shit.

—Did these encounters with your father continue?

—Again and again. And then one night I arrived and he took me into his arms and he said, god, so sweetly, "I've touched you with my fingers, I've tasted you with my tongue, I've smelled you, the deepest parts of you,

I've heard your breath in my ear. But I've never seen you. Let me put my eyes on you." And he lit a lamp and I—

—It's okay.

—His face.

—What was his face?

—Like he was sick. Like he'd just swallowed something rotten, like he didn't understand what he'd just eaten, but knew it was poison. And then it shifted. And he looked scared. And then right after that he looked furious. And he threw me off the bed and he came after me. If he'd caught me, he would've killed me. I ran. I ran and ran. I disappeared. I moved from one place to the next. I never stopped. Not for nine months. I knew my father's seed had taken hold. I knew it the very first night. My son would be my brother. My brother my son. My father would be both father and grandfather to this boy. This shared blood. I moved until I was too heavy to move.

—You're due soon.

—I'll name him Adonis.

—Your son.

—I want to be changed. I want to change. There's no bottom. The creatures are alive and there are more and more and they're getting braver. I don't want to be this anymore. Please. Can you help me? Can you please help me?

—What do you want to be?

—Not this. Not foul. Not a second hand snapping off the clock.

—It's okay.

—Can you make me a tree?

—I hear you talking of plants again.

—Can I be a tree? Can you help me be a tree? They talk. All of them actually do. But no one knows it and I could have my guilt without anyone knowing. Roots in the earth, bark skin around the shame.

—Mmmm.

—Please. Can you help me?

—We will work to find the tree in you.

—It's in me?

—It's in you. We'll find it.

—I can feel it.

—In time. You are brave.

—I am.

—We're going to explore the volcano.

—I'm ready.

—Let the creatures talk with you. Listen to what they say.

—They'll lead me to the tree.

—We have a lot of work to do together.

—I'm ready. I'm ready. I can feel it. Already I'm changing.

Io

PART I

On an afternoon at the end of summer, I walked home along the river. Jove approached and I believed him when he said, It's too hot in the sun, your pale skin, come into the shade, you'll be safe in the woods, come with me, no animals will eat you, no harm will come, I'll protect you.

I walked with him into the woods.

It was nice in the shade, cool, like flipping your pillow in the night.

It is still too bright, said Jove. I didn't know what he meant. He produced a fog and it surrounded us. It was cottony and dim. There were no more edges. I could not see the trees. To protect your soft pale skin, he said and he touched my soft pale skin. I did not expect this. His hand was too warm. I took one step away.

You're safe, he said.

He kept touching my skin.

You're safe, he said.

He touched the skin beneath my clothes. I stepped away. Not me, I said.

You're safe, he said.

No, I said. No thanks. I need to go.

Stop, he said. His voice was louder.

I stepped away. You stop, I said.

You're safe, he said.

No thanks, I said. Not me. I need to go. Stop please.

What was it like? Picture this: there you are and you're with someone else and there is an understanding. There is such a thing as things making sense and the feeling that you know where the other stands and both of you are operating under a shared system of how the world works. And then there is a moment when there seems to be a misunderstanding, when certain words aren't communicating what they're meant to. And maybe you try again. Perhaps you were not clear, or you did not say it in the right tone of voice. But then you see something different in the other person's eyes, something *gone*, and it becomes clear that it is not misunderstanding and it is not about tone of voice. The way you've understood things to be turns out to be very wrong and everything is upside down and out of control and words no longer have their power.

You grow up to believe that if you say, Please pass the salt, a person will reach toward the shaker, grab it in his hand, and move it in your direction. But then one day some of us might learn that it can happen that you can say, Please pass the salt, and a person will jam his hand into the mayonnaise jar and fling a fistful of it at your face. All at once, words don't mean what they're supposed to mean.

I am a girl. My name is Io. I say no thanks, not me, stop please. But all at once, words do not matter. I do not matter.

I am: Up against a tree. On the ground. On my belly. Split. All his body on all my body. The word is too small and too known and too tame for what took place. And it was only the beginning anyway. Another beginning. We begin again and again.

My words had no power. I was speaking the language of animals. I could not make myself understood. I was no longer the full human self I knew myself to be, who is friends with Linda and Daniel and Quinn, who loved grapes as a kid and hated socks, who drew pictures of castles and tigers, who laughs at rhymes and hates ice and loves milkweed pods. All at once that went away and I was a body and an entrance and a means.

Want is the only thing. One want eats the other. I want this to stop. Someone else wants it not to stop. Whose want wins? If we are basing it on duration, mine does. Because my want for it to stop does not ever end. If we are basing it on who gets what they want? His. My want was consumed by his want; it made his want bigger. My want was swallowed whole by a gaping, gulping mouth that spews and swallows at once.

Jove's wife saw the fog in the woods on that otherwise sunny afternoon and she suspected. And she knew what her husband was—except instead of saying, My husband is a rapist, she said, My husband is easily tempted and acts on his wants and she felt angry at the tempters for existing. The safer direction to aim the rage. Their shared life was eternal after all and he was not someone she could kill even if she wanted to.

And so she scorched down a path through the fog. Jove didn't want to get caught, didn't want his wife's wrath, he didn't want to hurt her. So the coward changed me to a cow.

He'd made me an animal already.

PART II

Begin again.

Low. I am a cow. All white. But not my eyes. The size of a baby's fist, they are the color of small ponds in fall. Io inside me. Her voice is lost. Low. My cry, my wordless bass-horn moan, the sound of it frightened Io inside me. The wordless expression of loss.

An all-white heifer to disguise Jove's crime. Juno knew. What's this cow, she said to her husband, his face still flushed, jewels of sweat sliding down his temples. She looked into my baby-fist eyes. Where'd this cow come from? It's nice, she lied. She didn't touch me.

Jove, his hand on my ribs and my muscles flickered beneath it. Juno's eyes and my eyes, we looked at each other and we both knew what we were. I saw her sad-ness. She saw mine.

Oh this cow? said Jove. This cow comes straight from the earth, if you can believe it.

She couldn't, of course. But she played along. We kept staring into each other's eyes and there we saw what the other suffered.

I would like her as a gift, said Juno. I blinked, lids so slow to lower. Blinked for the bad news that came in that wish. She's so beautiful, she said. Lie. Low. She wanted, too: see what he'll do.

Jove stood there, tried to smile, damp on his dick. Cock milk. Clear and white at once. Not the white of me or the milk that would come from the weight of my one own white breast below me, low. Swollen. I could feed so many mouths. All we do is hunger, from when we're egg and seed, before we're pulled from our original home. Each day after, all the days, hungering. It does not stop. I could pause your hunger for a moment with the white inside me. We are all so swollen low with want.

Jove, damp-dicked and trapped. What did he want? He wanted the cow that glowed like the moon which hangs in the sky like a drop of milk that fell from the breast of a star. He wanted not to hurt his wife. He wanted not to be caught. One could see the argument in his mind: give up this creature he wanted to possess versus please his wife. To deny her this request would be to prove his guilt— to give up the cow would be to lose something of his. Shame, potent motivator, lives low, pushes hard. Whose want wins?

Of course, he said to Juno. She's all yours.

But she did not really get what she wanted. And neither did he. And neither did Io inside me.

This was still the beginning.

I stood on hooves, four-legged, a tail at swish behind me, the new matter of flies. My hip bones sharp as arrowheads. Two lovers could sit within my rib cage, if each held their knees to their chests.

Juno knew what I was, she'd seen my eyes as I'd seen hers. Ban the tempters. Exile the enticements. As though Jove would mount me now. Maybe he would. I don't know how low.

Juno sent me off to Argus, a giant who had a hundred eyes. All time all-watching Argus. His eyes slept in pairs, ninety-eight left watching while two at a time took rest. He never took his eyes off me, suspicious Juno wanted it this way. His eyes held no sadness. They held the nothing of boredom: he had seen too much.

By day, I grazed. Chewed grass, flicked flies. Milk pressed up against the edges of my own low breast. There's boredom that comes in the back door: when one sees too little. The field, the grass, the fence. Mud puddles, dung, sun. Argus stooped, his everlasting leer, eyes shifted, flicked, rolled. Blinky blink blink. Gone wrong barnyard kaleidoscope. Io inside me. Somewhere the shape of her inside the shape I'd been given. White wide load low. One does not need to be jailed to be imprisoned, to be caged by something that happens. Memory lives in the body like Io lived in my body. I felt her there, caged by the moment when language lost its power, caged by the moment when her want lost.

Argus saw, did not talk. At night, he roped me. Put me in a pen. Tight hot place of wet dirt, stink. He jammed bitter leaves and thorned twigs at my face to eat. Chewed and chewed. Frothy cottony mouth. Sores from the thorns. Trough water mostly mud. At night he fastened a harness on me, perverse acrobatics to get it on, cinching it over my chest, pulling it tight around the space where my front legs met my body. Tethered to a peg. Always he found a way to touch my one own low white breast. Bumped it with his elbow, low, his hip, grazed it with his hand. This too-many-eyed monster. Sores where the harness rubbed me. Sores where the rocks dug into my flesh as I slept. Dreams about silence. Rid the low moan.

An afternoon, a fence post fallen, a way out. I followed the river to Io's home. Across one low bridge, paused, looked. In the water, wide white face, horn nubs, eyes the size of baby fists. Io in me. She could not bear to look. To see what she'd become. Reflected in the dark water like a distorted sort of moon. Hoofed off the bridge. There along the shore, Io's father, the sisters that were hers. They couldn't see her, but when she saw them through my baby-fist eyes, she urged me toward them, made herself more present.

There you are, I thought.

I nuzzled against her father. I ate soft leaves from his hands. Her sisters touched me. What a beauty, they said.

I tried to speak but low it was the same old sigh. To make them know, I steered my hoof in the sand of the shore and spelled out what I'd suffered. I wrote out the woe.

My father cried. No, no. My beautiful girl transformed. Ruined and muted. My sisters cried and pressed themselves against me. They kissed my eyes.

And then Argus appeared with the harness and my sisters clung to me and my father threw a stone at him and missed. They knew the massive all-seeing monster would take me away. And he did. He pulled me to a field and he sat on top of the hill and watched. I no longer lowed. Head bowed, lowered, couldn't lift it for the woe.

Jove saw the suffering and it panged him. It wasn't guilt that chewed his conscience. The gods exist without regret. Something beautiful was less so. So he schemed to save me.

Mercury, murder Argus for me, he said. Kill the cruel watchman.

Mercury winged his way to the hill. Shepherd-dressed. He played pan pipes to try to lull all Argus's eyes to sleep. When one set of eyes got drowsy, another set lifted its lids. Mercury stopped the song and talked instead. Told the history of the pipes he played, about Syrinx and her sisters. It's this—the tale, the words, the story—that lowered all of Argus's lids. The words worked. As soon as Mercury saw that Argus had drifted, the wing-heeled god grabbed his scythe.

The head bumped down the hill. Blood marked its trail. The hundred eyes blinked light dark light last sight the sky the ground the stars a swirl, eyelashes up, down, low, long night came to Argus, rest for the rest of time. Terrible to see: all his eyes were open, low, and they saw nothing.

But Juno saw it all.

She took the hundred eyes and spread them in the feathers of the peacock tail that pulled her chariot. Blind but iridescent.

What else?

She flicked her fingers and a Fury like a biting horsefly attached itself to my eyes. Low I raced and swung my head, pressed my face into the dirt. It bit and stung. I lashed and ran. Panted. Cantered. People moved away, a one-white-cow stampede. Wild-eyed crazed and wanting only for all of it to end.

Ran ran ran ran mad.

Bleached shadow on the world. Valleys hills forests meadows dawns days rains nights noons dawns suns dawns noons days clouds moons moons moons.

Spit-flecked jaw foamed white like the milk and the stars white like the absence of everything white the color of obliteration. And a cow with an Io inside but gone. So deep and small inside and a creature thuds across the world trying to escape the bites on the eyes, eyes gone white like the cow like the moon low and the whole world is an empty dark for the white to move through like a boundless cloud low the white cow is found in the desert the sun bleaching it to a white that blinds.

White wound moving through the world lakes storms apple pear plum oak elm owl the white cow is only a moving shifting pain. A desert. A river.

The language the absence the meaning and relief low it's being galloped after

In the world let me in, in the world let me out, let me leave, let me empty my one own low breast of its milk, into the river, let it be the sweep of stars, hey you, the bear, I see you burning white, I want to feed you with my milk, soothe you, fuel you, keep burning!

Want the world to pour out of me, want the milk emptied out of me, into the great wide white river made of milk. To flow low and low

A place beyond the pain made of milk, a milk with seed and yolk, all the possible lives inside it, a place past pain, passed pain, past form

Form low moves moves again, new forms stories and

Origins out of the cow low white like the nothing and the all the all

The voice inside Io Io Io endlessness silence

Wild mind and the stories told low without words in the blind eyes in the absence low low

The world made of sand and and and low the dune moon stars in the milk drink it drink it I know you're hungry I know you're thirsty you want it you want it low the river won't end so much milk from my one own low breast. Drink from it. Taste the endlessness eternity all over low it presses in on all sides all times

> all time in all directions
> and we are in the middle of it

The gods don't die low Juno Jove, Jove begs Juno, let her go, I am yours, low lie, for all time and it moves her because love blinds us makes us believe and she says yes I trust I believe she can go

And and and

PART III

I will try to speak simply. Now I was no cow. Girl to animal to god, in the desert on the side of the Nile. I was Io. I was a cow. I am Isis.

God is the voice inside that communicates without language through the dark expanse of time. The voice of god is the endlessness in you. The voice of god is silent and sensed at the edges.

So lie on your back in the woods with the birds and the birches the ripple of water milksap white tears like pearls bleed from the trees as one day gives way to another leaves on your skin and worms in the dirt and a spider in silk and a bear at a distance and a cow in the field and the reeds by the water and a spinning respinning story forms ongoing the origins annihilations that destroy the boundaries break the seed crack the egg and you again and again and again.

SCYLLA

Galatea lived across town at the time and she called me
one afternoon and told me she'd fainted buying seltzer
at the 7-Eleven. She'd been trying some fasting cleanse,
hadn't eaten anything but black tea for forty hours.
"Could you come over?" she asked. Her voice sounded
small. I stopped at the store on the corner, bought a
pouch full of raisins and nuts, an apple, and a sandwich
with mayonnaise and cheese. The sandwich was unbe-
lievably beige, but it seemed like the right sort of color
for the reintroduction of food.

I took a bus, and then walked quickly from the stop
to her place. The magnolias had opened. The air smelled
like bloom. At the door she looked wan, a sleepy smile
on her face, a fuzz about the eyes. "Have you eaten anything yet?"

We climbed the stairs. "I just feel shaky," she said.

We got to her bedroom and I laid out the options. We sat on her bed.

"What sort of sandwich is this?" she asked.

"Beige," I said.

She opened it, took a triangle in her hands and bit a corner off, a tiny bite. She closed her eyes and ate it, slowly, and picked out the cashews from the pouch and a few raisins. "It's all so good," she said. "I feel kind of feverish though."

"Let me brush your hair."

We sat on her bed. She sat in front of me and I un-braided her black hair, and it shined down her back, past her shoulder blades. I held the wooden handle of the brush and took a stroke through her hair. "Is it a rat's nest?" she asked. No, I said. I moved the bristles over her skull, she tilted her head back and made a quiet noise. I touched her neck as I collected her hair and saw the goosebumps rise on her shoulders.

We started to talk as I moved the brush through her hair and we found ourselves sharing stories we hadn't ever shared. Maybe in this way brushing someone's hair is like driving, the intimacy of a quiet closed space, no eye contact, the charge of nearness.

"I had a stalker," she said.

"What happened?" I said.

"We met at the end of a party. Polyphemus."

"The Cyclops?"

"Do you know him?"

"I know of him. I've seen him around."

"We chatted for two minutes and he said something about wanting to show me this link about my hometown and asked me for my e-mail and I don't know why I didn't just say no sorry that's okay. It was sort of like just riding along on the river of conversation and I didn't want to be rude. Why does it seem impossible to say no sometimes? Anyway, I gave him my e-mail and he e-mailed me later that night. Can I read it to you? 'Hey Galatea, really great to meet you tonight. Hope it's not weird to say, but you have really nice skin. A lot of women don't seem to take care of their skin but you seem to really take care of your skin. Like apple blossom petals! Here's that link I mentioned. Talk to you soon. Have a good weekend!—P.'"

"P.U."

"Exactly. Here, you should just read the whole exchange."

And Galatea handed me her phone. I stayed sitting behind her, holding her phone, the brush on the bed, my hand on her shoulder. I read.

```
From: Galatea <g.latea@gmail.com>
Date: Sat, May 10 at 11:51 PM
Subject: Re: Hometown!
To: Polyphemus <rolypoly@hotmail.com>
Hi Polyphemus, thanks for the link. Take
care.


From: Polyphemus <rolypoly@hotmail.com>
Date: Sun, May 12 at 12:24 AM
```

Subject: Re: Hometown!

To: Galatea <g.latea@gmail.com>

I'm glad you liked the link, Galatea. I
hope what I said about your skin didn't
make you feel weird. I was thinking more
about it. Maybe apple blossoms wasn't right.
Maybe more like the inside of seashells.
If I'm overstepping here, I apologize, but
you've got a really great body, like really
great. I can tell you think about what you
eat. It takes discipline to be slim like
you. I really admire that. To be honest,
it's been a long time since a woman has
caught my attention the way you have. Maybe
never as much as you have. Want to grab a
drink sometime?—P.

From: Galatea <g.latea@gmail.com>

Date: Sun, May 12 at 8:27 AM

Subject: Re: Hometown!

To: Polyphemus <rolypoly@hotmail.com>

Hi Polyphemus, thanks, this is flattering.
But I'm involved with someone. Take care.

From: Polyphemus <rolypoly@hotmail.com>

Date: Sun, May 12 at 8:31 AM

Subject: Re: Hometown!

To: Galatea <g.latea@gmail.com>

Someone told me you were dating Acis but I
wasn't sure. Bummer. You're beautiful and

funny and you have such a pretty voice and
again maybe it's weird but you remind me of
a lush garden, full of succulents. Hope to
see you soon.—P.

From: Polyphemus <rolypoly@hotmail.com>
Date: Mon, May 13 at 2:12 AM
Subject: Re: Hometown!
To: Galatea <g.latea@gmail.com>

Hi Galatea, I know you're dating someone,
but I just want you to know you're fucking
hot. Wanna know what would make you hotter?
If you weren't dating Acis. Think about
it. ;)—P.

From: Polyphemus <rolypoly@hotmail.com>
Date: Mon, May 13 at 11:21 AM
Subject: Re: Hometown!
To: Galatea <g.latea@gmail.com>

Hi Galatea, sorry to bother you. I was
thinking about it. And I stand by what I
said, about your skin and stuff and how
lovely you are. But also, just so you know,
you not writing back makes you pretty
rude, makes you a little bit of a bitch,
to be honest about it. It seems like maybe
you have the same amount of manners as
an animal. I got a sense that you were
kind of cold and prickly, and you're
definitely proving that true. It's a really

unattractive quality, actually. Honestly,
it's revolting. I think if you were to
actually try to get to know me, you'd
regret not being in touch, and you'd kick
yourself for keeping me waiting.

"Jesus. What a dick. Did you want to tell him to fuck off?"

"I guess I was hoping if I ignored him he'd just stop. That it'd be better than offending him, like I didn't want to give him more material to react to and be insane about. I wanted it to just go away."

From: Polyphemus <rolypoly@hotmail.com>

Date: Wed, May 15 at 2:41 PM

Subject: Re: Hometown!

To: Galatea <g.latea@gmail.com>

Galatea, just to tell you a little bit more
about myself since you don't seem to have
interest in asking yourself, and I think
maybe the more you know the more you might
realize what you're missing. First of all, I
own my own house and it's not small. And if
you like strawberries, my garden is full of
them. And if you like grapes, I have purple
and green. Do you like cherries? I have
tons of cherry trees. I make good money.
I'm not bragging, I'm just stating a fact.
And just so you know, if I gave you a gift,
it wouldn't be some boring flowers or a

pair of earrings for your perfectly pierced
ears. I know this area inside-and-out and
I'm constantly hiking, and I saw a pair
of bear cubs the other day and I thought
Galatea would love these. Just so you know.

And just to remind you what I look
like, because I was just looking in the
mirror and I was liking what I was seeing.
Probably you remember how large I am, much
larger than most men. In all the ways.
Just saying. And women happen to actually
love how long my hair is, that it comes
to my shoulders. And women also happen
to actually love the hair on the rest of
my body. For some women, it is a major
turn-on. Think about it: A tree is ugly
without leaves. A sheep looks ridiculous
without wool. Birds have feathers. People
say a man with a lot of hair is manlier.
My chest, back, neck, hands. And with the
one eye I've got I actually see more than
most people. Just so you know. I don't wear
contacts or glasses. I have perfect vision.

Also probably you already know this, but
my dad's a god, and not to get ahead of
ourselves here, but it's useful to have a
god for a father-in-law.

To be honest, I cannot understand what
you see in Acis. I've seen him and I've
talked to people, and he's a joke. Let him

know that he does not want to cross paths
with me. Honestly when I start thinking
about him, and when I start thinking about
him fucking you, it makes me crazy. What
do you even like about him? Is someone
with a smooth chest so sexy to you? Like
a little boy? Is that what you like? Is he
so good at fucking you? No chance he's got
a bigger D than me. No chance FYI. Does he
love going down? Galatea, I'd go down all
day any day. I don't even care if you are
on your period. Does Acis go down when you
are on your period? What do you like about
him? Honestly I think about him on top of
you and it makes me fucking insane. I just
pounded the desk here and a glass fell off
and broke all over the floor. I've got to
clean up the glass now.—P.

"He's fucking crazy."
"I know."

From: Polyphemus <rolypoly@hotmail.com>

Date: Thur, May 16 at 4:04 AM

Subject: Re: Hometown!

To: Galatea <g.latea@gmail.com>

You don't find anything there to respond to?
I find that surprising. It makes me think
there's something bigtime wrong with you.

From: Polyphemus <rolypoly@hotmail.com>

Date: Fri, May 17 at 3:58 PM

Subject: Re: Hometown!

To: Galatea <g.latea@gmail.com>

Nothing still? Are you a bitch.

From: Polyphemus <rolypoly@hotmail.com>

Date: Sun, May 19 at 11:21 AM

Subject: Re: Hometown!

To: Galatea <g.latea@gmail.com>

How's Acis, Galatea? Still a loser?

From: Polyphemus <rolypoly@hotmail.com>

Date: Mon, May 20 at 3:17 AM

Subject: Re: Hometown!

To: Galatea <g.latea@gmail.com>

Stupid fucking cunt.

"Jesus."

"I know. Like terrifying. My hands went all cold when I saw it. I couldn't get to sleep."

From: Galatea <g.latea@gmail.com>

Date: Tue, May 21 at 10:11 AM

Subject: Re: Hometown!

To: Polyphemus <rolypoly@hotmail.com>

Hi Polyphemus. Please stop e-mailing me. I'm not interested and your messages are frightening.

From: Polyphemus <rolypoly@hotmail.com>

Date: Tue, May 21 at 10:17 AM

Subject: Re: Hometown!

To: Galatea <g.latea@gmail.com>

Oh, Galatea. Sweet G. Thank you for writing. I don't want to frighten you. I'm just trying to make you know what I know: we are meant for each other. And I'm happy we're going to see each other soon.

"When I read that last one, I panicked. I got this sick, terrible feeling. That he was going to get me. That he was going to find me and get me. I knew. In my body. I knew it."

Her back still to me, Galatea was all tensed. I grabbed the apple from the bed and reached around her, a one-armed behind-the-back embrace. "Here," I said.

She took a bite.

"What happened then?" I asked, and I kept stroking the brush through her hair.

"I didn't hear from him for a few weeks. Nothing. Which in some ways was scarier. I started dreading opening my e-mail, thinking, Oh god, is he going to be in there this time? I had this terrible sense of dread. And I was with Acis one morning, and we were hanging out on his porch, sitting kind of tangled up together, drinking a coffee. I looked up, and down the block I saw this figure walking up the street. This massive, long-haired man. And I knew immediately."

"Oh god," I said. I kept brushing, trying to stay steady in my strokes.

"I said, 'Acis, I think that's him.' And he sat up. And I said, 'We need to get out of here.' And then Polyphemus started running, and we went sprinting and tumbling off the porch, and I went straight for the water, and dove in, and Polyphemus has these super long legs and he was there in what seemed like seconds and I was screaming at Acis to run, run, and Polyphemus started after him, and he was yelling stuff like I'm going to tear your limbs off, I'm going to fuck your asshole with your own foot, I'm going to rip your dick off and grill it on a stick, you're never going to fuck her again."

"This is fucking terrifying."

"And then he picked up this huge rock and threw it at him and it—it—"

Galatea started crying and I put the brush down and used both hands over her head, petting her, soothing her with my hands on her head and her back.

"It cracked his skull," she said. "His blood was all on the ground. But I turned his blood to water, and the rock that Polyphemus threw split in half and first a reed grew from it, then the form of man, it was Acis again, but larger, and his skin was blue-green, and now he was a god of the river. I changed him."

"You saved him," I said.

"I saved him. It's never felt so good to use my power. You just kind of take it for granted a lot of the time, but then something happens where it's there when you need it and you use it and it fucking works."

But she was afraid still, and she shook beneath my hands. I put my arms around her. "It's okay," I said. "You're okay."

"I don't feel okay," she said. "I feel scared all the time."

"I know, I know." Her hair shined. It smelled like mint and grass and bread. "It's so scary."

"Yeah," she said. She sniffed. "He was so awful. So disgusting. You should've seen all of his hair."

"I bet you could make a really warm sweater."

Galatea laughed. "God, that would be the most disgusting sweater. There'd be fleas."

"Also, what the fuck, he wanted to eat Acis's dick like a hot dog?" I said.

Galatea almost fell off the bed.

"I'm the only one who gets to eat his hot dog." When she stopped laughing she said, "I think part of why I wanted to do this stupid cleanse was to empty all this out of myself, get all this poison out. Like scrape out the insides of me."

"Sure, that makes sense. Probably talking is another way to get the poison out, too," I said. "You don't have to starve yourself."

"He didn't touch me."

"He didn't touch you."

"I'm okay. Acis is okay."

"Both of you are safe."

"In some ways I feel like I shouldn't even be complaining," she said. "We're fine. It could've been so much worse."

She stopped here and I brushed and we sat in her room in the quiet.

"But I can't stop thinking about it. I can't get him out of my head. It wasn't that bad. It could've been so much worse. But it's like he's moved into my brain and occupies like eighty percent of it. He takes up so much of my attention. I can't concentrate. No matter what I'm doing. Baking bread, sitting at the bar down the street with Acis, swimming laps. It's like I cannot escape him in my mind. All the time. Him. His stupid hair. The fear."

She shook her head. "Why did I give him my stupid e-mail address?"

"No, no, no, no."

"But if I hadn't—"

"No."

"It wasn't that bad. It could've been so much worse."

"Also, it was really bad. What happened was extremely scary."

"Yeah," she said. "It was really scary."

We talked for a little while longer. Galatea ate more nuts. I thought about how maybe the worst violence isn't the physical part, but what it does to the mind, hijacking the attention centers, recircuiting what the brain wires itself around. The ongoing fuckery of not being able to aim attention where you want. A violence greater than that to the body. "I can stay with you," I told her. She told me she wanted to sleep. She thanked me for listening.

"Thank you for brushing my hair."

"I will do that any time."

She walked me out and we embraced and maybe I was imagining it, but she seemed fuller than when I embraced her when I arrived.

"I love you," I told her. I had not said it to her before. She was my friend.

"I love you, too," she told me. "Thank you."

I walked home. The late afternoon was warm and I didn't want to ride the bus. I wanted to shake the feeling I had, clear it out.

I walked along the canal, the damp tang of mulch and daffodils in the air, and Glaucus appeared out of the water. Ours was not a large city, and once you live in a place long enough you start to recognize certain people, and you hear things. I didn't know Glaucus, didn't know much about him, but I'd seen him around. Seaweed hair that wrapped all the way down and around his torso. Man from the waist up. Fish from the waist down. I wasn't in the mood to talk.

"Hey, Scylla."

I walked a little faster. Maybe he wasn't a monster, but Galatea's story was coating my mind and it was making me wary, impatient, and mad.

"Hey, Scylla!"

I turned and looked at him again. Just stared. Broad shoulders. A cut middle. Definition in all the places you want it to be. Fish scales shimmering in the light, little oil slicks, rainbows on the pavement. He smiled and his teeth were straight and white. He was magnificent to look at. No one would deny it. I turned and kept moving.

"What good is being a god if I can't get your attention?" he shouted.

You had my attention, I thought, *I just stared at you for half a minute. You had all of it. I don't feel like giving you any more right now.* It's a choice I have, it's a choice we all have all the time—we are able to decide where to place our attention. You want to focus it on skateboarding? On watching TV? On drifting through the Internet? On examining the patterns of your emotional weather? On boys? On girls? On framing the photograph just right? On all those things on a single day? It's your choice. And we'll always have a thousand things that clamor for it. Me, me, me, look here, give me time, give me space, give me the most important thing you have to give. But we get to choose. And it is the project of a life to remember how valuable one's attention is, and the effort it can take to steer it where you want. Today, by the canal, I just wanted to walk off the feeling of monsters and fear. *Bad timing, Glaucus*, I thought. *Shitty timing.*

This was a problem for him. To solve this problem, he swam to Circe. He said, "Circe, I want Scylla, she isn't into me, you've got to help." Circe had an instant crush on Glaucus. "Why don't you stay with me?" she said and she touched his scales. "Forget her."

"I can't," he said. "She's all I want."

"I'm telling you from experience, it's a lot better to be with someone who wants you," Circe said. "It's a lot better when you don't have to beg. Be with some-one who can appreciate your beauty." She slid her hand down his scales. "I appreciate your beauty."

"I only want Scylla."

Circe didn't like this at all but she told him she'd help. She mashed up herbs, she pounded poisons together.

She took her tincture to the small bay where I liked to swim and poured them in. I headed to the water before going home.

It wasn't full summer but the sun beat down and I stepped into the water because the water can pull the poi-sons from you, like talking, like walking. I didn't know that Circe had contaminated the water. I went waist-deep, could feel the edges of Galatea's story smoothing out of me. I reached the line on my body where Glaucus becomes a fish. I stopped there, water to my hips.

Because that's when the dogs appeared. Dark bark-ing shapes all around my waist. Dark snarling gnashing dogs. I tried to chase them away but they were on me, they were attached to me. Huge dark barking dogs. A belt of dark and barking dogs with fire in their eyes. I bent and found that my legs were all dogs. A woman's body from the waist up. Waist down wild dogs. They growled and strained and thrashed. I stood on the backs of these beasts except I had no legs to stand on. A belt of black dogs. A snarling skirt of dogs.

I stayed where I was. I stayed for a long time. I trained my dogs. My dogs ate boats and all the sailors on them. You want more men, Circe? That's what you want? Tough luck, bitch. Glaucus cried, because of what

I'd become, and maybe for the guilt of causing it. You lose, too, fish man.

It's the most important choice of a life, where you aim your attention. Sometimes the choice is taken away from us, our ability to choose compromised. Over time, I hardened. I became a rock. I crush ships and drown the men so Circe does not get what she wants. Galatea visits. She sits on the sun-warmed surface of me. We talk. She scrapes the barnacles and washes the bird shit off of me just the way I brushed her hair.

I try to focus on this. On absorbing the warmth of the sun. On the rise and fall of the tides. On the children who climb on me and the waves that splash. I try to focus on the way the rain tastes, the damp caress of the fog. I try to ignore the ships and the men. I try to ignore the memory of what put me in this place. I try to ignore the sense of loss and anger. I try so hard. But ignoring does not mean gone. And the men and memories return like an army on the march and I find sometimes that I'm surrounded. Sometimes I win the battle—my attention on the seagull cries, the light along the horizon, the sound of a ship splintering against my edge—and sometimes I surrender.

SIBYL

In any life there are regrets and they accumulate like unpaired socks, taking up space in the drawer, doing no good.

When I was young, Phoebus wanted me. It's impossible to believe, I know; all that's worth desiring has long since seeped from this form. But it was true. And no, this is no glory-days rehashing, no sad longing for bygone time, no snare-drum bragging. You might think: the only direction she has to look is backward, all the good is behind. Yes and no.

Phoebus loved me. He desired me. I'm his prophetess, a translator between present and future. I give voice to mystery. And I liked what I saw in his eyes when he looked at me. How easily flattered we are. He gave me gifts—a wooden spoon carved of blood wood, a necklace made of hummingbird beaks, a song he wrote about the way my pupils contracted and swelled in pleasure. My body was a bag full of ripe peaches, hard pit in the middle holding seed.

Phoebus begged me. All those gifts to pry me, so I would hand him my virginity. "Please," he said. "*Please.*" I considered it. I imagined offering it up to him on a platter, a membrane red and gold, taut, translucent, strong, round as a cow's eye and thin as a leaf, held in a black velvet case. It's yours, press through, come see what's on the other side. Presumably, he already knew. But I didn't. What's it like when that wall comes down?

"I will give you anything you want for it," he said. It. This state, this condition, this prize, once gone, always gone. I am until I am not. "Make your wish," he said.

What do we know when we are young? I knew the heat I had, the glow, there, behind my eyes. The fire that brought people toward me. The other thing I knew is that I did not want any of it to end. It, all of this, life. I wanted it to go on and on, an endless stretch of possibility. I bent down and collected a small handful of sand, and I said to him, to a god that offered me infinity, grant me as many years as grains I hold.

Why did I think a handful of sand was infinite?

He put his hand on my cheek, he kissed my forehead gently. He exhaled and his breath smelled like laundry dried in the sun. But all at once there was sweat on my lower back, and breath moving faster for fear. A glittering image of offering something up on a platter is different from the raw fact of opening your legs.

He placed his hand on the hard part of my chest, below my neck. His eyes were closed and he said my name. His hand slid to my left breast and he and I both exhaled, our breaths pushing against each other in the space between us. I said it quietly at first.

No.

I didn't know what I was feeling. I didn't like what I was feeling. Fear seeped into my limbs and turned them to cold-hot stone. No, no. He kissed my cheeks, my lips, gently. He was so, so gentle. Everything pulsed too fast and all the world was spinning and all I could think of was wanting to be in my bed in my room alone. I can't, I said. He took a step away, his hands raised. "No?" No, I can't, I said. My whole middle quivered. "Okay," he said. And he looked me meanly in the eyes and touched my face once more and shook his head at me and then he was gone.

Why did I deny him what I owed for what he granted? Why so wedded to my purity? I've had so long to think on it. I changed my mind. I could not hand him my virginity on a platter. I was on one side of the membrane, he, another. The thought of that wall giving way, of the distinction between self and other dissolving, I could not go through with it. Or rather, I could not let him go through it.

He granted my wish, Phoebus with his gentle hands. He gave me all the years of those grains of sand. But I forgot one thing, I forgot the most important thing, I forgot to say, "And let me stay the age I am now, in my firm peach youth, for the whole span." And he was no fool, he knew what I'd asked for, and what I hadn't. So he granted me my wish, and he punished me for refusing what I owed him. Instead of letting me live out those grains of sand with my youth intact, he let me age. Instead of living out this existence with firm flesh and strong bones and full lips and full breasts and a laugh that came easily and joy that offered itself up to me readily, instead of sanguine strength, I embarked on an elongated withering. By the time I reached eighty-eight years old, for example, I'd aged at a human rate, was as brittle and decrepit as anyone who makes it to that advanced age. From there, the aging slowed, and I became more and more embrittled over hundreds and hundreds of years.

To see me now is to see the way veins swell across the birdwing-bones of my hands, inky ropes that shift closer to the color black with each passing year. The discolorations on my flesh, the splotches on my forearms, there below my eye, freckles that won't stop blooming. See the way my flesh hangs away from the bones in my arm? Flesh like pecked and sagging chicken skin. I make a person more aware of the concept of skeleton. And my chest? Forgive this slow unbuttoning (my fingers are not as deft), I'll show you. See? I don't know where my breasts went. I used to have them. Now, my chest, two empty pouches made of suede with a few grains of sand weighing down the bottom. Time enacts its wearing. It brittles and shrivels and drains. I am seven hundred years old.

Long ago, in my true youth, just before I turned

forty, the gray came to my hair. At first, the strands stayed clustered in the territory above my right eyebrow, a gray-white sweep like water falling over rocks. And they told certain facts about time. With years, of course, more came. But it was that first little bit that was so baffling—I would look in the mirror and think, how could this be? This gray says something that my mind and body don't believe; this hair is out of alignment with how I understand myself inside. I feel one way (young!); my body shows a different truth.

For a time, the bafflement morphed into a low-grade pain. I noticed going unnoticed. On the street, others' eyes no longer moved up and down me, or locked with mine in invitation. And I mourned that loss. But I still had my heat and wildness inside, the interest in what might come next, that certain wavelength that poured out of me. That did not go away, nor did I let it. Time moved me from the peach-flesh of youth and landed in me a deeper sort of smolder, one that had nothing at all to do with fruits and more to do with heat.

As soon as you believe it's all downhill, as soon as you close yourself off to curiosity about what each new age might bring you, and as long as you derive your sense of self from how much other eyes adore you, your light will go out, your heat, extinguished. The vital pulsing thing inside will dim and fade. Life's much harder without it. A much more miserable thing indeed. I knew that misery, and I climbed out of it, knowing it would be no way to spend my thousand years on earth. Oh, your hip has disintegrated inside its socket? Bone grinds against bone in your knee? No desire is aimed your way? Your hands tremble when you hold the pencil or the spoon? The paths of memory seem buried under deeper and deeper snow that no shovel seems to clear? All manner of bodily indignities come tapping at your door? It's terrible, all of it. Stay curious. You do not know what else there is to learn.

This was how I managed to move through my years. Seven hundred down, with three hundred more to go. I have been so many people in this life. And of course I asked myself, again and again, why did I say no? What would have been if I'd let him enter me? Would it have been worse than this prolonged state of drain? There are certain questions that press against you but the answers do not arrive, like passengers on a train that never, never stops. Those questions no longer come, and a more important one has taken their place: how to continue to make sense of yourself as time changes you?

Do I miss my firmer thigh, my fuller breast, my sharper mind? I do. What a wretched disappointment to lose these things initially. But the more important force lives on, I keep it burning, and people can feel that presence when they're with me. That force, I finally understand it now, is the continued ability to experience the beauty of this world.

To see me, from whatever state of youth you inhabit, is to confront a grotesque. It's frightening at first. The cobwebs in my mouth, the mothy texture of my skin. It's easier to look away from this hunched and wrinkled form, from my flapping loose-leaf flesh. But once you get past the initial horror, if you get close, ignore the smell, ignore the skull you can see below my almost hairless head, if you peer below the drooping flesh curtains of my eyelids, you'll behold new beauty. A beauty born of curiosity, of openness. Remember it. Take it with you. Keep it for when you'll need it in years to come.

We all wait for the long silence. We are all transformed by time. I will continue to disappear, from body, to whispers, to sighs. It is better this way, I know it now. All these years and I have come to know this above all else:

Immortality is the death of beauty. Beauty begins in endings.

SEMELE

"Fuck me like you fuck your wife."

Shaft of light light light light light light light light light
light light light light light light light light light light
light light light light light light light light light light
light light light light light light light light light light
light light light light light light light light light light
light light light light light light light light light light
light light light light light light light light light light
light light light light light light light light light light
light light light light light light light light light light
light light light light light light light light light light
light light light light light light light light light light
light light light light light light light light light light
light light light light light light light light light light
light light light light light light light light light light

light light light light light light light light light light
light light light light light light light light light light
light light light light light light light light light light
light light light light light light light light light light
light light light light light light light light light light
light light light light light light light light light light
light light light light light light light light light light
light light light light light light light light light light
light light light light light light light light light light
light light light light light light light light light light
light light light light light light light light light light
light light light light light light light light light light
light light light light light light light light light light
light light light light light light light light light light
light light light light light light light light light light
light light light light light light light light light light
light light light light light light light light light light
light light light light light light light light light light
light light light light light light light light light light
light light light light light light light light light light
light light light light light light light light light light
light light light light light light light light light light
light light light light light light light light light light
light light light light light light light light light light
light light light light light light light light light light
light light light light light light light light light light
light light light light light light light light light light
light light light light light light light light light light
light light light light light light light light light light
light light light light light light light light light light

light light light light light light light light light light
light light light light light light light light light light
light light light light light light light light light light
light light light light light light light light light light
light light light light light light light light light light
light light light light light light light light light light
light light light light light light light light light light
light light light light light light light light light light
light light light light light light light light light light
light light light light light light light light light light
light light light light light light light light light light
light light light light light light light light light light
light light light light light light light light light light
light light light light light light light light light light
light light light light light light light light light light
light light light light light light light light light light
light light light light light light light light light light
light light light light light light light light light light
light light light light light light light light light light
light light light light light light light light light light
light light light light light light light light light light
light light light light light light light light light light
light light light light light light light light light light
light light light light light light light light light light
light light light light light light light light light light
light light light light light light light light light light
light light light light light light light light light light
light light light light light light light light light light
light light light light light light light light light light
light light light light light light light light light light
light light light light light light light light light light

light light light light light light light light light light light light light light
light light light light light light light light light light light light light light light
light light light light light light light light light light light light light light light
light light light light light light light light light light light light light light light
light light light light light light light light light light light light light light light
light light light light light light light light light light light light light light light
light light light light light light light light light light light light light light light
light light light light light light light light light light light light light light
light light light light light light light light light light light light light light light
light light light light light light light light light lightlightlightlightlightlight
lightlightlightlightlightlightlightlightlightlightlightlightlightlightlightlightlight
lightlightlightlightlightlightlightlightlightlightlightlightlightlightlightlightlight
lightlightlightlightlightlightlightlightlightlightlightlightlightlightlightlightlight
lightlightlightlightlightlightlightlightlightlightlightlightlightlightlightlightlight
lightlightlightlightlightlightlightlightlightlightlightlightlightlightlightlightlight
lightlightlightlightlightlightlightlightlightlightlightlightlightlightlightlightlight
lightlightlightlightlightlightlightlightlightlightlightlightlightlightlightlightlight
lightlightlightlightlightlightlightlightlightlightlightlightlightlightlightlightlight
lightlightlightlightlightlightlightlightlightlightlightlightlightlightlightlightlight
lightlightlightlightlightlightlightlightlightlightlightlightlightlightlightlightlight
lightlightlightlightlightlightlightlightlightlightlightlightlightlightlightlightlight
lightlightlightlightlightlightlightlightlightlightlightlightlightlightlightlightlight
lightlightlightlightlightlightlightlightlightlightlightlightlightlightlightlightlight

so bright it was a darkness, so bright it was sound.

I said the words to Jove. He who'd come to me before, he who'd been inside my body, he who'd had a wife forever. He who'd made me pregnant. I wanted to see who he was. I wanted to see what he was. (There are some things you should not see. There are some things you should not know.) I looked into the black wall of light and saw the nothings that were there, only absence all around me. "Let me feel the truth of you." He thought he was so mighty. A light so bright it was emptiness. Oh, I realized, oh of course, you do not fuck your wife. And then, as fast as that, I was only ash.

MEDUSA

Translators build the bridges. The chasm between languages is a deep ravine of silence. So what can we do but trust that the translators' bridges are sturdy, will carry the weight of meaning from one side of the ravine to the other? But all these bridges are faulty. Hitches and chinks because one language cannot cross over to another language unaltered and unflawed.

And some of these bridges lead meaning into exile.

Which is where this story has been living. Far removed from its home. I am the home of this story. After thousands of years of other people's tellings, of all these different bridges, of the wrong words leading meaning and truth astray, I'll tell it myself. The story of how I got my snakes. It's short.

Let's be specific. These were the colors in my hair:

wheat, copper, and mahogany. It fell in waves down my back. See it. Wheat. Copper. And mahogany.

I was this tall and when I told people I was this tall they always said, you seem so much taller. I was one of those people who seemed taller than I was. I stood up straight and I carried myself with force. I remember how I was.

A certain sort of voice tells the story long enough and part of you ends up believing it. In hearing the telling of my story, I have heard the words "seized and rifled." I have heard the word "deflowered." I have heard the words "attained her love." The words have made me question, was I wrong? Was it maybe not that bad? Was I just not strong enough to handle it?

"Attained her love."

This euphemism, this shorthand, this *obscuring*. Let me tell you. Neptune, who smells like the sick, muddy rot of low tide, forced me into the temple of Minerva. He grabbed a fistful of my hair and yanked it so hard I screamed. The words for what happened next are not "seized and rifled." Not "deflowered." And not "attained her love." The word is force. The word is violence. Violation. Force. Chaos. Force. Violence. Chaos. Force. Violation. Rape. Rape. Rape. Rape. Rape. Let's say what it was. He put his body where I did not want his body. This is the moment I was amputated from myself.

Minerva stood there and hid her eyes and didn't help. Untouched, above it all, she was disgusted that this thing should happen in her holy place. This desecration. But she wasn't mad at Neptune. He went back to ruling the seas. Unscathed. Unpunished. Continued with his life as though returning home from a morning's errand to the butcher and the bank. Got what he wanted. Went on his way. Not me. I did not get what I wanted, and I did not get to continue on with my life. I was the one who was punished by Minerva. It started as a tugging, a tightness across my scalp, as though some large fist had grabbed my hair and pulled. My waves of hair, its rich color, its thickness, all of it tightened, coiled, twisted. I put my hand up to my head and ripped my hand away. Where there was hair now muscled creatures writhed and hissed, scaled and with eyes that burned. The snakes grew from my scalp like thick carnivorous vines rising out of the rich pulpy soil of the marrow of my skull. I became a serpent-headed calamity.

And Neptune rules the deep. He did not rifle me or deflower me and he sure as fuck did not attain my love, I'll tell you. He forced his body on my body. A tidal wave of foul water. And in all the tellings and retellings, no one got it right. And my words can't get there either. They're closer though. They're closer, I'll tell you that.

And another thing. It wasn't just the twine and snarl of the snake nest on my head. I deserved more punishment than that for the crime committed against me, vilified further for the wrong this so-potent god force did against me. So to look upon me, to see my monstrosity, was to be turned to stone. I watched as people's eyes would fall on me, and the horror in their faces as their limbs filled with wet cement, curing, hardening, stilling them for all time in stony rictus. My hall is a menagerie of statues, an exhibit of a perverse and masochistic sculptor carving different personifications of fear. I was too much. I was too much for anyone to bear. It was the most terrible thing, to horrify a person into paralysis, to know, with every encounter, that I am a monster too frightening for anyone to see, or touch, or love.

I am so lonely. I have been in exile so long. So many other people have tried to tell my story. For a long time, it made me disbelieve what I knew was true. Now, I tell it myself, with the force of the words that I choose.

And the last thing I'll tell you? It's not the snakes that are so petrifying to people. It's not the serpents writhing from my head that turn people to stone. Don't you know?

It is my rage.

I hope for a day when a fury as white-hot as mine can be held by another, accepted, understood, maybe even shared. I am not optimistic and in the meantime the statues in my hall grow in number and cast gruesome shadows on the floor.

CAENIS

I didn't "lose" my virginity. Someone took it from me. On a beach. I was young. He felt sorry afterward and said, more or less, I'll grant you anything you want. Anything I want? Why'd it take doing what he'd done for my want to matter? Why hadn't that mattered before on the beach? Anything I want? Now? As if there was something on offer in this world that could undo what had been done? As if I didn't understand that this was not remorse but another display of power? As if I didn't understand who he was and what he could do? Did he think being a god made a difference at all? Anything you want. As though I was a child with a skinned knee, kiss kiss, you're okay, here's a Band-Aid, you're all better. Why are we put on this earth? To experience pain and see where it takes us. Anything I want. "I never want to suffer like that again. Make me a man." "You got it," said the rapist. What else do you need to know?

ARETHUSA

I am my own microclimate. Forecast: too warm, probably humid, ever-present chance of flood. I used to get so embarrassed about how much I sweat. Not everyone understands what it feels like when your body is a swamp, drops slipping down your temple, or collecting at your lower back as you stand there chatting about the coming rain or the size of the moon.

I sweat when I laughed. The big full-body laughs that distort your face and remind you of the muscles in your stomach. I sweat sitting on the papered table of a doctor's office, no matter how air-conditioned those small and windowless rooms might've been. I sweat when I cried—or, maybe more accurately, I sweat when I tried not to cry, a prickle of sweat at my back a first signal that tears were coming, drizzle before the drench.

At some point, I overcame the embarrassment. I accepted my lot. This is the body I have, this is one of the things it does. So instead of trying to pretend it wasn't happening, I'd say out loud to anyone I met, first thing, Oh hello I'm sweating! or I'm probably going to drip sweat all over you! I'd hug people, knowing they'd feel the damp, and say, unselfconsciously, I'm soaked! What a relief, to shed that cringing sense of interior horror at myself. Plus, I was good at keeping people warm.

But this warm body of mine brought trouble, too. A summer hunt in the woods, and I'd pushed especially hard, run miles along paths in and out of shade, and I was hot and happy, my hair clung to my forehead, you could've wrung sweat water from my clothes. I came upon a stream, its banks lined with willows and poplars, the trees seeming to tilt themselves toward the water. I laughed at my luck to find this place and removed my shoes. After hours on the trails, each step a pounding down on earth, to feel the cool water surround my feet, cool each tendon, unswell each well-used muscle, a euphoric pleasure. I pulled up my dress and went knee deep, and a thousand tiny cooling hands rubbed the weary out of me. Knee deep, another step, my thighs, and I knew then I needed to put my whole body in the water.

I had this section of the forest to myself. It was around the time when Proserpina disappeared. There she was picking flowers in a field. Then she was gone. Everyone in the woods was talking about it. A lot of people were looking. It was a hotter summer than usual, maybe from the heat of Ceres's fear. I removed all my clothes and draped them over a low branch of a young willow by the water's edge. What a pleasure it is being naked outside, to feel the air touch parts otherwise covered by clothes. Air and sunlight touching the belly, the lower back, the full length of the legs. But something felt different. I'd spent a thousand summer afternoons stripping off my clothes and swimming, but this afternoon I lingered for a moment by my clothes. Proserpina's disappearance haunted the back of my thoughts and I wondered, am I maybe not as safe as I think I am? But we cannot live our lives in fear.

Ankles, shins, knees, I paused. Thighs. Mid, inner. Higher. A clench, a ripple, goosebumps. Water around the waist and I lowered myself in. I dove around like the dolphins do, hair slicking down like an otter's tail. Sweetest reward to surrender yourself to a body of water. Body because it is something to enter and be absorbed by, because it offers a certain release, in a way not possible on mountainside, or forest path, or dune. The water holds all of you.

And then the noise. A squelching burble rising from deep and breaking through the surface, a glotted sticky heaving, the noise the big animals make after you've slit their throats and they are gulping on their blood. Fear leaked down the back of my spine—this was not a noise that signaled something good or right—and I splashed out of the stream onto the opposite shore. I paused for a moment, saw my dress on the limb across

the water, and listened again, my heart thumping inside me.

Then the bubbling rattle became clearer.

"Don't go," said a hoarse, choking voice. Each of my
muscles tightened at once. Especially the ones around
my ribs. Especially the ones in my calves. "Join me
again." River god, Alpheus. "Back in the water," he said.

In the bad dream I used to have again and again,
I'd find myself someplace and realize I had forgotten
to put on shoes. Everything fine and familiar and then
everything *all wrong*, a sense of chaos and doom, a vul-
nerability, a humiliation. The horror is twofold. One:
something is deeply wrong with my mind if I have forgotten such a basic thing. Two: I won't be able to run.
The combination brought a sickening fear.

Here on the bank of a stream, my nightmare was real.
"Don't leave," said the muddy voice again. My clothes
on the other side of the stream moving in the breeze like
laundry on a line. And there in the shade my shoes, still
as stones, their leather straps waiting to be laced. But
they would not be laced. And my clothes would remain
on that branch. I had to run. Bare bodied, barefoot. My
legs, which I'd used so much already, found speed and
strength, and I whisked away from him. "Why are you
leaving?" he yelled. "Don't leave!"

My naked flight only increased his excitement and
he took human form—slick skinned, glistening—and
began running after me. Twigs snapped beneath his
steps. His breath was steady and quick. He called my
name.

For a moment I was reminded of being a child, of the feeling of pure fright that comes when running up the stairs with a darkened house below, sure there's something there behind you. The giddy fearful leap into bed and the pulling of the covers all the way over to render you invisible to the force that pursued you up the stairs, absorbed into a cloud of undercover safety.

I ran without shoes, without clothes, unaware of the leaves against my skin as I raced by, unaware of the stones and sticks beneath my feet. I ran to the east, the sun at my back. Over open flat fields, up hills and down. Faster than him for miles. Until I couldn't, and the god of the river was close behind me. So I used my voice and I cried out for help. I pleaded to Diana, my mentor, my goddess, to protect me, please.

Diana heard me. She pulled a single cloud from the sky and steered it earthward so it wrapped itself around me, obscuring me from Alpheus. Inside this thick damp fog I stood, still except for the rise and fall of my chest as I tried to catch my breath. This muggy mist held me, the moisture all around, particles dense and close, like the humidity from breathing too long with your head under the covers. A gray-white nothing all around me, the color of blindness, I imagine. Not dark, but a muted, glowing gray. A shadowless cloud. It almost felt like drowning.

Alpheus couldn't see me, but he was close. He moved around the cloud, circling me—he'd seen that my footprints had stopped, he knew I was nearby. He waved his hands through the mist and the minuscule pearls of vapor shifted around them. He said my name, the sound carried to me on tiny beads of moisture, his voice bursting in my ear with every droplet. I couldn't move, or cry out, and here, now, from running, from fear, from being enclosed in the clammy hold of a cloud, I began to sweat.

Every pore opened and on came the water. Drips slid like an army on the move down my back. Broke through the stormwall of my eyebrows and slid into my eyes. Beads rose and collected around my wrist. Ran down my chest and slicked over my breasts. A cold dread sweat, and water dripped from my shoulders, from my hair, from my fingertips, and the drops hit the dirt and darkened it. I shifted my feet and felt a puddle and the puddle grew as my solid form dissolved, the bones that held me up, the muscles that helped me move, each fingernail, each tiny strand of hair, the slick red insides of me, my teeth and jaw and tongue, all melted away into water. My whole self liquefied.

I still wasn't safe. Water is drawn to water, and Alpheus recognized me in the water I'd become and returned to his river form so that he could join with me, so that we could mingle and run together, one whole flow.

Diana rescued me again. She cracked the earth and I sped into the chasm she created, cascading down deep into the dark undercrust. I moved quickly in the dark places, and lost Alpheus behind me. The world below was new to me. The things I saw underneath. Underground mountains, creatures that glowed with blind eyes that dangled off antennae, butterflies with bodies the size of bread loaves and wings the size of kites whose abdomens throbbed a jewel-like blue light, plant blooms that lived off the inner waters and the earth's internal heat, feathery leaves that spread across warm rock. Other creatures, furred and fierce, skulked about, with long claws and long jaws lined with mean teeth. These demons hid in caves, in the darkest parts of the world below. The thing I felt as I moved through this dark new place: in the depths, I am getting close to something important and true. I saw the small furred clawing monsters who slipped around in shadows. I saw the glowing bits that brought small light to a pressing sort of dark. If I kept going farther down, I'd come upon something I needed to know, that maybe not everyone could access. The pull was strong and I went darker, leaving the world I knew behind. There was so much to explore here. Altered now as water, I went down.

I slipped through worlds I don't have the words for, where the gloom and dread pressed, where gravity tugged with more muscle, each step an effort, each blink testing the limits of your energy, when it's all you can do to keep from placing yourself on the ground and letting yourself get gobbled by the dark creatures, how that, in some ways, would come as a relief.

Darkness has its own gravity. It has its own ways of seducing. Just a little lower, keep coming, you'll find something extraordinary. Painful, maybe. Frightening, maybe. But just stay down here long enough and you'll reach it. That's the promise of the dark, that eventually you'll hit something real.

I shifted and moved and slid and finally edged into the trickling tributaries of the River Styx, into its gray-watered eddies. I raised my head and that's when I saw her. Proserpina, slumped in a large dark throne, looking small and wan. Her eyes were aimed at some non-distance, the static of fear buzzed off her. She sat in nervy stillness. She'd been stolen by Pluto, it was clear, snatched from above and made unconsenting queen of the land of the dead. What a land it was—the color of ash, a dim untouched by dawn, all noise muffled, a strangled inchoate whispering, the shifting shades of sentient body-shaped mists, mouthless, drifting, an orchard with trees bearing gray fruit, spoiled before falling from their stems, every plant looking strangled, small animals darting in the shadows, each breath in my chest became more and more of an effort against the oppressive, unrelenting gloom. And Proserpina, a stranger in this world and a stranger to what her underworld king wanted of her.

I watched her for a while. She looked so alone, and so young, her eyes dull and darty, the color absent from her cheeks. I couldn't carry her back to her mother, but I could tell her mother where she was. And so I made my way back up.

On the surface of the world, her mother, in mourning, had salted the earth with grief. Crops withered. Livestock starved. A spreading state of barren. Ceres, I called. Ceres. You can stop making the world a wasteland, please. I know where your daughter is. I saw her with my eyes. And I told her where she was and Ceres stood like a statue, a stony rage took hold of her, as though the news had paralyzed her. But her senses returned. She looked at me with fire in her eyes, nodded, and aimed her chariot toward Olympus to take it up with Jove.

Now, above again, I see the stars I had forgotten. I feel the tree limbs bend and skim my skin. The whole broad sky opens itself above me. Even in the dark, bits of light shine. I lift my head, I wring the water from my hair. There, the moon. The white light of it dances on my surface. I'm made of water. I dance with the light.

THE HELIADES

Parents set up a circus tent. Parents—these clowns, these trapeze artists, these lion tamers, these strange ringmasters trying to control the show underneath the tent. Parents or their stand-ins, the different forms care-takers can take. As children, we live underneath this tent, and we watch the highwire act, we see the acro-bats fling their bodies over their bodies, we touch the trunk of the elephant, we get roared at by the sad, scared lion, and we think, *This is life, this is regular, this is how it looks for everyone.* In time we learn that's not true at all, it's different under every tent. But what's the same? It's probably strange for each of us. The strangeness of learning how to be alive from the people under the tent with you, who brought you into their tent even as they were trying to set it up, doing the best they could maybe, but fumbling with the ropes, hitting rocks when they plowed in the stakes, still learning how to balance on someone else's shoulders. It's their first time through being alive, too, and they don't recognize the power they have in the miniature world they build. It's useful to have brothers and sisters, people who know what it's like under your specific tent, because it can be a hard thing to make sense of, and it can be hard to make another person understand. Brothers and sisters can sometimes make things feel a little easier. Sometimes they are protectors.

But sometimes they can't protect.

There were four of us under our tent. My two sisters, my brother, Phaethon, and me. Our parents, Clymene and Phoebus, made six. I'm the oldest so I'm speaking on behalf of the three sisters. We were a gang, the four of us kids, and sometimes we kicked and punched each other and stole things from each other, and read each other's private diaries, and there were tears and shouts and we were sometimes monsters in the way that children are monsters. It was a strange circus, with a faraway mom who lived in a nest of her own self-obsession and dread and a distracted dad who wasn't around because he brought the sun to the world every day.

We worried about Phaethon, we always did. He was sensitive and proud and defensive. He was sad but wouldn't say so, maybe didn't even know so, and he made all of us laugh when he wasn't being sullen.

Some so-called pal started teasing him, told him there was no chance Phoebus was his dad, that our mom had been lying all these years. Phaethon went red in the cheeks and pretended not to care. "You're full of shit, Epaphus," he said, "and all the girls talk about how your breath smells like a sewer." But he came home and cried to our mom.

If only he'd come to us instead.

We would've said: "Who cares, Epaphus is a nothing, a jealous worm, you don't need to listen to him, you know what you know and you are what you are. Trust us. We say the true things with force. Let's play catch in the yard." And five minutes later we would've been laughing. And the next day we would've found Epaphus and surrounded him and said, "Hey, little worm, are you so jealous, are you so small and jealous? If you touch him we will rip your fingers off and eat them." And that would've been the end of that. He's our brother and we're ferocious and we protect each other.

But he went to our mom. And instead of wrapping him in her arms and assuring him and telling him not to listen to jealous bullies, she took Epaphus's words personally as though this child had insulted her. She read it all wrong. She thought: *People think I'm a liar? That a god wouldn't want to sleep with me?* She didn't try to calm poor Phaethon, not even for a moment. "You go up to your dad and you tell him to prove it to you. He'll show you, I promise, ask for anything you want." She riled him, fanned the flame of his hurt, showed him he was right to be upset.

And up he went to find our dad, and Dad said, "Of course, my son, to prove that what your mother says is true, I'll give you anything." A vow we all wish he hadn't made. No god can refuse what they've promised. Phaethon was excited but didn't know what to do, he was too young to know anything, and he thought of how he could rub it in Epaphus's face. And he saw Dad's chariot and he said, "Let me drive." And Dad said, "Oh no. No, no, no. I'm the only one. It's too much for you. It's too much for anyone but me." But Phaethon loved the thought of zooming over Epaphus's head in the chariot that brought the sun, and he persisted. Over and over our father tried to dissuade him. "Phaethon, no, not this. Jove himself can't carry out this task. It's too dangerous for you, a mortal, and young. Let my worry for your safety be proof that you're my son." But Phaethon wouldn't be persuaded—once he'd had this idea he couldn't give it up, stubborn and seduced by the danger, the power, the trying to do what only Dad could do. He insisted on exactly what he asked and our father had to agree. Phaethon hopped on and took off.

You could say he lost control, but he never had it in the first place. The horses sensed a different pair of hands at the reins, and they tore through the sky. And what's hard for us is thinking about him up there, getting dragged and tossed, and how terrified he must've been, so scared, maybe crying, maybe shaking, trying to pull the reins, not knowing what to do, regretting his wish and just wanting to be home with us in the backyard playing catch, just one more game of catch after dinner as the sun goes down. We think of him ripping through this nightmare, past the monstrous creatures who live up there, nearly gutted by the horns of Taurus, stung by the Scorpion's tail, pinched in half by the Crab, clawed open by the Lion. Our brother, alone up there, so afraid he can't even cry, gripping the reins as tight as he can, making small noises, whimpers. He must've felt so alone. This is the thought we can't stand. Because we saw him as a baby and we saw him as a boy with his stuffed animal dog. And we heard his voice crack when he was growing into himself. And we saw when he wanted to be tough. We saw when he fought tears. We saw him sad and lonely, the three of us sometimes excluded him even though we loved him, and we wish we hadn't left him out, and we wonder if maybe that's what made him sad. We teased him and he teased us and we all laughed and played catch and it was nice because we could tell he loved us, and we loved him.

Up there, he couldn't stop, he couldn't get control, the horses dragged him this way, that, up high enough so he careened against the stars, and low enough so that first the earth's peaks lit fire, and then the heat of the sun burned away all moisture in the soil. Trees were cinders; fields were dust. Rivers, streams, and lakes boiled, evaporated to their beds. Whales wouldn't breach; to surface was to burn. Towns, cities, the world became a furnace, smoke so thick Phaethon lost his way even more. Earth herself begged Jove to make it stop, and choked on smoke as she cried out. Jove did what needed to be done. He threw a thunderbolt at Phaethon, direct hit, and our brother fell through the sky like a shooting star, ignited by the bolt, all the way back to earth. Our father put his face into his hands and in his grief, for one whole day, there was not a single ray of sun.

We three sisters found the place where his bones were buried and flung ourselves upon the ground. We lost ourselves in grief. We wailed and mourned and were helpless in our sorrow, our young brother gone gone gone. Who were we without him? Incomplete.

Brothers go away sometimes. Our poor scared brother all alone in the sky where we couldn't help him. Our poor sad brother who was urged on by a small-headed mom. And after a month of mourning at his grave, the three of us began to be rooted to the earth where Phaethon fell. In our grief we started to change into a three-tree grove of poplars. Mom rushed around and tried to pull our bodies from the trees we were becoming, and every twig and branch she broke was breaking off a finger, an arm. "Leave us, leave us," we screamed, blood dripping from our branches. "You and Dad are both useless! You can't do anything right! Leave us alone!" we yelled as we hardened further into our new forms.

Now, just this once I will not speak for my sisters, because I do not know if they share this feeling that I have (but if I know them, which I do, I bet that I am not alone): I think about wrapping one of my branches around our mother's throat and pressing there until she's dead.

We make a new tent with our boughs. It's all that we can do. There will be no children here, not under this tent, only the small soft animals of the forest who take comfort in our shade.

ALCMENA

I did everything right. I took being preggers *very* seriously. You've got to! The way I ate, the way I exercised. Weights, yoga, and pilates for expecting moms. Lots of brisk walks. And foodwise, I probably caused an avocado shortage in Mexico. I'm not kidding! I was buying them by the case. Those omega-3s, baby. Lots of Brazil nuts, lots of those lush and leafy greens—kale, chard, collards, broccoli rabe—do you pronounce it *rabe* to rhyme with *abe* or *rabe* to rhyme with *rob*? Spinach, dandelion greens, jeez, if it was leafy and green, I sautéed it with garlic or made it into a smoothie. In the mornings I drank this superfood babybrainbuilder slurp. Homemade yogurt, peanut butter, grass, tinctures of nutmeg oil, anchovy oil, and, what else, cinnamon, boiled chicken chunks, dried myrtle root, powder of bear claw, and these pills my Chinese healer gave to me. Who knows what was in those! Whatever it was, it worked because I could feel this baby *growing*. I allowed myself to eat exactly what I wanted while also focusing on ingestibles with the highest density of nutrients. Like, if I wanted a bowl of peanut butter chocolate chip ice cream, I'd say hell yes, and get myself a spoonful of peanut butter and a square of vegan stevia-sweetened chocolate. I don't want to say it's about indulgence, but in some ways, that's exactly what it's about! But I did get a lot of comments. Because of how big I was. Most women go by that fruit-and-veg chart, like the little nugget is going from lentil to lime to bell pepper to spaghetti squash (love those!) to cabbage to coconut to pumpkin. For me, more like, watermelon to beach ball to hay bale. And people would see me on the street, taking my brisk walks, and be like, *How many people you got in there?* And *You giving birth to a teenager?* And *Do you fall on your ass when it kicks?* I usually tried to laugh. The kicking was an issue, to be honest. I mean, that kid was *strong*! I wouldn't fall on my backside, but it could stop me in my tracks, that's for sure. I tried to laugh those comments off. Probably people were jealous, is what I figured. Big baby, child of a god, Jove's son, everyone knew, and my hair and my skin looked great. It's a responsibility bringing any new life into the world, and that responsibility increases two million percent when it's a demigod growing inside you. And believe me, I felt the weight of that responsibility in a literal way. There were mornings I'd wake up and think, *How is this my life? How'd I end up here?* And not in a grateful way, necessarily. And I'd think, *Oh, one drunk night, one bad decision I don't remember making, and my whole life is different.* But don't get me wrong. I also felt really proud, knowing that the person inside me had the potential to be something truly important, an actual hero of the world. And maybe all expectant mamas feel that way. I don't know. But I guess feeling like a vessel of someone else's potential felt, well, exciting on some days, most definitely, but also maybe a little isolating? Like maybe it felt a little harder to locate my own self? Also, there weren't a lot of women I could talk to about it. There weren't a lot of women who understood. I found the friends I had, the girls I hung out and partied with, well it felt like we were moving in different directions in life, and I wasn't really understanding them and they weren't really understanding me. And people get weird when they're jealous. And then there were the people who touched my belly without asking. Like they'd place their palms on my body. Without asking! Strangers! I'd grab their wrists. "Do I *know* you?" I'd ask. I'd look right into their eyes. They'd blush, apologize. "Don't you ever," I'd say. "Do not ever." "You think you can just *touch* me?" It's like when you're holding another human life inside yourself, suddenly you belong to everybody. I get it, I really do. It's exciting, but it's my body and you can't just touch it because you're excited. That's just a rule of thumb. Don't go around touching pregnant ladies you don't know. For one thing, already, with a baby inside you, you sort of feel—I mean, I definitely felt a little like my body was no longer my own? That suddenly not only was I sharing it with someone else, I'd sort of given it over to someone else? If that makes sense? I didn't feel that way all the time, but sometimes. But there was this one time, at the market, I was buying ginger root and chia seeds and, you guessed it, avocados, when he started kicking, and for once I wanted someone else to feel. And there was an old lady sniffing cantaloupes and I said to her, "He's kicking. Do you want to feel?" And she looked at me and maybe because I looked so fit and my belly was so big she felt nervous. "It's okay," I said, and I took her wrist to place her hand on the spot where he was kicking. She snatched her wrist away. "What are you doing?" she asked. "Why would I want to touch you?" And she kept squeezing cantaloupes and sniffing them. Probably it was the hormones, but I started sobbing when I got outside. Pregnancy is a roller coaster, that's for sure! I guess maybe in that moment, I just wanted to be touched. But I went to bed looking forward to my big morning baby-brainbuilder slurp and told myself, new morning, fresh morning, there's a baby of a god growing inside you. I don't know, maybe every mama thinks their baby is going to be great, but I really knew it. I really knew that the force inside me was going to be great. And I still know it! Look at him! Little Hercules. He's about eighteen months now. Sometimes I look at him and think, *You came from me?* He's just that beautiful. His hair's a little messy now—I need to give it a trim—but the way he romps around and he shares so well and has so many words already. Hercules, be careful on the slide, please!

I mean, talk about good genes, right? Sometimes I see the other mothers and their littles and I think, *How does she* deal *with that child*, the way it grabs or tantrums or throws its little snack-pack container of Cheerios on the floor. I try not to be judgmental, but it's hard. Or I see the parents giving their children M&M's or those dried cranberries. I want to tell them, *Don't you know what's in that?* And sometimes I do tell them. But it's none of my business and all I can do is control my choices. And I know my choices don't involve sweetened dried fruits or, my gosh, industrial candy. It's like, oh, yeah, good idea, let your baby play with the spray cleansers that live under the sink, or let them lick the subway poles, great idea! Herc only wears organic cotton. From a skin stand-point and an environmental standpoint, it's the only thing that makes sense. Ethically. His toys are made of natural materials. Wood, wool. It was the same with breastfeed-ing. I mean, you have breasts, you have a baby, isn't it obvi-ous what you're supposed to do? I shouldn't be judgmental, but also, every study ever done says it's so much better for the baby—nutrient-wise, allergy-wise, bacteria-exposure-wise, bonding-wise. And speaking of bacteria, that makes me think about natural childbirth. Honestly, I knew from the start that I wanted my birth plan to involve a natural, vaginal birth, even though I knew the size of him might do me right in. I wanted it in a bath. No drugs. No epi-dural. No C-section. Again, not to be judgmental, but everything the doctors say confirms that the baby needs to pass through the birth canal, like the process is in-complete if it's just pulled straight through a slice in the abdomen. The baby doesn't get essential bacteria that way, ones that keep it healthier, stronger, less allergic to nuts, less likely to get autism probably. I mean, I'm not positive about that, but it's probably true. I get it, it's a personal choice. One woman's neighbor, when she heard the woman was getting a C-section, said, "That's right, stay tight for Ted." I mean, yeah, great. Stay tight for Ted, but what about the bacteria your baby needs? What about the most natural act a woman can take part in? Stay tight for Ted, but at what cost to your baby? It's shocking. I was nervous for the birth, obviously. This was going to be a huge baby, and I wasn't sure my body could handle it. I've told so many people the story of his birth, I hope I'm not boring people. I was walking downstairs into the kitchen when my water broke and I thought, *Okay, here we go.* And I called on Lucina, deity of childbirth, to come and help the process, standard operating procedure. I had a doula and a team of midwives, too. And as I waited for the contractions, I put the kettle on to make red raspberry tea and started humming my calm song, just like they'd taught me. And Lucina arrived, and she pulled a stool from the kitchen and sat down outside the door of my home birthing room. I was pretty distracted by the whole being in labor thing, so I didn't think much of the fact that she was staying outside the birthing room, sitting there with her legs crossed and her hands clasped. I hadn't done this before, so I figured that's just how she did things. But eventually it became clear that this was *not* how she just did things. So I go into full labor. I'm sweating, I'm pacing, I'm lying down, I'm squatting, I'm trying to sing my calm song, I'm crying out, I'm wailing. I'm calling my herbalist in a panic attack. I'm feeling so deeply alone in the pain. Like I was entering some new realm. And it goes on and on and on. I try pushing. I push with every single muscle in me. All the muscles I've worked over years of running and yoga. Nothing. All the while, Lucina is sitting in the hall, her right leg crossed over her left, and her hands clasped over her right knee. She sat and sat and I thought I was going to die. I'm not kidding. At a certain point, I thought, *I can't do this. I'm not going to make it through this.* The pain was—well my gosh—there just aren't words for it really. If you know, you know. I'm serious when I say I was in full labor for seven days. Seven days! I laugh about it now, but it was *no joke.* Somewhere around hour a hundred and fifty of full labor, in a complete delirium, I finally realized what might be happening. Jove was the one who got me pregnant, it was just the one time, and I barely remember it. I used to drink a lot more than I do now. Though, these days, I have been drinking a little more again. But I wondered if maybe Juno was super jealous, which I get, her husband getting another woman preggers. Of course that's not cool. And I began to wonder if maybe Lucina and Juno were in cahoots, and that she was trying to kill me because of loyalty to her friend. I couldn't express anything at that point except grunts and howls, so thank god for Galanthis. She was this young woman on my midwife team and she was a sweetheart and tried to say all these kind, coaxing things, and she smudged sage around the room and fed me eggplant and had me do this bouncing thing, all to try to get that baby *out*. But nothing was working because Lucina was outside the room with one leg crossed over the other and her hands clasped. I was wailing, and honestly, I barely remember this point. I was totally delirious. Like honestly, maybe I was a little insane. But Galanthis knew about the whole deal with Jove, I'd confided in her, and she realized that Lucina was doing Juno's bidding, and so she closes the door for a little while and I'm screaming away, who even knows at this point, and then Galanthis goes rushing out the door and says to Lucina, "Oh my gosh, great news! She did it! It's a boy! She had a boy!" And Lucina, furious, unclasps her hands, and uncrosses her legs, and thereby undoes the lock that had kept me in labor for days, and that, for real, is when it happens. Lucina flies off, and right away I *know* it's happening. I lay down in the bath and the pain of this baby rips me in two. Herc was just over fifteen pounds, and my body hasn't recovered. Eighteen months later. I say ripped me in two, and I mean it. He tore me apart. But oh my gosh, it was so worth it. To see his head in the bathwater, with flower petals floating around? I'll never forget that. I saw him and I was more in love than I'd ever been. Honestly, maybe it was the first time I *was* in love! It sounds ridiculous, like totally woo-woo, but I'm serious: it transformed me. Motherhood has made me something else entirely. I am the mom of Hercules. That's not all I am, there's other stuff, too. But a lot of the time, it's all I feel like I am. A mother.

Sometimes it's enough. I mean, really, most of the time it's more than enough. My body is still not my own, and it never will be, as long as he and I both walk the same earth. Total transformation. I look at him and I just feel awe. The one hard thing though, Galanthis, when she realized she'd really been able to fool Lucina, she laughed. And the gods can be so catty, you know? She shouldn't have laughed. But she did. And before Herc was all the way out, Juno turned Galanthis into a weasel. A slim blond little weasel who slithers close to the ground. And, weirdly, when she gives birth to her littles, they come out of her mouth. I was grateful for what she did, so she lives here with me, I mean right here, on me. All of my clothes have a small pouch for her, so I can feel her sort of squirming around. She's so soft. She really likes to be pet on her belly. I like having her. I take really good care of her. And she squeaks in my ear sometimes. She's my friend. Honestly I've been a little lonely. I mean, I have Herc. But everyone needs adult companionship, right? A friend? She's my friend, soft little Galanthis, aren't you? Ouch, please don't bite. Aren't you?

PROCNE AND PHILOMELA

Have you ever ridden on a swallow before? No? Oh. I hope you'll like it. Some people get a little airsick, I'll warn you, the darting and swooping, and speeds that might surprise you. So if you start to get queasy, find the horizon with your eyes and just hold your gaze there. And here's a pack of wintergreen Life Savers. They can help, too. Ready? Use the step stool there and just climb on and sink in. My feathers will wrap around you, that's right. Just let yourself sink in. Right, yes, yep, they'll absorb you. If you get too warm, just let one of your legs dangle, like you would in the bed, out from under the comforter. We'll be moving shortly and you'll find the air all around you—most people don't get too warm, but I always like to say it just in case. The tour lasts about forty minutes, and, as you know, some of what you'll hear will be challenging. Maybe more so than you're anticipating. Good, no, I know, I know, that's why you're here. I understand, and I'm glad you're here. I just need to say it—some people have complained. Yes, I mean it. Oh, just that it's *too much*, and that I should've warned them, and that if they'd known how awful it was going to be, they never would've signed up. I want to respect each one of my guests, each person who climbs on and sinks in and *listens*. It's hard, believe me, I know. It'll get harder than you think. So. There you go. You've been warned.

So now, as long as you're settled?—good—we'll ease into things. You'll feel a bump and then a lift then it's on our way.

All right now, oh, it's beautiful. You're lucky to have such perfect weather. It's about sixty-one degrees up here right now, about twenty degrees cooler than on the ground. The winds are coming from the southwest, and I think we're in for a real stunner of a sunset. Oh, I can tell it's just going to be a beauty. There's that milky late spring air that always gives me hope. As we head toward our first stop, I'll start with some facts. We'll ease in.

There are eighty-four species of swallow. It's said seeing the first one of the year means good fortune comes your way. I've been a swallow now for, well, you don't need to know how long! Let's just say it's been a while. We make our nests in places with wide doors, places like stables and barns and sheds. On average, it takes about twelve-hundred back-and-forths to make a nest. And it's the work of the female swallows.

Hoopoes, in the Upupidae family, have this hideous flare of feathers on their heads. Sometimes it's pointed back like a crown, other times flayed out, and the tips of the crown are black, like it'd accidentally dipped its head in tar. The rest is a peachy orange. Yes, but not as vibrant as that. And the wings are bold striped, black and white. Ha, yes, a little like a prisoner, you're right. They've got long beaks and I don't have to tell you what that's a stand-in for. They use it to probe. I hate that word, don't you? They eat creepy-crawlies like cicadas and earwigs and ants. And they're aggressive. In finding and securing a mate, they battle, men and men, men and women, stabbing at each other with their long, sharp beaks. Do you know how many one-eyed hoopoes there are because of this? A lot. And the female makes a secretion that stinks of rotting meat while she's sitting on the eggs. It's to keep away predators. And, ugh, the most horrid thing, the babies, once hatched and living outside the egg for less than a week, hiss at threats like they're snakes, and if an intruder enters the nest, they aim streams of feces at them! Yes, I mean it! Oh, ha ha, yes, that's another way to say it. Oh dear. But I will say they have a nice call. *Thwoo-wooot. Thwoo-wooot.*

Nightingales build their nests low, close to the ground, not high in the trees, and they eat insects and seeds. When I was young, I used to imagine nightingales as having purple heads and green breasts and yellow bands and flowing long tails and the most beautiful eyes. Not like a parrot, they're too thick and showy. But a bird out of your dreams, like a fairy in a nightgown that's also a bird, with flowing dangling feathers that went for miles. Have you ever seen one? No? Well, if you're like me then you're in for a shock if and when you do—they look like any old warbler or finch or thrush! Just a boring brown bird like you'd see anyplace. Light brown like a mouse, sometimes with creamy feathers under their chin. Beak, not so long. Just really unremarkable. I don't say it to be mean. I don't know how people can tell them all apart, all the different small brownish birds. They're known for their song, a quick pep of notes high and low, *wheet wheet wheet wheet wheet, tnk tnk tnk, whirripwhirrup.* Oh yes, I've been practicing my mimics. Nightingales sing at night. The males are the only ones that sing. The females are mute.

So we're going to dip to the east here and swoop in toward where I used to live. Hold a little tighter as we'll be riding at some angles here. Yes, you can grip the feathers with your hands, no, don't worry, they're hard to pull out. And you can also grip with your thighs. As though you were riding on the back of a motorcycle. Right. Use your legs! All right, so below to your right you'll see the place I lived with Tereus. I came from Athens; he was from Thrace. Athens was at war and Tereus, well, the phrase is *came to the rescue.* He had money and he had power and he brought in his troops and won against the invaders. We were all grateful and impressed. And in thanks, Dad offered me up as a bride. It was exciting. It was a moment when the whole city let their shoulders loosen, let the tension of being under attack dissolve, and Tereus was a powerful figure, broad and dark-haired and commanding. It's amazing how different a person can end up being, isn't it? When they let you see the darker part of themselves? At this point I believe everyone's got that shadow in them, and that it either eats you alive or you learn to acknowledge its presence and try to stay on civil terms with it. That's a little beside the point though. As we dip to the right, you'll see a balcony there, on the third floor, overlooking the sea. Tereus would stand there for hours looking out. I used to ask him, "Hon, what are you thinking out there, you seem a million miles away." "I could try to explain but I don't think you'd understand it, so why should I waste my breath," he'd say. "Try me," I'd say, newlywed, trying to be sweet and kind and game. "You want to know? I'm thinking about the shit I took on the face of the man I killed in battle two weeks ago. I'm thinking about how frightened he looked right before I killed him, how he looked left and right to see what could save him. I got an erection from seeing that fear. My dick got hard. I was thinking about that erection. And I shit on his face because of that fear. If he'd been less afraid, I wouldn't have had to do it. It was amazing, his fear, and it was disgusting. I was thinking about that. Squatting over his face. Letting my balls dangle above his throat. He was dead already, but I liked the thought of him suffocating in my shit. That's what I was thinking about, standing out there. Are you glad you asked? Sometimes I think about business and what to say to who to make them do what I want. Sometimes I think about bending you over the worktable in the kitchen and pulling your hair back and grabbing your throat as hard as I can so I can feel all the tendons tight, and then surprising you by ramming my dick into your asshole."

Oh, oh, I'm sorry, you're right, I get carried away sometimes. That was more than you needed to know! Here, we're going to dip close and look in my old bedroom window. Hang on as we descend a little here. The new owners kept the bed. I used to be embarrassed but what can I do, yes, those are chains on the bedposts. That's how Tereus liked it. "My dirty prisoner," he used to say to me. I admit, it could be exciting, sometimes. And he could occasionally be quite gentle. Oh, but I should tell you, at our wedding, Juno, wedding patron, was absent. She had other places to be maybe. Hymen didn't show, neither did the Graces to give their blessing. You know who was there though? The Furies. Three of them, black-winged like bats, that strange stretchy wing material, not like feathers at all, and red-eyed— we'll be flying over the courtyard where the ceremony was held, see down below, and the forsythias all in bloom all around it!—with their gnarled hands and stinking breath and dog teeth in their faces. I didn't know it then, but it's right that they were there, deities of vengeance, holding torches they'd brought from a funeral. They stood at that corner, on the stairs leading into the house. That night, a screech owl sat on the roof above the bedroom, that tawny bird whose screech broadcasts calamity. These were the beginnings of the marriage. That night I conceived. Yes, bad news is one way to put it.

We're going to make a sharp turn around the back of the place. And I'll point out to you little Itys's room. That window there, with the bars on it, that overlooks the crags and the woods, that was the nursery. I'd sit in the rocking chair with him at my breast night after night. Tiny helpless little Itys. And oh my, look over your shoulder to the west at a particularly lovely bank of clouds. You're warm enough? Comfortable? Good.

Ooooooh, we're dipping down along the first floor. I'd like to show you the kitchen. I can't make promises, but occasionally the door is left open and we can get a look around inside. Oh, yes, good luck! Okay, please do hold on as we're going to have to be quick, I don't want anyone smashed with a broom by an angry cook. There, that oak worktable filling the center that Tereus talked about. And there's the set of cook's knives. I know, you wouldn't think you'd need as many! And the hearth with the spit there, oh, I can remember the crackle of fat as it dripped into the flame and hissed. And the massive stove. And from the ceiling, oops, close call! From the ceiling you see the pots and pans, notice that large one, big enough to bathe a baby! They've cleaned it up nice. New floors, got rid of the stains. Painted the walls, got rid of the stains. All right, out we go before we get caught.

So, back out into the light. We'd been married a year, and I was deeply homesick and missed my sister Philomela. I was a new mother and a new bride and far away from the world I knew and the people I loved. And so I said to Tereus, "Please, can she come stay with us for a while?" And Tereus agreed and took a ship to get her. He arrived in Athens and bowed at my father Pandion and said, "You know how women are, Procne wants her sister's company." And apparently that's when Philomela entered the room and everything changed.

We're heading east now back into the woods. Poplar, ash, oak, pine, beech. I promise we won't hit any trees. It'll get a bit dimmer soon—we're moving toward a particularly dense part of the forest. Look, you can see penny bun mushrooms at the base of some of the trees from this morning's rain.

Tereus saw Phila and wanted her, instantly. She's beautiful! She had long, wavy chestnut hair and big eyes and she was fresh and young. She was also, I want to emphasize, a *child*. And Tereus immediately changes his tune, going from "Ugh, women! Right?" which never would've won my father over anyway, to pleading with Pandion, professing how much he loved me and how there was nothing in the world he wanted more than to make me happy, and the one way he knew he could do it was to bring Philomela back to me for a time. Tereus could be compelling when he wanted to be, and he could make himself cry, so to seem even more sensitive and pitiable and soft, he let the tears come.

My father bought his pleas, reluctantly. He had never loved Tereus, and had this itching sense that something wasn't right with him. But Tereus was hugely grateful, and Phila was excited to go for a trip and come see me. The pure excitement of a child.

Look down on our right as we pass over a sacred

spring. Even prettier from up here, don't you think? The way the light hits it, and the way the branches are reflected?

The next day, before they set sail back here, my father pulled Tereus aside. And sometimes, well, sometimes this makes me cry so if that happens today, please bear with me. No, no, tears don't affect safety of flight in any way. Dad sat down with Tereus and put his hand on his shoulder, and you need to know, my dad was a quiet man. He was the kindest man. On our birthdays, he'd sneak into our rooms before we woke up and leave flowers so we'd wake up to blooms. He kept track of how I loved parsley, but Phila hated it, and that she liked to eat shrimp, but I thought the texture was gross. And the morning they left, Phila told me, he looked older, like he'd aged ten years overnight, with a deep sadness in his eyes. He held on to Tereus's shoulder and said, "I'm calling on your loyalty here. Please, please, guard Philomela lovingly, as a father would. And send her back as soon as you can." And then he turned to Phila and said, "Please come home as soon as you can. I already miss your sister so much. To have both of you gone—"

Oh dear. I'm sorry. You'll just need to give me a— dear dear.

Thank you. I'm okay, yes.

It will be cooler for the next little bit as we get deeper into the woods. You'll see the tree cover is thicker and there's that foresty smell, that earthy vinegar stink of rotting leaves. I agree with you, it definitely feels gloomier.

Now that I've gathered myself. Goodbyes are said. Phila's giddy; Tereus is descending further into monsterhood in his mind; and they set sail. Tereus didn't touch Phila on the boat—close quarters, too much risk of a scream and getting caught. But Phila says there was a moment when she knew things were not right.

She was leaning against the rail, looking out at the sea, at the point in the voyage where they'd slipped out of sight of the land they'd left, and couldn't yet see where they were going. Open ocean. Tereus comes up behind her and grabs her waist and does that thing where you pretend you're tipping someone overboard, when you play at pushing them and then pull them back. Phila squealed, thought he was just being playful. Tereus laughed, too, and said, "It would be so easy to push you in." Something in the way he said it made Phila's guts go cold. And from then on, she just wanted to get to shore, knowing she'd be safe once she saw me.

Notice how there are no real paths below us, how thick the bramble and brush are. There are thorns everywhere. If I let you off here, you'd be sliced to bits by the plants.

Phila counted the hours until the ship reached land and when it came into sight, she felt a sweeping sort of relief—she'll make it, she'll be reunited with me, she was just being silly about Tereus. She didn't know. When they pulled into the dock, she bounced on her feet, so eager to step foot onto land, to find me! It was late in the afternoon, getting dark, she wondered what we'd have for dinner, whether I'd remember that her favorite dessert was brownies with vanilla ice cream and chocolate sauce. I *did* remember, and I had made brownies for her that morning. These were her child thoughts.

"This way," Tereus told her, and they started in a direction away from the rest of the crew, and away from the lights of the city. He led her deeper and deeper into the forest, along the way that we've come. She kept asking, "When will we be there, isn't the palace the other way, is Procne meeting us somewhere?" Tereus didn't answer, just kept pulling her along. All Phila could do was hope she was being led to her sister.

Grip tight now as we're going to swoop low. Yes, here you'll see the hut. This is the hut where he brought her. This hut in the depths of the ancient woods. The door is broken off now, and the walls have started crumbling. Yes, we'll go inside. Hold tight.

Give your eyes a minute to adjust to the dim. It smells awful, I know. Now here is a moment in the tour where I ask you to hop off for a moment, stretch your legs, as we stand here in this hut.

Tereus brought her to this place, to this rank room we're standing in. He brought her to this hut, my young sister with her chestnut hair. She'd begun to cry. And I hate thinking of that because I knew Tereus loved when I cried, he loved when I seemed weak or fragile or broken. And the thought of him looking at her, as tears fall down her smooth cheeks—oh dear.

"Can I please see my sister?" she asked.

"Do you know how much I want you?" he answered. "Do you know how hard it was not to touch you all these days? The delay has just made me want you more. Phila, you beauty. Your father said to take care of you as a father would a daughter—when I saw Pandion embrace you, I envied him, and I thought, If you were my daughter, I'd embrace you in a way that wasn't what anyone would consider fatherly. I waited for his hand to drop down your back, to grab your little ass and press it into him. He didn't, but I would've, if you were my daughter. You're not my daughter though, and you have no idea what's in store for you. I get to touch you now."

And she didn't know. She had no idea. She didn't know what it meant that he got to touch her now. A hug maybe? But he could've hugged her before. Holding her hand? She would've welcomed a comforting hand on the rough seas. He approached her, here, in this hut. Please imagine him, a tall man with cold eyes and a dark beard, standing here, and please imagine my sister, Philomela, a girl, slight as a broom, her face wet with tears, just wanting to eat brownies with me.

And now please imagine Tereus taking three steps toward her. One two three. And touching her hair first, running his hand down her soft hair. And then touching her neck. And then using both hands and pressing them against the place where her breasts would be if she were old enough to have them.

And please imagine her starting to shake in fear.

And please imagine Tereus lifting her dress and roughly pulling it off her body. And please imagine her shivering and please imagine the feel of this dirt floor against your bare back. You see the stones. You see it's damp and cold. Touch it if you—no, all right. Please imagine Tereus tossing her to the floor, pinning her easily because she is a child, and spreading her, here, on this spot, where you stand, and holding her throat as he puts himself inside her. And he doesn't cover her mouth because, as you can imagine, there's no one near enough to hear her scream. And he likes the sound of her screams anyway. It makes him feel big. It makes him feel like he's got something that she can feel.

She screams for me. She screams for our father. She screams to the gods. And once he's off her, she pulls at her hair and cries out, "Don't you remember what you said to my father? How he asked for you to take care of me? Don't you remember that?"

Tereus laughed.

"What you've done, Procne will kill me for my crime. You made me betray my own sister. Everything is wrecked!" And the young thing worked herself up more and more, frenzied and terrified. "I'd rather be dead than this. But if the gods have any power, they'll hear me, and someday you will answer for this. You will pay and pay, I promise you. I will tell *everyone*. I will call it out from every rooftop what you did. And if I'm trapped here in this hut, I'll scream at the trees until they spread the message. The rocks will hear me and they'll cry, too. And heaven will come to know the truth. I will tell!"

Phila, poor powerful helpless Phila, my sweet sister.

There's a poet who says, there's no anger without fear. I believe it. Tereus would've said that Phila's words made him *angry*. What they did was make him afraid.

And a man whose fear has made him angry is one of the most dangerous kinds of men.

Please imagine Tereus pulling his sword from its sheath. Please imagine him grabbing Phila by the hair and yanking her head. Please imagine him tying her hands behind her. Here, right here where we stand. And please imagine Phila saying "Go ahead, go ahead, just do it," as she offers up her throat to his blade, hoping to have an end to this misery. "Just do it!" she cries. Please imagine her shaking. And please imagine now Tereus taking her tongue from her mouth, pinching it tight and tugging it as far out as it will go. Please imagine Phila's soft pink tongue. Please hear her cries as she continues to call the names of our father, and me, and the gods, the sound garbled and caught in her throat, her pink tongue wriggling between Tereus's dirty fingers. And please imagine Tereus raising his sword and bringing it down and severing Phila's tongue from her mouth. And please imagine how it's not a clean cut and how he has to saw at it until it falls to the dirt floor, there, where you're standing, and please imagine how it continues to wriggle, how it twitches and moves on the dirt floor. And please imagine the blood pouring from Philomela's face. And please imagine how pale she is and how she chokes on her blood. And then imagine, though it is hard, please imagine Tereus propelled again by lust for this tongueless, bleeding child. Imagine him on top of her, there, in the corner, on the floor, pounding away at her body.

```
A A A A A A A A I I I I I I E E E E E E E E E E E E E
A A A A A A A A A A A A U U U U U U U U L L L L L L L
L G G G G G G G G G G G G G G A A A A A A A A A A A A
A A A U L L L L L L L L L L L L L L L L L L L L N N N N
N N E E E E E E I I I I I I I I I I I I I I I E E E E E E E E E E E E
A A A A A A A A A A A A A A L L L L L L L L L L L G G
G G G G G G G G G G G G G G G G U U U U U G G G G
G U U U H H H H H H H H H H H U U U U U U U G A A
A A A A L L L L L L L L L L L L L L L L L L L L L L L L L L L L L L
```

This was the sound of her scream. I've been working on my mimics. Does it hurt your ears? I'm sorry.

```
A A A A A I I A I I I L L L L L L L L L L L L L L L L L L
G I I I I I I I I I I I I I I I I I I I I I I I I I I I A A A A A A
A A L L L L L L L L L L L L L L L I I I I I I I I I I I I I I I I I I I I I I I I I I I
I E E E E E E E E E E E E E E E E U U U U U U U U U G G G G
G U U U U U U U U U G G G G G G G G G G U U U U U U U
U U U U U A A A A A A A A A A A A A A A I I I I I I I I I I I I I I I I I I I I I I I
I I I I I I I I I I I I I I I I I I I I I I I I I I E E E E E E E E E E E E E E E E E E
E E E E E E E E E E E E E E E E E E E E E E E E E E E E E E E E E E
```

Please, now, climb back on and sink in. We're going to leave this place. Yes, just step back up. You feel weak in your knees? I understand. Do you want a minute? All right. Yes, have a Life Saver. All right. Ready? The feathers will absorb you. Let yourself be absorbed. A bounce, a lift, and on we go.

Yes, it's good to feel the air again. What I might do

now, as I can sense from the way you're holding on that you're feeling a little bit tense, I'm going to go higher than I normally would, above the tree line. Here we go, up and up. And back to the late afternoon light! It's a relief, isn't it? The sun still shines, there's warmth to be had. Oh, good, I can feel you calming already. The way the light hits the top of the trees, the way they dance in the breeze, wind the great choreographer. Yes, we'll take a moment just to enjoy it in quiet.

We're heading back toward the city now. Back toward the home Tereus and I shared. And I'll tell you what happened next. Tereus returned from his trip to Athens alone. "Where's Phila?" I asked when he walked in. "Oh, Procne. It's awful," he said. His eyes shined with his tears. "She's dead," he said. He made this lie in front of me, her blood and her body all over his skin. I collapsed and could only half hear his fabrication. Fast illness at sea, fever, madness, death. I was lost. My one sister gone. It was the worst pain I'd felt, a depthless sadness. The brownies in the tray and never one more chance to laugh with Phila, hug her, hear her soft feet coming down the hall. Gone.

And to your left, down near that large sharp rock, you'll see where I made her tomb. It was empty, of course, just an echoey sepulchre, vacant chamber. And you'll see the bones of the animals I offered in sacrifice, honoring her death, the Shade she was, gone somewhere in the deep sea. I wore mourning clothes and never smiled.

It was for nothing, this tomb. Though something in her had been killed, Phila wasn't dead.

Now we'll hug the cliffs and you can look out to sea. Breathe in the air, there's nothing better than a lungful of ocean air. Good for the body, good for the brain. What a beautiful late afternoon! You could not ask for better. We're closing in on low tide but the sea is swollen from the full moon which should be rising shortly. This section of the tour is for breathing easy and enjoying the views. Enjoy!

A year went by, and life continued, and my grief clung to me. Then one day, a Thracian serving woman arrived in the city. If you see the pillars of the temple there, and the small bakery beside it, that's where I was standing, out with little Itys for a walk. The woman bowed to me in the street and handed me a thick cloth, rolled tight. I took it from her and waited until I was home to unroll it. I've stashed it nearby. I'll ask you again to hold tight as we're going to do a little more dipping and swooping, yes, here we go. Just a little more up-down back-forth, and you can see that great oak? Rising above the rest of the trees at the edge of the park? I've hidden that cloth there, up in the tree, and will show you firsthand what I saw when I unrolled it.

Now, grip tight with your legs because I'm going to be a little more vertical as I work to spread the cloth. Nope, I've got it. Thank you, no, I'm all set. I said I've got it.

Okay, now, you can see. Big as a bedsheet. On a crude loom, Phila made this, she sent me this message.

She wove these words in purple thread. See them, in that rich color. Read each word. Read her story. Read the way she tells all that I've told you. These are her words. She wove her story. It's the only way she could find voice to tell. I'll give you a moment.

Now read it again.

No, you cannot touch it.

I had this spread before me on the floor. I stared at it. I read it. I read it again. First in my heart: She's alive. My sister's alive. And the joy was dizzying and took the strength from my knees. And then the sickness took hold. I stood and I was silent and I was still. Some people can't believe this. Some people ask, "How could you not have immediately started screaming for help? How could you have wasted another minute of letting Phila stay in her horrible den?" Well, you don't know how you'd respond and the way these words slammed into me stripped me of my own words for a time. And believe me, I searched for the words that would rightly name my rage. There were none.

I did not shout. I did not cry. I did not speak. A tunnel presented itself in my brain and I burrowed into it. I sunk into myself. You know about that? About sinking into yourself? Have you thought about revenge? Yes, you're probably right, at least one time or another.

The route we're taking now follows the path I took the night I found the hut. It was the feast of Bacchus and all the Thracian women gathered at night to engage in the secret rites. I stood in my room beforehand, door locked, and I adorned myself. I wrapped vines around my head, a crown of leaves that trailed down my back and over my shoulders. I slung the deerskin over my left shoulder. It smelled of dust and leather, and weighed heavily against my arm, its face peering out of dead eyes at my face. We were twins, joined for this one night. I looked in the mirror and saw fire in my eyes.

Out into the streets I went. I joined in the wild parade. We cried and shrieked and it was a chaos of vines and fur and women's bodies and women's voices rising into the night. Animal pelts and the secret spells and vessels of wine passed around and around. We followed the side streets you'll see right below, the narrower streets. Then, feigning frenzy, faking that I was wholly taken by Bacchus, I veered a sharp right, away from the crowds, away—Oh, I'm sorry, I should've warned you about that turn! Get your grip back? Good, good. Back to the facts. Far from frenzy, I had never been more clear-eyed in my life. From the streets I made a path into the forest. We'll dip in, back into the bramble. I strode through the woods and my fury propelled me without care of prickers. I moved with more force than I'd ever moved in my life. Like my body was not my own. Here, by this brook, by this stone, by these pines. And now, back at the hut.

It's hard to be back, I know. People get surprised that we go back here. We won't go inside—unless you want to again—no? Okay. We will simply circle above. You see the way the door is ripped off, you see the way the stone walls around it are crumbling. I did that. I demolished these barriers and flew into this stall and wrapped myself around my sister.

AAAAAAAAAAAAUUUUUUUULLLLLLLL
GGGGGGGGGGGGGGAAAAAAAAAAAAAA
AULLLLLLLLLLLLLLLLLLLLNNNNNNNEE
EEEEEIIIIIIIIIIIIIIIIEEEEEEEEEEEEAAAAAA
AAAAAAALLLLLLLLLLLGGGGGGGGGGG
GGGGGGGUUUUUGGGGGUUUHHHHHHHHH
HUUUUUUUGAAAAAALLLLLAAAAAAAAAAAA

I did not know if it was her voice or mine or both that howled. I know it hurts your ears.

I dressed her in vines so her face was hidden. I draped a pelt over her shoulders. And I led her back home.

And so yes, as you can guess, we'll move *back* in that direction and I'm going to show you a different part of the house. As we head back that way, with the wind in your ears, I'd like you to imagine for a moment how your voice would sound without a tongue.

That's what a lot of people say. Like the sound in a nightmare.

To be in the home of the man who'd done this to her, it pulled the color out of her cheeks. Her hands shook and she kept her eyes on the floor. She couldn't look at me! Her own sister! Her shame was too big. I held her face in my hands and told her I was so happy she was alive, that I loved her so much. She started crying then and I told her, "Listen, I know, this is all too awful for words, and we have work to do, no time for tears. Now's the time for making him pay. Now's the time for re-venge. I'll cut out *his* tongue. I'll gouge out his eyes. I'll saw off the thing that shamed you." (I couldn't bring myself to give it name.) "I've thought of so many differ-ent ways for him to die," I told her. "I just haven't landed on the right one."

I'll just sort of swish back and forth in front of this window. Inside, this was the room where I brought Phila, a spare bedroom, one I used when I didn't want to share a bed with Tereus. You're holding on a lit-tle tighter—are you nervous? Okay, thank you for being honest. No need for nerves. I understand it's uncomfortable.

As I was saying. I was thinking out loud all the ways to punish Tereus when Itys, my beautiful little Itys, wan-dered into the room. He padded in in sock feet, his hair rumpled, and something in my heart went cold. It was like I was seeing him for the first time, or maybe more so that I was seeing how much there was of his father in him. Tereus was there in the spread of his brow, the way his nose wrinkled when he laughed, the mean shape of his mouth. And this is when my mind began to go horrendous.

Okay, you're gripping a little tight. Could you loosen a little bit? Thank you, that's better, yes.

Little Itys climbed on to my lap. I felt the weight and warmth of him against me, he put his arms around my neck and I held him, his heart against my heart. My little Itys, my warm little Itys. There's no weight like a child's weight. You could hold the same amount of pounds of a container of milk, warmed to human temperature, and it would feel nothing like it. Little Itys all against me. He smelled like butter. His cheek was so soft and he curled himself into me with a purity of comfort that I wish I could feel myself again, I wish all of us could know that sort of comfort again in our lives. My throat clenched in a gaping tenderness for this small warm creature that had come from me.

But I didn't want to be swayed. I opened my eyes and I looked at my sister. I looked at Phila, thin and pale, wordless, the scarred stump of a tongue in her face. She'd never taste a brownie again. She'd never articulate from her mouth I want you, I love you, I'm hungry, I'm scared. This boy can say mama, but she can't say sister? Think, Procne, I told myself. Don't you waver. Don't you waver.

And I didn't.

Now we'll dip back down toward the kitchen. I didn't show you before, but there's a room behind it, a storage place, dim and separate. I brought Itys here. I grabbed him and the only way I can explain is that I left my body. I was a tiger dragging a fawn through the forest. I was gone from myself. I knew that Itys was crying out, Mama, Mama, but it registered the way you hear an alarm in the distance. A noise, a disturbance. One that has nothing to do with you.

So you've got a peek inside this room, you see how small and dim it is, through that narrow door at the end of the kitchen. I brought him here and Phila followed us.

You remember all those knives from earlier? I grabbed the largest one. Itys sensed something had gone all wrong and tried to put his arms around my neck again, reaching up for me, wanting the comfort he'd had just a minute before. I was gone.

And I took the knife and I sliced him. My baby. My soft, small baby. I put the knife through his skin and I opened him up along his chest and down his soft little boy side. When he was born, the blood was black. Thick and dark and clotted. Here, it was the alivest red I've ever seen—how could a color like this have come from something I made inside me? I felt the warmth of it on my fingers and my wrists. It soaked my sleeves. I never looked away. I saw the inside of him. I saw his eyes go dim then dark. That quick, and he was gone. Phila wanted in. She grabbed a paring knife from the block and made a wicked smile across his throat. And then we sisters, together we cut the little thing apart. We ripped arm from shoulder socket. Thwop thwop! We pulled and tore. Legs from torso, feet from legs, small soft dimpled hands from wrists. Blood. Blood. There was so much blood.

Dizzy? Oh, I'm sorry. I forget that some get squeamish at the thought of blood.

Look there at that large copper kettle. I pointed it out earlier. That huge one, yes. Fine piece of kitchen equipment. We filled it with his parts. Other pieces went on the spit there over the hearth. It sizzled and spit and crackled as his flesh melted, as fat dripped away from body. *Tssszzz*. *Tssszzz*. Like that. *Tssszzz*. Child fat hitting flame.

You don't want to know about the smell.

Oh dear. Okay. Like I said, try to find the horizon with your eyes, and now might be a good time to have a Life Saver. The mint really does help nausea. Yes. Good.

We cooked a feast of him. When we'd finished, I found Tereus, and made up a story. "Tereus, hon, in Athens there's this special sacred night where wives make a feast for their husbands and they're the only ones who can take part in the meal. It's tonight! I've been cooking all day. I can't wait to serve you."

So we'll move now to the hall where Tereus sat on his throne waiting to be served this sacred meal. I brought out platefuls, bowlfuls, steaming and savory. "Eat, eat," I said, but I didn't need to tell him. He ate it all. He slurped it down, every bite. Grease coated his lips and the suckling noises he made, the chewy squelch, made vomit rise up my throat. I turned so he would not see me gag.

"Where's Itys," he said, wiping his mouth with his sleeve. "Bring him here."

I couldn't contain my joy. I started laughing. "He's here," I said. "He's right here. He's closer than he's ever been to you." Oh, I laughed. And here now we will move away from the palace and toward the sea. You're gripping my neck a little—could you—no, no, I'm sorry, we're almost done. There's no getting off now.

I kept laughing. Imagine it, please. Please imagine my laughter as I told Tereus that our son was right here. And now please imagine Philomela rushing in and please imagine how her hair is matted with blood and there is blood underneath her nails, on her neck, she is wild-eyed and covered with blood. And please now imagine the head of Itys in her hand. Imagine his small head. Skull with face attached, a terrible purple-gray color to his cheeks, his eyes dull like coated in wax paper and lilting up into their corners, his soft mouth hanging open as though in sleep, a bit of spine poking out from his neck, a jagged, dripping piece of severed spine. Please imagine this. And please imagine the weight of a child's head in your own hand. Are you imagining that? Imagine it. Its hair between your fingers, the hardness of its skull against your knuckles, knowing that a quarter inch below is the brain that told his heart to beat, that let him learn words like *mama*, that held his small boy joys and sadnesses. There it is, in your hand! And now please imagine throwing it. Because that is what Phila does. She hurls the head of Itys right at Tereus. She takes his small head and she hurls it at his face.

AAAAAIIAIIILLLLLLLLLLLLLLLL
LGIIIIIIIIIIIIIIIIIIIIIIIII
IAAAAAAAALLLLLLLLLLLLLLL
LIIIIIIIIIIIIIIIIIIIIIIIIIEEEEEEEE
EEEEEEUUUUUUUUGGGGGUU
UUUUUUGGGGGGGGGUUUU
UUUUUUUUAAAAAAAAAAAII
IIIIIIIIIIIIIIIIIIIIIIIIIIIIIIIIIIIIII
EEEEEEEEEEEEEEEEEEEEEE
EEEEEEEEEEEEEEEEEEEEEEE

She'd never wanted more to be able to speak. To be able to form words with her tongue. To shout out. To be able to sing her joy.

The child's head flew, Tereus's face went gray with horror, he dodged being hit, and the head cracked against the wall like a cabbage and thudded to the floor.

Right, yes, sorry, your ears will ring for a day or so. You might feel dizzy. I said you might feel dizzy. Yes, but it won't be permanent. No, I promise.

Tereus lost it, of course. Tables flipped, him raving about being a tomb for his own son. And he came after us with his sword. And at that moment is when we three are changed. Phila, a nightingale. Me, well, you know. And Tereus a hoopoe. We flew our separate ways. And now we'll head back to where we started, and we can— oh, oh dear. You want off now? Just a few more moments. Find the horizon. No, but I warned you. Yes, but you were warned. Have another Life Saver. Let yourself be absorbed by the feathers. I know, I understand. But it's starting to get to me. People want to know. And then they don't want to know. That keeps happening. It's so horrid, it's so gross, people say. It's too loud. But it was horrid, and it was gross, and it was loud. And either you want to know or you don't want to know. And it's easier not to know. It's easier never to have to imagine the weight of a child's head in your hand or how it would feel to fling it. It's easier never having to imagine a blade against a pink tongue and the mottled scar tissue on the root. It's easier not to think about a grown man putting himself inside a child whose mouth is pouring blood.

It's so much easier not to know. Well, right, yes, but you see, I did tell you it would be hard. I told you it'd be harder than you thought. But not like this? What did you expect?

No, really, what did you expect?

We'll land shortly. You'll be able to gather your things. Look over your shoulder first. To the west. I told you! I told you. The sunset was going to be beautiful. Look. I told you it would be and it is. It's so beautiful. It's just so beautiful.

BAUCIS

Do you remember that day? We were sitting in the
kitchen after the morning chores were done. We were
drinking tea. We were talking about how short the days
had gotten, closing in on the equinox, and we were talking about the shorter twilights, and I asked you if you
remembered late one summer so long ago, we were by
the beach, and we'd fought that morning, and you went
down to the ocean alone and came back and said, You
need to come, and I was still mad, but I did, and you
said, Feel the water, and I did. And it was so warm. So
much warmer than it should've been at that time of year.
Do you remember how we took off our clothes? How
we were naked on the beach, how we shared it with the
seagulls and the spider crabs, and that one small fishing boat not far from shore, who saw us, I'm sure. Do

you remember how it felt to swim? How it washed away all the morning's poison? I remember, you said. We ate clams that night, you said. That's right, I said, remembering sitting on the porch in the dusk, swallows flinging themselves across the sky in front of us. We ate so many clams. And we were both laughing at the memory when there was that knock on the door.

We looked at each other, paused, surprised. We had guests from the village now and then, but people didn't usually arrive unannounced. I put my mug down on the table and moved toward the door. You sat up straighter.

I turned to look at you before I opened the door. And I can see you there, the way the light was hitting you from the kitchen window, lighting you up from behind so your hair glowed. It was those days when I'd see myself in the mirror and think, Who is that old woman? Who is that old woman with her white hair and the lines around her eyes and cheeks that hang off her face? It was a shock. Who was this old person before me? When inside I felt as I did at twelve, at thirty. And I'd wink at myself in the mirror and think, That person, those people are still inside you. But when I looked at you, even when your hair glowed gray in the light that morning, I didn't see the old man before me. I didn't see the slumped shoulders and your knuckles bulged with arthritis. I didn't see the untamable white hairs whiskering out of your ears, your eyebrows. I didn't see the changed slack way skin hung from your face and your arms. I saw you as you were at twenty-five, at thirty. I saw your cannon legs, thick as oak trunks. I saw the waves in your light brown hair.

I saw the broad spread of your shoulders, and the line of muscle that cut beautiful trenches from your torso to your waist. I loved that part of you. And that's who I saw when I turned around before I opened the door. You, beautiful and full of blood, fifty years before.

Not all lives are large. Not all stories are sad.

I opened the door to two men, one taller than the other, both with bones that framed them to look like they came from elsewhere.

"We've knocked on a thousand doors," the tall one said, "looking for shelter. Looking for someone to take us in, even for just a night."

"And we've had a thousand doors closed in our faces," said the shorter one. "We're not from here, and we're hoping for just a little bit of warmth. We haven't found it yet."

"Come in, come in, please, come in," we both said. You stood from your chair, and I cringed as you cringed as it pained your knees to rise. Our visitors ducked through the low door, and I could see the way their eyes had to adjust to our small, dim home. We were so used to every inch of it, knew all its cracks and crannies, all its creaks and crevices. It wasn't large. People asked, How can you live in a place so tiny? It was large enough for us. You shook their hands.

And then we worked together, you and I, the way we'd done again and again, for guests, for ourselves. I pulled the bench away from the wall toward the hearth, fluffed the cushions and welcomed them to sit. You brought them water right away, without asking if they wanted—any traveler needs to slake their thirst.

I shifted the coals from the prior night's fire and there was heat there still. The embers glowed. I kneeled and added leaves, sheets of dried bark, I blew and the embers gave life to flames. One can keep their own home at whatever temperature they want, but let a guest feel warm. Let a guest not hold their shoulders by their ears in chill. Warmth in the body opens doors to warmth in the heart, to making one feel comfortable, safe, and welcome. You were the one to build the fires. I'd sit and watch as you placed kindling and logs. You had your methods. You'd light one corner, then another, and lean back on your heels, watching as the fire grew. It gave you pleasure, I know it did, and I liked to watch you do it, to see the light grow in front of you, you becoming silhouetted against the flames, to feel the warmth as you were feeling it against your face and chest, to hear the leaves crackling, giving way to the lower roar of the fire taking hold, and the hissing and spitting, and above that, a quiet whine, one that signals a form in transition from one state to another. And once your knees made it too hard for you to bend that way, I took the job, and you taught me how to place the logs, and I came to know what a pleasure it was to bring warmth into the home.

Once the fire was lit for our guests, I started another under the stove below our little copper pot that you kept shining all those years. You'd brought deep greens in from the garden that morning, beautiful fans of chard with their fuchsia veins. I cleaned them, stemmed them. And cabbage heads, too, dense and fresh. I began slicing the bottoms off and peeled away the outer leaves. You chopped an onion. In another pan, darkened by years of use, I heated the olive oil brought from our friend with the olive grove up the mountain and let it warm before placing your sliced onions there, and soon their fragrance filled the room. I never tired of that moment, when the smell of onions heated in oil rose and spread. A moment of promise, the promise of warm food cooked with love, of sated appetite, of home. Onions in oil, and a little salt.

As I kept watch on the stove, you used your two-pronged pole to grab the slab of smoked ham hanging from the rafter, one you'd aged with care, and you sliced some off for me, for our guests, for you, and placed the pink flesh in the pot to boil. The noises of an active kitchen made good concert. The sizzle of the onions, the bubbling of the boiling water, storming all around the pot, the thunk of the knife through cabbage leaves into the thick board below. And as we made the food we talked with our visitors, asked them how long they'd been traveling, where they were heading, where they were from. They were vague! And they asked us about our lives, how long we'd lived in our small home, if we had children—No, we said, we don't, and they seemed embarrassed to have asked. I paused my chopping. "Don't worry," I said. "It was our choice. Our love for each other was enough."

Our visitors seemed at ease. They were generous with their thanks, even before the humble meal was set before them. Conversation rolled and it was good to have these strangers here.

With a handful of mint in my hand, I rubbed the

surface of the table clean. The mint leaves rolled beneath my hand and their fresh smell—spring, growth, green—rose and filled my nose, and our guests'.

I pulled the cloth from the shelf, the one we used for feast days, celebrations. It was shabby, tattered by years, softened by time, and showing the stains of many meals enjoyed on it beforehand. The embroidery of oak and linden leaves that ran down the center in cream-colored thread looked as fresh as when I'd first had it in my lap. I always liked to spread the cloth across the table, the way I'd spread a fresh sheet over you remaking the bed after washday. That gentle *thwap* sound as it's snapped into the air, and the soft way it falls, on the table, over your body. I liked to see the contours of you below it, valleys, fields, and hills in snow. It fell silent as light over you. It turned you to a child. You remember? Those were summer days, the light sheet, the dark blue cotton blanket.

The cloth down, I noticed the table wobbled slightly. I took a fragment of a broken plate and slid it beneath the spot where the floor had dipped. I pressed on the table: level now, and firm. Four knives, four forks, four spoons, four plates, and four wineglasses, I laid out. My hands had started shaking by then. And then we started eating.

I placed a dish of olives, green and black, on the table, and a tiny bowl for the hard pits within. It's the right way to begin a meal—the scent of the mint lingered in the room, mixed with the savory smells of onion and ham—and our tastes were opened by the bitter salt of the olives sitting in their oil. The light in the eyes of the shorter of our guests came on, the light that said, without words, delicious. We'd pickled cherries late last summer; I opened the jar and spooned some out. A red so dark it was almost black, a soft sweet tang to complement the murky depth of the olives. Our new friends praised the cherries. You said you'd show them our small garden after we ate. The purple and white endive in their missile-shaped bulbs I'd roasted. Their edges charred and the flavors sweetened by the time near the fire. Fresh raw radishes. Their bright crunch danced with the softer chew of the endive leaves. "All from your garden?" the tall one said. You smiled as you nodded. "It's nothing large," you said.

I placed the cheese out next, the cheese I'd strained myself, let curdle, from our old goat. It was smooth and the purest white, like clouds in September against those bright blue skies. You never loved the cheese, I know. Something in the texture. I loved it though, and hoped our guests would, too. From the ashes, I pulled two eggs that had been roasting slowly there, meant for our own humble lunch, and now shared. We all sat around the table and enjoyed. Peeling the shells had gotten harder for my shaking hands, but I was able to and sliced them in half to reveal their golden yolks, the gooey sunshine within.

"Perfect!" the shorter one said when he saw it.

When this first stage was done, you cleared the plates, our plates that we'd eaten off of for decades, sturdy earthenware, they felt like friends, some chipped, others showing cracks, still with us. You poured us wine into our beechwood cups and we toasted the coming season, new friends, the meal. It wasn't fancy, our wine. It wasn't aged. Our table wine, and I could tell you were nervous it wouldn't please our guests. There were times when our humble tastes didn't seem to match what others wanted. But the mood was grateful and pleased and I hoped you'd see it, too.

And you did, I think, when you placed the steaming dish of ham and cabbage on the table. We all ate and drank our fill, and I told you it was delicious and I meant it, as I meant it every time. You nourished us. All along you nourished me.

When we'd had enough you rose to clear the plates away and I rose to bring on the final stage of the meal. I set dried dates on a small plate, they looked like nothing special, with their thin waxy skin and the coppery-brown flesh below, but they were sweet as small cakes. A dish of nuts. And, my favorite, figs. No fruit more beautiful on the inside. Soft as the meat of my thumb, and dark skinned. Inside, that pink-flecked flesh with its cream seeds, and the rim of white around it. You barely had to chew them, just press them with your tongue. We had a few ripe plums, skin taut and shining deep purple, and purple grapes as well. You set a bunch on the table and our guests plucked them off their stems. Little blasts of juice as they broke the skin with their teeth. An ant crawled on one, and the smaller guest took care in removing it. He did not squish it against the table, but walked it to the door and let it go outside. Just like you'd do when spiders and other crawlies found their way into our home! And I sliced an apple and we shared that, too. Last of all, I placed a honeycomb on the table. The amber liquid pooled on the plate, its stick coming slowly from the waxy combs, each chamber a small mystery our bees had built together. It was the last of the season's comb, and we shared it gladly. The taller guest pulled a piece of apple through the honey and a noise came from deep within him of pleasure.

"I can taste hyacinth," he said, "and lilac. And, and maybe a little bit of rose?"

"You'll find those flowers all around us," you told him. "It's inside those petals our bees do their work."

"It's almost as good as ambrosia," the shorter one said. We all laughed at the kindness, to be compared to the gods' own nectar. But it was as the tall one pulled another piece of apple through the honey that we noticed. Remember that moment?

Both of us at once. We'd been enjoying the meal all afternoon; the sun had followed its curved path across the sky and was on its way toward its nightly rest. We had poured glass upon glass of wine. And yet, do you remember, it was as though none had been had. I hadn't refilled the vessel; you hadn't either. Neither of us had opened a new bottle, nor had our guests, and yet the bottle was full, as though it was replenishing itself.

Remember how frightened we were? I laugh about it now, but we leaped to our feet and kneeled and raised our hands to the skies and begged forgiveness for how humble our home was, and how humble the food was. And then you had the idea that one way to make up for it was to kill the goose and serve *that* to our visitors. So out we went, and you tried to chase it, and it flapped and honked and you'd lunge, and just miss it. And you were panting, and I couldn't help but smile, the way it outran you, and I think our visitors were smiling, too.

"Please, please," they said, "you don't need to do this. We've had so much! We're so grateful for all you've done, especially compared to your neighbors who shunned us."

"There's punishment in store for them," said the other. "Not for you."

"Come with us," said the tall one. "We're heading there," he said, pointing to the peak above the olive grove, a distance away. I remember thinking of your knees, and your fear of heights, and my heart still pounded from seeing the wine bottle filling its own self, coming to know who it was we had sitting at our table. But what could we do but obey, so up we went, you and I together, following these two gods. We stepped carefully, slowly. "Watch that root," you'd say. "Careful here, it's slick," I'd say. That way, we made it to the top.

Right before the summit, we turned. It's funny: I remember the day so vividly, the softness of the figs, the saltiness of the cheese, the bright flares of pink in the leaves of the chard, the tiniest moments that could've happened any day! But this part, my memory feels blurred. We turned around to see that our whole village was drowned below a swamp. Low, dark waters where once our neighbors had lived. And thinking about it now, looking down on that scene, it feels like the way one might remember a dream. I remember water everywhere, and having no idea where we were or what we were seeing. But then you pointed: "Our house," you said.

And there were tears in my eyes and tears in yours, for all that had changed, for all that was lost, for all that was behind us, for every moment that led up to this one. We stood with our arms around each other and I do remember the noise you made when our house starting shifting shape. It was a noise I'd never heard you make before. And it was that, more than seeing our small house rise and turn into a gleaming temple, streaked marble, glittering gold, tall columns. Here was a noise I'd never heard you make. How lucky, for there always to be space for surprise. All those years. And this, now, new.

Our small, humble home, the place where we'd shared our lives, it transformed before us. We understood the honor, but our holding of each other spoke our sadness, too. Our home had held us and held our love and kept us warm for so many years. We did not need to speak, and we did not want to seem ungrateful to the gods, but we held each other tight and let the tears come, and we understood what the other was feeling. The loss, the years, the small corner of our world.

And then the larger god turned to us and thanked us again and asked us what we wanted most in this life. We held each other as we whispered to each other. Do you remember what we said? We barely had to say anything at all; we both knew the answer. I remember the warmth of your breath on my neck, and the feel of your arms against my hands, and knowing then, as I knew over so many years, that we were for each other.

"We'd like to guard the shrine you made of our home," you said. They nodded. You went on. "And also—"

You paused and swallowed tears. "And also, we would like—" You couldn't complete the sentence. I held your hand and squeezed and I continued for us. "Please, when one of us dies, let the other die in the same hour. Let him not have to bury me. Let me not have to see his grave. Let us continue on together and unparted, please."

They were kind to us. We lived out our many years tending to the shrine, and then that morning, you remember? We were talking about the meals we had when we were visiting the small village of your grandfather, the rabbit, the wild boar, the steak with the ribbons of parmesan on top. We were laughing. And I looked over and saw that you were growing branches, growing leaves, the lobed leaves of the oak, that your body was becoming trunk, and at the same time I saw from the look in your eyes that I was changing, too. I looked down to see that I was also becoming tree, a linden, with its large, heart-shaped leaves. "It's time," I said.

And just as our mouths were covered by this new skin of bark, we said, "Farewell, farewell, my love, my true lifelong love, my friend, my love, farewell." And our roots went deep into the earth and they entwined there, and we grew tall in the sun next to each other, close enough that when your leaves flutter in the soft breeze I can feel them against me, and you feel mine against you. And sometimes, *sometimes*, I imagine I can feel us embracing in the earth, our roots wrapped around each other and giving a little squeeze. We were so alive together. I like the windy days the best now, when we feel each other most.

IVORY GIRL

Pygmalion hated women. He thought they were disgusting. Their voices, their laughs, their hairs. The way they sweat, smelled, stepped. "You Cyprian women get so wet," he said. "What's with that?" No one told him. No one told him what the wetness was.

So it don't hurt
Because we like it
A way of saying getting there
A way of saying ready
A way of saying more
A welcome
A compliment
An invitation

Between the fingers it spreads like thread, a glow, a
word: silm, the shimmer
You know how lucky?
To feel that?
From a woman?
On your knees
The rivers, the ocean, the rain, tearfall
The rivers that do not make it to the sea
The ocean that's absorbed again by the skin, wash of
brine on the body
The rain before it reaches the earth to evaporate
Tearfall unfallen
Detour the moisture
But it's not like water at all
Moves better than blood
It's got its own light and the light is a mystery
Have you ever even made out with a mango?
You feel it on the inside of the thighs and not know
what sort of prize that is?
That's another thing entire when it gets to the legs
What's with that? There's so much that we want
And otherwise we'd drown

"You Cyprian women get so wet," disgust dripping
off his tongue. So he carved one dry as stone. "Ooooh,
you're perfect," he cooed and splooged—she's mute!—as
he groped her ivory breast. He clasped necklaces around
her neck, beads and jewels between her breasts. He
placed her in his bed; stiff; under the covers he warmed

the stone. "Cold toes," he'd say. Women knew he hated women. Women know when a man hates women. It hides in their smiles. It hides in the smiles of surprise each time a woman shows she's funny, strong, or wise. The men who hate women are surprised at this. Pygmalion hated women and all the women knew. A man who hates women builds one with a juicy ass and giant tits and no belly and a face that's foreign and empty and dumb.

And when Pygmalion begged Venus to make her real, and Venus granted his request and put moving blood in her body and gave her breasts that squished if you gripped them, we teased her, but only because we wanted to make her know.

Where's your stretch marks, sweetheart?

Where's your peeeeeer eeeee odddddd?

Where's your laugh? Don't you laugh?

Where's the one hair at your nipple?

Where's the flesh crease on your back?

Where's your smells, sweetheart? Don't you smell, sweetheart?

Where's the strength in your legs?

Where's the muscles in your shoulders?

Where's the wetness? Where's the rivers, oceans, rain, tearfall?

Where's your sag?

Where's your power, sweetheart?

We'll tell you, sweetheart.

It's in you, sweetheart. All over you. It fills every curve and swell. Find it, sweetheart. Know it, sweetheart.

He doesn't make you who you are.

Time separated her from her statue life. "Smell this," she'd say and lift her arm. We laughed! You got it, Ivory Girl! You stink! She sweat and seeped like all of us, less perfect every day. "There's nothing duller than perfection." She'd learned! "Really, it's a myth." That's right! We loved her more and more. "There is no love in loving the ideal. Pyggy doesn't love me. He loves an idea in his brain." Pyggy is a shit, she knew it. "We're made of mess," she said. Sweetheart, yes. That's exactly what we're made of.

DRYOPE

I figured it was my fault. I was young, he was the god of the sun, and I didn't know what to do except scream, but that didn't help anything. I didn't tell a soul and I didn't know till later that the sick I felt was shame. Not the flu. Not Lyme. Not some undiagnosable nonbelieved neuro-degenerative disorder. All I wanted to eat: banana cream pie Blizzards from Dairy Queen. That's all. Sometimes, fried egg sandwich. Sometimes, peanut butter. Mostly vanilla ice cream all swirled up with banana chunks and Nilla Wafers. Or maybe it was Vienna Fingers. I can't remember now. I guess you could say the experience made me shame sick. I thought my life was over.

I knew a girl who was taking oxy. I was crying to her over vodka and 7UP one afternoon at Paddy's and she said, Here, try this, it'll soften all your edges. That's exactly what it did. When I see pictures from that time, I don't even recognize myself. Just dead behind the eyes. Just greasy strings for hair. Gone, dulled, bad. I'd take a pill and it would feel like crawling into a basket lined with feathers, a splintery wicker basket big enough for me, with feathers on the inside. And inside this feather basket, absolutely nothing mattered and that's why I liked to go there.

I was sick. All the way. Then my friend Celine came to my house one day and brought pasta with broccoli in it and lots of cheese and she said, You're going to eat. And I said, You don't tell me when I eat. And she said, You know how this ends, right? This ends one of two ways: you quit or you die. If you don't do it for yourself, do it for the baby you got inside you.

And I did quit. Not that day, but soon. Her words landed on me and lived in me. I quit and I started working again and lost a lot of the DQ weight, but then gained it back because sweet things were a good replacement for what I'd been taking, and the thing about giving something up is that you have to retrain your brain about what's good. It took a little while to learn. And I started telling myself that everyone is broken parts, and I was no better or worse than anyone. I worked hard to fix what was broke. I did it for the baby, and I did it for my own self. I was walking taller and smiling more. And then me and Andraemon started spending more time together. We'd known each other since growing up and I always liked his hair, how he wore it a little longer than most of the guys, and he always smelled like he'd just come in from a snowstorm. And the thing was, he made me laugh. All the time I was laughing with him. When I told him about what had happened when I was young, and what it was like being a single mom to a little baby boy, he just put me in his arms and said, Jesus god, I'm sorry. He didn't drop me. He didn't hate me. We got married and my life was on track. I'd climbed out of the bad place, and I had a lot of love around me. I laughed every day. Every day!

But if bad luck can find you once, it can find you again.

I was down by the river with my baby one morning. I was showing him plants and bugs and flowers and frogs and all the weird little creatures that crawled and fluttered around the riverbank. And I spotted a lotus flower. Oh sweet pea, look, it's a lotus. Purple lotus. And I picked it for him. I was trying to teach him colors. Purple, I said. But then things went bad.

I looked at the flower and saw blood dripping out of the place where I'd plucked it and I thought, Oh hell no, did someone slip me something? Why is this fucking plant bleeding?

I found out too late. It wasn't a regular flower. To escape being attacked by Priapus, that creep with the arm-length dick, a nymph named Lotis had changed herself into this plant, to protect herself. I didn't know. I was just trying to go about my life and show my little guy what purple was. How was I supposed to know? I wouldn't've picked it if I'd known, man, doesn't anyone understand that? Me of all people? Of all things,

I understand about wanting to escape that shit. But I made a mistake. I thought I'd made a mistake before, that I'd asked for something I hadn't asked for, but that wasn't a mistake, that wasn't *my* mistake. That wasn't my fault. And I paid for it anyway, and then I pulled my life together out of a shitstorm that could've drowned me. Picking that flower, making it bleed, it was an accident. I didn't know it was Lotis, I didn't know it was another girl doing what she could to protect herself. It wasn't my fault. Bad luck finds me and keeps finding me. I paid for that accident, too.

So what's next? For picking the wrong flower, the gods turned me into a tree, a black poplar, imprisoned inside a cage of branch and trunk, with deep-furrowed, rough, brown-gray bark. In those first few minutes, as I'm hardening up and down, my poor baby kept trying to feed, but there was no more nipple where he could latch, no soft, full breast for him, just thick, dry bark. Oh sweet pea, sweetie no, I said. Oh no. No milk. No more milk, just splinters for his small tongue. He wailed. And his cry, I didn't feel it in my ears, it hit my actual heart.

For a little bit of time, my face stayed in the tree. Just enough time to tell Andrae when he arrived to make sure my baby would know it was me here, that he'd make sure to tell him who I was, and I told him that they had to come visit, come sit and play beneath me. I said, You've got to tell him about the dangers, you've got to make sure he knows about all the shit that can go wrong. Don't let him drink. Keep him away from the drugs. Keep him away from the bad kids who do the drugs. Don't let him play near pools or ponds or springs or rivers. Don't ever, ever let him pick a flower. Any bush or tree or rock or flower—he has to be careful, he has to be so, so careful!, because you don't know whose body might be in there. In the rhododendron bush, or the laughy brook, or the honey locust, you don't know who might be in there, every blade of grass, every cloud, there might be someone in there, keeping safe, or being punished, you don't know. You don't know.

CANENS

Thank you. Thank you so much. Let's have one more round of applause for Delia Spritz on drums and Susannah Hubbard on bass guitar.

Thank you. Thank you all for being here tonight, for spending your time with us here on this beautiful night on earth. But really they're all beautiful, aren't they? Even the lonely rainy ones. Tonight I'm feeling lucky to move through a bit of time with you, to have shared part of this night with you. You've been so lovely. It's all been so lovely.

For our last song we're going to do an old folk tune. Told and retold, spun and respun, sung and resung, age after age. It's "The Ballad of Canens and Picus." Legend has it that Canens had a singing voice so beautiful she could enchant the rocks and trees, that rivers would stop moving to listen to her sing. She loved the handsome Picus and he loved her, too. But then one day in the woods, a goddess witch named Circe tried to seduce him. He spurned her love, and because goddesses can at times be wrathful, she punished him by turning him into a woodpecker. In her grief, Canens wandered the woods singing until she dissolved into air itself. And legend has it, this was the song she sang. It's a sad song, on a beautiful night. Thank you all again for being here. It's been an honor, to share our songs with you. And now, "The Ballad of Canens and Picus."

Ride well, ride well, my one true love
Ride well, ride well, did he.
In purple cloak and javelin armed
He went to the woods to see.

The morn' was fair, the morn' was bright,
He went hunting boar,
My Picus left on his stallion tall,
He left for evermore.

Circe she stalks, Circe she roams,
She sees Picus on his horse.
She's struck at once, and wants him now,
Unwav'ring in her course.

He flees her fast, he flees her swift,
Off down the path he goes.
Her sights are set, it's him she wants,
Her choice has now been chose.

The witch, she morphs, the witch she shifts,
A boar's shape she takes,
And lures him on foot to the deepest woods,
Where she'll try to claim her stakes.

She shows herself to be who she is.
She's driven by her lust.
"Picus, I'm yours, Picus, be mine.
Give me your love, you must."

Back on his horse he galloped away,
Hooves thundering his reply,
"Not me, not now, I have a love,"
He shouted to the sky.

A woman's want is a dangerous thing
If you are to spurn.
Immortal hunger is bottomless
As my poor Picus did learn.

"Hurt me, you'll pay, you'll know my rage!
Forget hearing Canens's song.
A bird you'll be with a drummer's soul
For the choice you made was wrong."

She turned to the West and turned to the East,
She touched him with her wand.
Then Picus flew on wings so red,
His new life it had dawned.

I'm wrapped in grief, I'm wrapped in woe,
Sorrow becomes a veil,
As you who know who've lost a love,
My song becomes a wail.

Tap, tap, my heart, tap, tap, the clock,
Tap, tap, bird's beak on wood,
They count the moments of my loss,
Now I, too, am gone for good.

Fly well, fly well, my one true love,
Fly well, fly well, did he.
I join you now as air so soft,
You can fly your way through me.
Oh fly your way through me.

ALCYONE

Now: there's a place called Folly Cove. Granite bulging at the shore. Tiny eyelid of beach. Shells and crab parts on the sand. Snarled heaps of seaweed. Coarse white barnacles suctioned in clusters to the rocks. Fog in trees. A crust of salt. Rock outcroppings a swimmable distance out to sea, depending on what sort of swimmer you are, and what state of push or retreat the tide is in. Islands at low tide. Swallowed at high. As though they never existed at all. So that each low tide brings the surprise of their existence. There's no way to know what's down there then, except we know what's down there. Storms come and make the water white. But for seven days and seven nights on either side of the year's shortest day, the seas are calm and the winds pause. Halcyon days. The solstice-close time under a cold bright moon when all is ease. Stars do their nightly sweep across the sky. Days bright and the clouds nothing but playful. Waves lick, don't bash. Take five, Aelous says to his winds to allow for the kingfishers to lay their eggs in safety. So I lay my eggs in safety, living for that calm that comes. I wait until the nights are long and the days are bright and still. Egging in the quiet. This is the way it is now, how we stay together. I wasn't always a bird. I was a woman once who loved a man and he loved me. Oh the calm. Oh the deep dark calm. Seagulls cry and beak the beach. Seagulls are what become of our confessions.

Once and Always: there's a cave where Sleep lives. Poppies on the way in. No entry for the sun. A dim place thick with silence. Sleep sleeps limbs strewn on a feather bed weighted under blankets, clouds of down. In his chamber, un-alone. Surrounded by shape-shifters, more than anyone can count, all the different forms a dream can take. They wait in silence for direction. You to this dream—be his grandmother spreading egg yolk on her elbows. You to that dream—be a house on fire that feels familiar the dreamer has never seen. You—a falling tower. You—a figure in the shadows. You—a sexual river. You—a throbbing pulse of light. You—an alligator in a muddy stream with baby chickens on its back. You—an antlered child. You—a tidal wave. You—a laughing mother in a lawn chair throwing dirt clods at her daughter crawling toward her on the grass. They'd shimmer, slip out the cave, and travel through the night to drift in the window of that night's dreamer. "Be her husband," Morpheus was told, he most skilled of all the shifters, highest hero of this world. "Make her know about the storm." So this mottled and beautiful transparency, this fiction form, came to me in sleep, my love, naked, kneeling at my bedside, ocean dripping from his beard, seaweed clinging to his shoulder. He made me know the ship was smashed to splinters, that he'd been swallowed by the sea. He made me know it all in two words, such is the language of dreams, and the shared language of our love. I won't tell you what they were. That's private.

Then: there's a harbor from which they all sail away. Fishing boats. Lobster traps. Striped buoys by the jetties. Seals slip. Fog on the docks. Blang of rope on poles. In mourning the morning after he told me in the dream what was true, I went down to the shore, near where I watched my husband's boat disappear on the horizon. At sea, a little ways off shore, a floating thing, a body. His, I knew. The waves carried him to me. He was blued and grayed. His lips pulled the way they did when he was angry. Fights swept through our home like storms, battered every wall. I waited for the calm. Oh the calm. Stormless peace. But like the dark rocks hidden at high tide, danger lived below the surface. There's a state of too-close, of getting bashed against the rocks. There's such a thing as too much love. It's possible to lose yourself. I saw my husband's body limp and swollen in the sea and

I ran to throw myself off the high storm wall onto the rocks, into the waves that blasted over them, spraying up the cliff. I leaped, so we'd be together still because I could not be alive without him. I believed this lifelike fiction. I believed in the illusion of two-as-one. There would be no me without him. I jumped. The damp cold sea air. Locked neck. White foam. Black rocks. Roar of fall. But I did not land. I was turned into a bird, and he was, kingfishers, both, a pair all but identical. We weather storms, we weather storms yearlong and wait for calm. Oh the deep dark fleeting calm.

THETIS

I can tell you what I am. I'm a goddess of the waves. I can tell you what I do. I wink and change my shape. I ride naked on a dolphin. My legs astraddle its rain-gray body, gripping its slick between my thighs, we race the spray. We leap, roll, rise, soar, and splash. My clitoris against its dorsal fin, the cartiligean press, a yield and pulse with the rise and retreat of the sea. I am with the tides. The briny murky depths. The swell and crash. I am always changing. Sea foam against your ankles feels like whispers, telling secrets you thought you knew, but didn't. I have my secrets. You have yours.

I can tell you what I know. There are prophecies. There are truths from the beginning of things. There are situations we arrive at knowing or not. Proteus told me: "Were you to get pregnant, you'll bear a baby boy, one who will outdo his dad." Jove wanted me. But he didn't want to be outdone. He sent Peleus, his mortal grandson, in his stead. *Take that virgin as your bride*, Jove told him.

I can tell you where I was. There was a cove. The water there was clear. An eyelid of sand in various states of blink depending on the ebb and flow of the tide, the phase of the moon. Among the rocks along the shore, a grove of myrtle trees, their berries purple-red, hid a cave. I went there to rest. I dismounted my dolphin and took deep sleep. It was a hidden place. I slept naked in this cave.

I woke one afternoon in living nightmare. Peleus on top of me. He pleaded, begged his case, this fragile creature who knows of ends. *Who do you think I am?* I wondered without saying. No no no no no, I said out loud. It was not the answer that he wanted, and so he moved toward force. *Don't you understand?* I thought. *I'm not like the women that you know. I can change myself to anything.*

I shift my own shape.

And as he pressed upon me clumsily, this awkward mortal man, I showed him.

A bird at first, I fluttered, tweeped, and beaked his skin, nono, nonono. He didn't heed, kept lunging for me, grasping. I shifted to a beech tree, wide trunked and mighty, and my bark bloodied his knuckles as he groped and grabbed. He did not stop. I changed to a tiger, muscled, clawed. My roar dizzied him. He saw the points of my teeth. And because he knows about ends, he was afraid, and fled.

And he asked the gods for aid. *What do I do?*

Proteus told him how to get his way. He outlined my torture. "When she sleeps, tie her up. Bind her hands. Knot her tight. Stay on top of her. She'll take a hundred shapes. Each one is a lie. Ride her until she can shift her shape no more and returns to her nude truth."

I can tell you how it looked. I woke in my cave with my wrists bound, tied wide to each side, Peleus's weight on my body. First I shouted my objection.

Then I began my bestiary.

I went from woman to

Elephant   legs like beech tree trunks tusks aside the snuffle, wise eyes with sadness for the graves to

Squirrel   gray comma curled tail scattering up trunks click of mischief to

Weasel   soft wild sock with fangs to

Ladybug   five black spots against the red acrid odor when there's fear to

Mourning dove   color of dawn, coo coo the color of calm to

Raccoon   burly masquerading night beast, small palms grasp the way we all do to

Vulture   wide-winged eyes aimed toward rot toward the splay of viscera on the sand riding thermals between infinity and death

Which are the same thing after all to

Pelican   deep beaked on the dock to

Camel   sand dune bump humped two-toed soft stepped what's water to

Ibis   round-backed bird long black beak deep dusky red a splash of grapefruit juice added to the cranberry to

Horseshoe crab   spike-tailed like a spade prehistory in the feathers of the feet to

Great blue heron   on stalks stoic in shallows feather tint of morning sky to

Buffalo   dark wooly thickness a gallop like thunder and a dry blue tongue to

Scorpion   whether insect or other who knows poison in the puncture lurking in your shoes to

Possum   pale and always looking moist babies on the back pointy-faced to

Goldfish   loyal sparkling swimmer glitter like coins near the surface to

Beaver   furred dentata saw-toothed gnaw your bones to grind my teeth to

Fox   flame across the backyard sleek and fleet as fire to

Rooster   dawn's strut feather flay like a spray of sparks ruler of the morning to

Boa constrictor   thick serpent wrapping tighter hug gone suffocating but I imagine this is a nice way to die to

Goat   devilish rectangular pupils do you want to live deliciously I do I do I do to

Catfish   whiskered scum sucker grab 'em right out of the polluted canals hold them in your fists to

Rat   flattened on the roads squeezed in cement's cracks leathered baby-biters plague-makers to

Otter   a water poem a dark brown sleek a back-
stroke of small paws water joy

And I pant and twist, keep changing, and Peleus remains
on top of me, hanging on to my outsides, his entry into me
blocked by my ever-shifting shape

Then to
Walrus   sand slug lardy tusked bayer on the
beach to
Snail   shelled slug slick on the sidewalk my shin-
ing sluction to
Bat   black-skeletoned black velvet night angel to
Swan   white slide on the water with the proudest
chest in the animal kingdom to
Squid   fingerling pulse with no bones a thready
throb of milk muscle to
Frog   at algal squat by the pond a tinny song and
great green leaps to
Alligator   amber-eyed at lurk on the surface full-
length spike to
Hummingbird   glittering green about my neck
tiny heart thidthidthidthidthid one thousand miles a
minute to
Moth   dust-winged by the porch light to
Eagle   mean-faced wide-winged more bullet than
bird to
Cricket   tunes the violin tucked at the back of
my thighs to

Sheep   sink your hands into the coils of oily cream wool to

Moose   steeple-heighted loomer to

Gecko   seedling green rappelling up walls chirp like a toy to

Porcupine   a creature made of cactus spines a prickling pelt to

Anaconda   fifteen coiling uncoiling feet thick as a football when there's a toddler inside to

Egret   white where black river meets shore like the color on the collar of the habit of a nun to

Ant   blistery go-getter to

Jaguar   jungle sleekness pads of silence to

Chicken   prancing clucker color of caramel to

Iguana   almost unblinking spiked a low-down dragon with no fire to

Rabbit   cabbage-bodied nibbler by the bushes on the run to

Jellyfish   luminous throbber party streamers swaying below to

Crow   a winter caw and a black so black it's purple green and midnight

I am changing faster faster the panic builds it feels a little bit like drowning

Cockroach   armored and ongoing to

Swallow   darting swooper in the evenings to

Boar   stubbled tusked muscled ferocity to

Octopus   tenticular sentience inky three-hearted elegance to

Horse   hoofed mover canoe hull rib cage to

Owl   history in the span of wing in the silence of my eyes

Groundhog   tubby tunneler to

Giraffe   endless necked bending down to kiss with arm-length purple tongue to

Dragonfly   midair fucking on gossamer to

Rhinoceros   sad-eyed jouster to

Robin   blush-chested sign of spring to

Pig   muddied bristled pink snout slopping to

Daddy longlegs   orb on walking threads to

Peacock   emerald purple splay to

Zebra   black like the bars of a crib or a cage to

Mosquito   song of insomnia to

Seahorse   curled tail undersea cavalry to

Skate   wide white sheet of underwater muscle, all wing, all wave to

Musk ox   densest sweater to

Mouse   shadow scurrier to

Bee   honey-combing pollinator to

Ram   heavy-horned skull basher to

Polar bear   yellowed on smalling ice floes to

Wolf   a dog jawed wildness to

Badger   grumpy in the den to

Cardinal   red light to

Seagull   shoreline mourner to

Turtle   leather and shell, crust and the dough to

Penguin   arctic wobbler to

Spider crab   pinching warriors to

Swordfish   a sleeker sort of unicorn to

Hippopotamus   furless behemoth with a mouth that can swallow the world to

Snow leopard   mountains hiding in my tail to

Manatee   giant solid dust mite to

Civet   lithe pointy-faced feline secretor to

Skunk   an odor more solid than the light-and-shadow form to

White-tailed deer   leaping my flash of snow behind me to

Firefly   light pulse by the bushes at the edges of the yard to

Olm   blind in double darkness pale squirmers in underwater caves to

Mongoose   slithering egg eater to

Barnacle   sessile filter feeder take the skin off of your knuckles to

Electric eel   socketed shocker in the current to

Clam   pouch of brine flesh sealed inside a purse of shell

Exhausted, the beasts become no longer of this earth

A sheet of golden color like the surface of the sun hard-edged blinding yellow to

A woman with tree legs, leaf waist, lion arms, six breasts whose roar is the wind to

Headless, holeless creature crawling on hands,

knees, sores on the skin oozing weeping weeping weeping to

Hatchling out of a massive egg too-wide human face, stump legs, low bird-feathered body and under each feather another tiny bird emerging, wide-mouthed featherless blind needle-beaked hundreds and hundreds and hundreds of tiny mouths to

Moon-eyed fish face with a gasping gaping mouth where tiny men on fire come rushing out in scream to

A bristled thrashing yowler with no eyes and eight legs walking on human hands to

A woman legs splayed giving birth to a woman giving birth to a woman giving birth emerging in blood from between the legs again again again to

A shadow to

A scream to

A sigh to

A puddle to

Myself again, dissolved. I had nothing left in me. My wrists bound, a woman's form again, and in that moment Peleus entered into me. He'd clung tight, and when I was back to a woman's form he pushed in and sprayed himself up into me, and I lay there like a corpse. It was the final shape I took that day, and for the first time afterward, I did not choose the shape my body took. Over the coming months, a slow swell, a growing, my body not just mine, and out came Achilles, who will have no trouble outdoing his dad who bound my hands and held on. Each shape a lie, said Proteus. Wrong. I can tell you the truth. Each one is in me, every part is true. I'm a shifting shape flickering between the trees, over and under the waves, shadowy and swift, a moving intertwine of forms. I've got all the animals inside me, their blood moves in my blood. I take any form I want. Raven, moss, or church. Stone or snake or light. The one form I didn't choose, the motherhood forced upon me, I absorbed into myself as well, powerful as all the rest. Stillness is the only trouble. In our changing, we trick time, proving that once being does not mean always will be. I choose my shape. You choose yours. We don't always know what's inside of us, or what it might take to free that creature from its cage.

SALMACIS AND HERMAPHRODITUS

S: All the women of the woods they told me. Pick up the bow. Run the paths. Hunt with us. I saw them. Sweaty. Bruised. Snarled hair stuck with burrs. Animal blood below their nails, dried like ash on the private part of their wrists. No thank you. It's good to challenge yourself, said the naiads. Rest feels better when you work for it, they said. I worked for it. The women of the woods chased animals. I had a different hunt.

H: I was fifteen years old.

S: While they chase boar, deer, rabbit, beaver, bear, while their skin is snagged on prickers, while their muscles burn from crouching silent and unmoving so not to startle a stag, I lounge by my spring. I comb my hair. I touch myself. I wait.

H: I'd never left my parents' home on the mountain before.

S: My spring is unmuddied. No dead leaf murk. No slick surface spread of algal green. No clog. No floating twigs or leaves like little paddle boats. I keep it all the way pristine. I comb my hair. My skin is smooth. These breasts of mine, they're massive. I look into the water. My reflection pleases me. The robe I wear is a silk the color of the clouds; it drapes off of me like vapor. I leave it open most of the time—I let the wind have its way. The air touches all my body.

H: I'd never kissed a girl.

S: I positioned myself in the morning on moss. My robe ate the dew. My breasts are big as beehives, not like the other naiads, who sweat and run all day, who end up with little lemon breasts. Lying on my side, the softness of my belly dropped, the wide roundness of my hip rising as result. My right-hand fingers in my hair, my left-hand fingertips on moss, sunlight through the trees dancing on my body. Pure allure. The birds and small soft creatures look upon me. They don't get close. The eyes of the squirrels are black. The nervous birds' bones I could crush in my palm, crack their little twig ribs and mash the air right out. They don't get close enough.

My body rises and falls slowly with my breath. I watch the sky move on the spring.

H: I'd left my parents' home to see the unfamiliar parts of the world. I didn't know where I was.

S: And then he arrived. He came through the trees into the morning sun by the spring, tentative as a fawn, and I liked this. Son of Aphrodite, son of Hermes, are you lost? Let me help you feel at home, beautiful boy. Let me distract you from your fears. I looked at him and oh, this beautiful young man, this meat. All verge. All cusp. Any minute he would fall from the high ledge of boyhood and land in the bristled plain of being man. And I liked this, too, this almost there but not all the way, this in-between. Long legs with muscle bulge above the knee. The bones of his ankles like arrowheads. The spread of his chest and its smoothness, I imagined no hair yet on this young man. His clavicles across his shoulders like sticks to bang a massive drum. The juicy swell of his lower lip, that bulge, the perfect seagull M of his upper lip. Eyes not black like the squirrels but pristine as my spring, and revealing him right away untouched. Already I was too excited. I needed calm. I smoothed my robe, positioned it off my left shoulder, pulled my long hair over my right. I bit and wet my lower lip.

H: There was a lady at the edge of the water. Her legs were thick, a lot of her beneath a robe. I was seeing too

much of her. She did not look like my mother. There was
something hungry in her eyes.

S: Your mother is lucky to have had you inside her,
I said.

H: I don't remember what that was like.

S: Your brothers and sisters are lucky, too, if
you have them, to be able to look upon you as their
sibling.

H: I don't have them.

S: And very lucky was the wet-nurse whose tits you
tongued and sucked, whose breasts you emptied. And
here I moved my hand down and absently touched my
own, felt my nipple firm against my palm, just the way
I wanted it. And I saw his eyes follow my hand, just the
way I wanted it.

H: I don't remember—

S: Luckiest of all is your girlfriend or your bride-
to-be, because I can only assume you have one. It's all
right. Oh, it's all right. Don't worry. We can love each
other secretly. No one will know except the birds and
the squirrels and the leaves, and they're voiceless when it
comes to this sort of thing, I promise.

H: This sort of thing?

S: The blood rose to his cheeks. And I suspected that blood was gathering elsewhere as well. And my stomach dropped into my hips in that expectant throb, that heated pulse that precedes the best thing.

H: I watched my mother butcher a rabbit once. She punched its head to break its neck and the lights went out of its eyes, and then she knifed it open and tugged out all its guts, all those dark wet interior parts. She tossed them to the dogs. They lapped the floor for so long. I didn't like it. I was seeing more than I should see. I didn't want to know. I had a queasy feeling. Now I felt this way again.

S: Here. Don't worry. Here. Just a small kiss.

H: I hadn't seen looks before like the ones she gave. They reached into my guts with fingers on the inside that tickled. It didn't feel right. And also at the same time it felt like something I'd been approaching, maybe since the beginning, and I had a sense somehow that this is what I faced, this was what was coming for me, this new realm was opening to me, these looks and swells and smells. But I wasn't ready.

S: Like this. Here. Just a small kiss. Like a sister. Like this.

H: I don't think I—

S: Here. Just quiet. You don't have to worry. Like this.

H: I took steps back.

S: He took steps back. Though the hunt had begun as soon as he stepped into the clearing, now in earnest it began. They don't know it, and I don't tell them, but the naiads' pleasure in the hunt is the same as mine— tension and the release of it. That's all I'm ever after. They chase and stalk and aim and shoot and if they do it right, they catch their game and kill it dead. Thrill born out of effort. If in the woods you were to pause on the path and a deer emerged from the trees and instead of leaping away in frighted flight, it walked toward you, brown dew eyes glittering all fearless, and it offered itself to you, displaying its flank in easy range—where would be the challenge? And there- fore, the satisfaction? Better to leave the eager deer standing there offering itself and try to find one that will make you earn your pleasure. I've never wanted the ones that offer themselves up to me, who beg to touch my beehive breasts, who tell me they want to lose themselves in my soft thick curves. Too easy. No eventual moment of surrender when the fight leaves them and they're yours. This is what I live for. I do not need a quiver or a bow.

H: I kept stepping backward away from her touching and kissing.

S: Those steps back, that resistance, it heated me and made me juiced more than any sort of beauty, more than any sort of sculpted form or shining smile or brains or smell.

H: She just kept coming.

S: He stepped back and I felt the wet between my legs. You don't want it? I will make you want it. Here. Just let me—doesn't it feel good? There? Doesn't that feel good? Like this? So gentle, so slow. Let me—

H: Listen, if you don't stop I'm going to leave.

S: Okay, okay, okay. I stepped back.

H: She stepped back.

S: It's all yours. Enjoy the spring. I leave you to it. I slipped away. He thought me gone. He couldn't see me and that was fine. I crouched like the naiads do, my knees on the leaves, waiting for my meat the way they wait. I opened my robe and felt the weight of my breasts in my hands. I peered between the leaves. He paced the lip of the spring.

H: I paced the lip of the spring. I tried to calm down. She left. I was glad when she left.

S: He paused, dipped his foot into the water, I could feel him feel it.

H: I touched the water with my toes. I wanted to be in it.

S: He wanted to be in it.

H: I pulled off my shirt.

S: He pulled off his shirt and folded it and placed it on a stump. A pimple on his right shoulder, raised and red. Young men, their oils.

H: I felt the sun on my shoulders. I missed my mother.

S: He bent and he undid his pants and he slipped out of them and I saw all of him.

H: I took off my pants.

S: My teeth clenched to trap the moan.

H: I dove in.

S: He's in! His whole naked self. Now was the time. I let my robe fall and dashed waterward and slipped in.

H: There's a rippling in the water.

S: I swam quickly.

H: What's there?

S: I wrapped myself around him.

H: She's wrapped herself around me. All at once all around me. I didn't want it. Get away. I tried to get away.

S: He was everywhere against me, and he was trying to get away. I moaned to feel all his muscles tensed against me, fighting me off, trying to swim. I wrapped round tighter. Like this, just still, like this, I'm yours, be calm.

H: She's all around me and I felt sick. It's too animal. I didn't want to know. It's as though she's all tentacles, some massive octopus, pulling at me, tugging me in toward her, her legs knot themselves around my legs and she opens herself and is rubbing all over me. I don't want this. STOP.

S: STOP, he said, and I held him tighter. I pressed myself into him. We both breathed heavily. I knew any second would come the surrender. I have to hang on a little longer, a little tighter. I've been here before. They always surrender. They always give in. Like this, like this. Just relax. You're going to like it. I know you'll really like it. Trust me, you can trust me. Relax, it's all right. Just give it to me.

H: No no no no no. Stop. STOP.

S: I rubbed and rubbed myself on him and I was so close, I was so so close, and his arm was pressed against my breast and trying to push me off and I opened and tightened and all the muscles in my hips were tight and clenching and it was almost I can feel it almost there there there there oh god, I cried out, oh god please, let us be joined forever, please let us never be apart.

H: What's happening?
S: Oh he's in he's in. I'm all around him.
H: She's everywhere.
S: He's in. I'm in. He's entered me I've entered him, the gods gave exactly what I'd wanted. We're swimming in each other now.
H: I've entered her. She's entered me. Some strange combining.
S: Entwining.
H: And entwined.
S: Our bodies joined in the deepest way.
H: We're one.
S: We're both.
H: This changed home, two forms one body. A she becomes me. Becomes him. I a he become her.
S: We fondle ourselves

H: Our self
S: Like this
H: Wait I like that
S: Just like this
H: Touch me
S: There
H: Keep touching
S: My beehive breasts. His waist-down manhood.
H: We are both,
S: Blurred and joined,
H: And neither.

EGERIA

People think they know. People think they know all sorts of things. People want to tell you what they know, like all of them have PhDs in being alive. One thing to know: no one knows shit.

It doesn't matter what my husband's name is. You don't need to know. It doesn't matter how he died. It doesn't matter the way he cooked lamb with garlic and rosemary on special days. It doesn't matter that the word we had for caterpillar was fur worm. It doesn't matter that sometimes he cried out in his sleep and that I'd reach for him. Not to you it doesn't. You don't need to know. You don't need to know very much at all, actually.

He died. That's all anyone needs to know. My grief was bottomless. I cried and cried and cried. People at home said, Okay, it's okay, stop crying. I couldn't stop crying. So I couldn't be home and I left and I cried in the woods. Shhh, shhh, it's okay, said everyone and everything that lived in the woods. It's okay, it's okay. Stop crying. It wasn't okay. I couldn't stop crying.

I kept crying in the woods and a man came to me, you don't need to know his name, it does not matter because he could be any man. And he said, Oh jeez, oh dear, wow, gosh, I'm so sorry for your loss, I'm so sorry your husband passed. He's in a better place. Don't cry.

I kept crying.

And he kept talking, this man.

"You're not alone," he said. "You're not the only one who's gone through this. Other people have had things happen that make them cry. Hard things have befallen a lot of us. Maybe if you think of those people, the ones that have also lost someone, or maybe had something worse happen, you'll stop crying as much. I have a sad story myself. Maybe it'll give you the perspective that you need?

"My stepmother told my father that I tried to seduce her. She told him I tried to climb into her bed and touch her. I didn't even do this. I didn't even think about what she looked like when she got out of the shower and I barely ever noticed when she'd come into the kitchen in the morning in her silk robe and she'd let it open while she looked in the fridge for the orange juice and then turn and her nipples would be all hard under the silk. I barely noticed that at all! She was the one who wanted me! She was the one who wanted to climb into *my* bed and touch *me*! She was the one who noticed *all the time* about my pants! I have no idea whether she did what she did because she was mad that I told her get out of my bed, or if she was afraid I was going to tell Dad myself. Who knows. But already this was a shitty situation. So I left my home, I got out of there, and on the way, riding off into exile on my chariot along the coast, a giant storm came, and this huge bull rose out of the waves, snorting seaspray and flinging his horns back and forth and crashing toward us at huge speed. My horses freaked, of course, and went galloping off in all different directions. I didn't care about the bull, all I could think about was getting away from home and my stepmother and the way her hair fell over her shoulders which she wanted me to smell and like, but I didn't even like. My horses went nuts and I tried to steer and rein them in, and I would've been able to because I'm strong enough by far, but that's when one of the wheels hit a tree and cracked off the axle and I got thrown out of the chariot. And I'm not sure if you've ever experienced something like this, I doubt it, but time dilated. I flew through the air and it felt like I was in the air for two weeks, and I had time to think about being a kid and my real mom and wanting to marry her and how we'd hold little pretend weddings until Dad got pissed. And I thought about the day he married my stepmom and how it rained so hard that day and I had to play with my cousin who was damaged and couldn't talk but drooled a lot and how I wanted to make him talk to me instead of drool on his small chest. But he didn't. And I thought about the way he waved at me as we were leaving the wedding. And I thought about the color of my stepmom's robe, a deep blue that you only get to see in the sky the twenty minutes before dawn. And that's the last thing I remember because I was ripped apart. My bones snapped. My guts were torn out from in me, some landed in a pile like a gray-red heap of earthworms, my sinews tangled themselves around a tree, one leg got ripped off by the reins, all my parts were strewn. I was completely unwhole. One big wound. Blood and bone bits and dark snags of entrails. I think about that, and then I think about you, and yeah I'm sorry for your husband but really? You cry? You cry and cry about this? You think you have it bad? Imagine having your pancreas land fifteen feet from your shoulder. Imagine seeing your pancreas. If you have a stepdad, imagine him accusing you of wanting to suck his dick. You're crying? I saw the underworld. The bright blue of the robe gave way to the lightless dim where the shades go. And the only reason I'm here talking with you today is because Diana took pity and restored me, though not to what I was. She put some years on me and changed my name and deposited me far far far away from my stepmother looking for juice in the morning. So that's just something you should know and maybe it'll make you feel a little better about your own life. And maybe it'll convince you that all the boo-hoo-hooing is out of proportion to what's happened. I was a pile of guts. I'm not crying. You don't see me crying."

He didn't know. He didn't know a goddamn thing. Anyone wants to tell me how much worse it could've been? Don't you know: not a single person in the history of the world has ever felt better hearing "it could be worse."

I went on crying because that was the form my grief took. I didn't apologize to him, and I won't to you. I lay on the leaves and the twigs and I cried for my husband because I loved him. He was part of me and when he died, I died, too, and you know what? That's sad. Having your guts ripped out of you, that's not sad, that's bad luck, that's gross. Wanting to fuck your stepmother, that's natural. Getting brought back to life by a goddess, you're lucky and of course you shouldn't be crying. I wept, wept, wept, and Diana took pity on me, too. She turned me into a spring. I was only tears anyway. She made me what I was. Come dip your feet in, drink. But if you tell me how bad it could've been, I will drown you.

NYCTIMENE

The crow will tell you it's because of a monstrous thing I did. The crow will tell you, with its charcoal-throated caw, this tree-branch gossip, that I'm an owl because, well, because—please, closer, come closer, I need to whisper, it's not the type of thing I can say to anyone— because I convinced my father to—because I seduced— because I convinced—because I lured him—here, closer—the crow will tell you that I fucked my father and then retreated to the woods to hide away in shame, which is where Minerva took pity on me and changed me to an owl, exiled to fly in darkness when sleeping eyes won't see me for the foulness of my act. She turned me into a wide-faced feather barrel, flight as silent as the grave, and she pulled me in under *her* wing, so to speak, and made me her bird.

Don't listen to the crow. It's jealous. It's the one who used to be Minerva's favored bird. The crow had been a beautiful girl, walking on the beach; Neptune saw her and had instant heat. She tried to flee and Minerva heard her cries and turned her into an ink-black crow to keep her from the violation that was coming. But the crow was talky, a gossip, always spilling the wrong secrets, and Minerva downgraded her, didn't want such a servant of rumor riding on her shoulder anymore, and I took its place. Jealousy came to live in the crow, eating it from the inside out like maggots in meat, and so it tells the story a certain way. It wants to make me look like the monster. There's more than two sides to a story—the doers, the done-tos, and the ones who interpret who's who.

Closer, here, in under my wide wing. Let me be the one to tell you what happened, horrific as it is. My father arrived in my bed, at night, in the shadows, so that each night I lay shaking in my bed hoping not to hear the stairs protesting his weight as he climbed them toward my small pink room. And each night when the stairs cried out, it was as though a bees' nest broke in my brain, and they all started stinging. They buzzed loud and stung, and—here, closer, let me tell you— their honey was bitter on my tongue. I did not go to the woods in shame. I went to escape. Minerva helped me more. Now, an owl. A feathery movement between the trees. A flurry and then form. I'm the movement. Then the owl. To see that wide squall of wing, that blur, is to see a state of mystery, to witness the moment before a form becomes what it is.

LEUCOTHOE

The sun sets. Bands of color spread themselves across the sky. Violets, fuchsias, peaches, golds, and even some strange faded green. The whip-poor-will trills from a branch nearby, evening song. Night comes. The first star has just emerged, shy at first, gaining courage as day retreats, more and more outgoing as darkness deepens. Sky fangs of the crescent moon. With the last blast of color on the horizon, it's as though Helios brags: *Well, I did it all again, and here's the full spectrum of my skill before I do it all again come morning.*

Some things belong in darkness, better never brought to light. What is pressed down gets darker, gains force, and rises from the shadows, knuckled and fork-tongued.

Now it's not a secret, but it was: Venus and Mars. The flowing-haired goddess of love, the armored god of war, pressing together in a passion they tried to keep hidden from everyone. Helios arrived on the chariot that brings day to the world, and saw the two entwined, and told Venus's leather-skinned husband, Vulcan. He relished the telling, and juiced it with detail. Vulcan, thick with muscle, turned weak to hear the news. The swage he gripped seemed to take on more weight and he dropped the tool on the floor of his forge; the sound echoed up to the sky. With a clang that rattled the walls of heaven, his shock and hurt gave way to anger, which steered him toward revenge.

He worked by night in his darkened forge, and the heated glow of metal lit his face as he bent over his work. He fashioned chains of bronze into a net so fine no eyes could detect it. He positioned it on the bed where his wife had opened herself to another man. And like a spider catching a fly, Vulcan caught Mars and Venus in the midst of their coupling.

He kept them trapped there, joined and pressing like two thrashing fish pulled from a pond, and he opened the wide bedroom doors and invited all the gods to look. They gathered, pointed, laughed. Venus turned her head away and tried to shift her hips to bring some modesty to the scene. Her maneuvering only made it seem that they continued their press and grind regardless of being exposed.

Once amply shamed, they were released. Thin lines of netting marked their flesh. Venus, furious in her embarrassment, aimed her wrath at Helios for shining light into a place that belonged in darkness.

This story is easy enough to tell. It's not hard because it's not mine. But this is the moment when my story takes root with theirs.

I was a girl and my dark hair was long and it shined in the light. I lived far from Mount Olympus alongside fertile Persian pastures, and to walk the streets was to be swept along on clouds of scent, saffron, rose water, dried limes, the lemony musk of sumac. I was home inside these smells. I wish I could linger here.

But the story goes on. Venus cursed Helios so that the god of the sun, the one who watches all the world, could only aim his eyes on me. So the light rushed to the eastern sky above me and lagged in moving west. Our winter days grew longer. One night, while his horses grazed, feeding and resting to gather strength to pull the sun across the sky again, Helios arrived at my home. I will tell this part of the story in as few words as I can. I was in my nightgown brushing out my hair; the women of the house were with me. Helios, disguised as my mother, told the women to say good night, that time alone with a daughter was needed. As soon as the door shut behind them, he revealed himself as who he was.

"*I am the world's eye*," he said. "You look especially beautiful when you're scared."

And then, just radiance. A light so bright it entered all of me.

Is it rape if you don't realize what has happened until afterward?

I vowed to never, never speak of this. If no words were given to it then it could stay less real than a dream.

But I wasn't the only one to know what happened. Pouring all his light my way meant that he left other loves in shadow, like Clytie, who missed feeling the sun god's warmth. In her jealousy, she spread the word of my shame. Something I wanted locked in darkness, she pulled into light. It was my secret to keep, not hers to tell. But she told and told and told. And she made sure to tell my father.

I kneeled at his feet and begged. I used the word *force*. I used the word *trick*. I used the word *rape*. Raising my arms at the unrelenting sun who wrecked me, I pleaded with my father. Please, please, it was not my fault. He said nothing. He looked at me and there was nothing on his face. Not pain. Not rage. Not love. Nothing. He stood in silence and walked away from me. I followed at a distance, and begged.

Then he grabbed a shovel and it was as though a door was slammed on the room that held my words, a room now locked and inescapable. All the words, all my pleas, echoing off walls with sound that would never penetrate. My words entombed by horror.

The sound of the spade eating a hole into the sandy dirt, metal through the earth, lasted from the afternoon deep into the evening. My father grunting as he plunged the shovel. The blisters on his palms. The sweat through his shirt. The hole was deep and dark. I watched my father dig my grave.

I lay facing up into the night sky, hands bound, small rocks digging into my back. Some feet above me, my father stood, leaning into his shovel. The stars blinked

at me. I couldn't see the moon. The first shovelful hit
my shins. A dusting. Pebbles and dirt. It smelled like
rain-damped garden where I was, my face so close to
the walls of dirt. It smelled like roots and ash. It smelled
like childhood. Another shovelful. The dirt riding down
my feet, collecting by my ankles. He aimed his load at
my hips, sent it sliding off the shovel and down onto me.
A pelting on my flesh. I looked at the stars. I breathed
in the dirt. It fell in piles. And at first it was nothing.
Like sitting still in a snow flurry. A dusting. But with
each shovelful the heap increased. Soon dirt filled my
ears. The weight of it pressed my chest. My hip bones
felt about to turn to dust themselves, pulverized under
the weight. Soon to breathe was to fill my mouth or nose
with dirt. Soon the weight was too much for my lungs
to fill with breath. The stars disappeared. Shovelful after
shovelful. Scoop, slide, fall, pile, press. The rhythm of
the night, the song of my death. My grave filled. My
body crushed in darkness. My body buried in darkness.
Permanent night.

Helios, sorry and still fixed on me, took pity. The
next day, he shined his rays hot enough to burn a path-
way through the dirt that I might free my head and
breathe again. Too late. He tried to warm my gone-cold
body. Too late.

He grieved. He wet the earth with nectar. It seeped
down, darkening the soil, to where my lifeless body
mingled with the dirt. My skin drank it in. A changing. Limp crushed body turning, coiling, twisting and
twisting, harder and tighter, round and round. Then a

rising, a gnarling, a rooting, and a pushing. Part pressed up through the dirt, back into the light—too bright, too bright—spreading up and out as a knotty low-flung frankincense tree, all knucklebone. And the roots went down as though pulled by the strong gentle hands of the man who keeps his feet in the core of the earth. The spread of my branches is not my arms raised in exultation or relief; they are not opening up toward the light. It is more a dismissive flick of the wrist. I keep my tears inside.

People come to take them. They make an incision into me, they cut a gash, and tears of milk run thick right toward the opening. Once they reach the light, they harden like pearls. And the human hands pluck them like the jewels they are, and the tears scent the air.

As for Clytie, the Sun was repelled by how she'd told. Deserted and bereft, she sat naked on the earth and set her eyes on the sky as the Sun arced every day across it. She did not eat or drink. She just stared at the Sun until the earth started to swallow her, grow around her, and she changed into a flower, pale and violet-shaped, that turns its face to follow the light.

Me, I dread every sunrise. I spend each evening wishing night will never end. Shame lives inside the body as hot rough hands made of tar that close around the throat, a tar so pitch it repels the light. I wish I could've stayed buried lifeless with my secret, there in perpetual night. Now, I know my violator with every sunrise; each dawn reminds me of my attacker, of my father, his shovel, his blistered palms, of the growing weight of the sand on top of me, of my shame. It is no surprise that my tears, molten and alive inside me, harden when they are touched by light. It is no comfort either.

Each dusk: let this be the last night. Let this begin darkness without end. Each dawn: come cut me open then, come release my tears.

ATALANTA

I had Olympian thighs.

You wanna race? You wanna race? You wanna race? A starting line drawn in the dirt with a stick. The finish line marked by a juniper branch. Warm. The blood moves. On your mark. Muscles ready. Get set. All tensed. Every sense awake for the word *Go*. Press against the earth, push through the air with the arms, and then take off. Or that's how it felt. Each step leg thrust foot land arm swing. Two things in consciousness: where can I find more speed; that finish line.

Where can I find more speed? I'd ask. Sometimes it lived in the big muscles of my thighs. But usually it was in the space between the belly button and the mound, the dark hollow of lowest, deepest guts. That place held more when I needed it. Go faster, Atalanta, I'd tell myself.

Go a little faster. You can, can't you? Where's the speed? There it is, low down, get it. A hollow where the speed lives. No one's feet were faster.

I liked to win.

One coach I had trained me this way: forget marriage. You are not a wife. If you marry, you will lose yourself.

I did not like to lose.

Unwed. I was. But plenty pursued. To end the ongoing chase, I made a contest. You want to marry me? You have to race me. If you win, a wedding. If you lose, you die. I made the rules.

Unbeatable. On race day. All these men hoping to cross the finish before me. People cheered and yelled. I could run across a pond so fast I would not sink below my ankles. Men came. Men raced. Men died. They got into what they knew they were getting into.

Then: "You wanna race?" A young man from the stands asking to compete. Hippomenes with wide strong shoulders, strong long legs, a wild reckless smile. Great-grandfathered by Neptune. "You wanna race?" he asked again, because silence had been my first answer. And all at once, everything slowed on down. All except the strong muscle in my chest which thumped at a pace only running had brought it till now. His voice vibrated in a certain way. It hit different. Young, he was, but with wise eyes. Bold as a lion. I was myself, but in myself something whoa so new. And it sent my mind down two different roads, each one ending in a question mark. Each one ending in pain. Do I want to win? Could I want him to?

That question—that it even came into my own head—brought other questions. Does he have a death wish? What do I lose if I lose? What do I win if I win? What do I lose if I win? What do I win if I lose?

Brave and young. He knew it: *the gods help those who dare.* All the posters in all the coaches' sweat-sock-stinking offices. Can't win, don't try. Fortune favors the brave. Second place, first loser. Sometimes the finish line is only the beginning. Forget me, I thought. I did not want him to die. Go find another wife, don't waste your beauty and youth on a race you won't win. But also, he makes his own decisions. I am not in charge of his mind, same way no one but me's in charge of mine. I liked the way it felt to stand near him. I heard the words of coach: you lose yourself. Before I race I keep my mind clean. Now, my mind was cramping like a hamstring. My mind, racing.

In some part of myself I hadn't known, some dim hollow of my body and my brain, came some unfamiliar sense. I want for once to be outrun. I want him to run faster. This small hollow is where love lives and in me it's felt for the first time and it fills and fills and fills and there is no bottom to it. No bottom to that hollow at all.

I saw Hippomenes kneel before the race, lips whispering in some prayer, some humble plea to Venus, bowing down to her because she's the goddess who most loves love. He spoke sweetness she couldn't resist. She gave him strategy and tips to win. She nestled herself close to him and handed him three apples made of gold from her sacred grove and told him how to use them. Was it his sweetness that swayed her to help? Or was it that she was eager to force a love-shunner to un-shun love? I have my own mind, though, is the thing. I knew what I was doing.

On your mark. Starting line drawn in the dirt. Get set. I could smell his sweat and I liked it. Go. I did not know how to lose. The race at first as they always were: leg foot arm lung full flight. Where's the speed? There it is. A little more? There it is. And more? Get it. Hippomenes was fast. We both knew I was faster. He held my pace but I knew from his breath he wouldn't for long. It was then that he tossed a golden apple in the path. It glinted in the sun as it rolled, and I grabbed it. So many gold medals hung on my mirror, here it just took a different form. But to bend and swift it off the ground, I sacrificed a step, lost some of my composure. But I regained it, found my feet, and passed him once again. I was myself. Only myself. I knew where to look for more speed. I knew what my body could do. I knew so well my own mind.

He threw another golden apple in the path and I understood that this was his way of winning, this was how he'd been coached. Another gold medal, another trophy for my mantel, another gleaming testament to my speed, a souvenir from another win. I leaned to reach it, grabbed it in my hand. I knew my speed and knew I could play his game and win. I lost a step, another. I saw his back. Atalanta, you're unbeatable. And I found the speed and he saw my back.

He threw a third apple, this one way off the track.

Two choices. Win. Or get the third apple. I had the power and the energy and I knew how to execute the race. I could cross the line first if I wanted.

I chose. Veered. Dashed. Grabbed. Apple. Hand. Blazed back to the track and saw the line. I felt young and light and fast. There was more speed, get it, it's the only thing I knew how to do. But this other hollow, the one newly swelled with love, checked my pace by a step. What will it feel like to lose? I wanted to see.

His back. Across the line. I one step behind. I lost. Streak broke. Who was I if I wasn't winning? A moment panting panicked, everything I'd known about myself shattered when his body crossed the line before mine. Who am I? My breath slowed. I was myself. I had lost. A race. I had won. A love. A hollow newly filled.

A wedding and all was right and I was who I was. But who was the man I married? He had Venus to thank for his victory, for coaching him the way she did, for showing tricks. But he didn't thank her. He forgot all about it. As though he beat me on his own. As though any man could beat me on his own. Why couldn't he have just said thanks? Lit a stick of incense? Kneeled in prayer? Where's his gratitude? Aim it right. But he didn't and who could blame her for her anger.

After the wedding, we went for a run together. No race. Long and slow, our muscles moving, keeping pace with each other, each able to dip into the other's strength. Love, I thought. That's what it is. Each able to dip into the other's strength, each made stronger by the other.

We braked, weary, and our sweat dried quickly in the sun.

I want to kiss the salt off you, Hippomenes said. Love high, body spent. Venus, in reaction to his lack of gratitude to her, filled his body with desire, immediate, unfightable, in this place where she knew it was a crime.

Not here though, I said. We were in a sacred place. Just as Venus had planned.

Here, he said. And he pulled me toward a cave. Inside, small wooden sculptures of the gods lined the walls.

Not here, I said.

Here, he said. And he ran his tongue along my neck. Salt harvest. That was enough and we gave ourselves to each other. In the shadows, the sculptures turned their heads.

We sullied the place. We profaned what was sacred. Cybele, the goddess whose cave it was, in fury at what we'd done there, dissolved our human forms. Hair turned fur, tongues roughened, two-footed to four-pawed, fierce-jawed. Not enough time to say: *Why didn't you just say thank you?* I lost myself.

Now, I bite. I eat prey whole. I put claws into the low dark guts and pull the insides out. Roar and race, we drag Cybele's chariot, lion and lioness.

Unbeatable. I was. And am. Will be. Worse fates. Could've been turned into a mountain unmoving. Could've been turned into a snail.

IPHIS

"Thanks for doing this with me."

"It's okay."

"Your father still doesn't know what happened."

"I don't have a problem with that."

"Do you think I should tell him? It feels strange not to tell him."

"I think he would freak."

"You're right. He would freak out. You know before you were born, he said that if you came out a girl, he'd kill you."

"Mom, you've told me that literally a thousand times."

"We didn't have the money for a dowry. He said we couldn't afford a girl. Does that make you hate him?"

"Do I hate Dad? No, of course not. Does it seem like I hate him? They were different times."

"They were different times."

"I'm glad he didn't kill me."

"I saved you."

"I know, Mom."

"You wouldn't be here if—"

"I know. Mom. I'm not sure I can thank you in a way that will make you believe that I'm grateful."

"When you came out of me, I felt like I'd just been absorbed into a cloud made of love."

"Gross."

"Not gross. Really nice. Maybe the nicest thing I've ever felt. And when I saw you were a girl, I thought—or not even thought—I knew that I wasn't going to let him take you away from me."

"I'm really glad about that. It's hard to imagine."

"I told the doctor and nurses to tell your father you were a boy. We were so happy. I'm telling you, I've never seen anyone as happy as your dad the day you were born. We were so happy!"

"That's really nice to hear. You hadn't told me that before."

"And it wasn't hard to keep the sugar. I kept your hair short, and I dressed you in little boy clothes and we gave you a name that could've been for a boy or a girl and you were a boy."

"I wasn't a boy."

"No, I know. I mean, everyone understood you to be a boy. And you had this face, these high broad bones, those dark eyebrows—"

"That's still my face."

"No, I know. Just that you would've been beautiful if you were a boy or a girl. You don't say thank you to that?"

"It doesn't actually feel like a compliment, so."

"Well, it is a compliment, sweetie. You're beautiful."

"Please stop touching my hair."

"For heaven's sake."

"I thought you wanted to have this conversation so you could know better how all of this has been for me."

"I do, I do, I just thought it'd be good to establish the history."

"Don't you think I know the history?"

"Well, you were a baby. You were just a little boy. I don't know what you remember."

"Girl."

"Okay. Yes."

"If I was a boy—don't you understand?—we wouldn't be having this conversation. I don't think you understand how hard things were."

"I do, sweetie, I do."

"No. You can't."

"But it all worked out."

"It all worked out? You asked me to tell you what this has all been like for me. Not how things are now, but how they were. If you want to go on believing everything was fine and the regular amount of hard, go ahead. They weren't."

"Things were hard for me, too, you know. Keeping this sugar. From your dad. From everyone."

"I hated that we called it that."

"You did?"

"Why couldn't we just say *secret*?"

"It was our secret language. Our code. It was our way of talking about it. *Secret* can sound so dirty. So shame-y. I didn't want you to feel like it was something dirty."

"We could've said *secret*."

"It was hard, keeping it, whatever you want to call it. And it was hard when you got to an age where you couldn't hide certain things."

"Are you talking about breasts?"

"I am."

"You can just say breasts, you know."

"I didn't want to make you uncomfortable."

"Why would that make me uncomfortable?"

"Please, you don't have to get tense."

"At the age where I started to grow boobs, yeah, that sucked. That was awful. Taping myself up every day so tight I couldn't take a full breath."

"You couldn't breathe?"

"Obviously I could breathe, I just couldn't take a full huge deep breath."

"Sometimes I feel like that with my jog bra on."

"That's not how it feels."

"You just said it was so tight you couldn't take a full breath. I feel that way when I wear my jog bra. I *do* know."

"Your jog bra? That navy blue thing that's lost most of its elastic? Are you joking?"

"It's tight."

"Okay. Imagine it tighter. Imagine if your boobs had sprained their ankles and needed to be immobilized. Imagine wrapping yourself up so tight your ribs can't fill with air. That is not the way your fucking jog bra feels."

"Common ground. I'm just trying to find some common ground here."

"You haven't found it yet."

"Why don't you tell me more about what it was like."

"When I was thirteen? That hell? Sure. Imagine you're a human kid—"

"I was."

"—and you have two legs and two arms and skin and hair on your head—"

"I had all these things."

"—and a brain and heart and guts and a mouth and a tongue."

"Got it."

"Like you're just a human like the rest of us and some days are fun and some days are boring and sometimes you have to go to the dentist and they give you a giant balloon and some days you get to play soccer and some days you get yelled at for getting paint on the rug and some days you eat Popsicles."

"That sounds like a really nice childhood."

"And then right around thirteen, your skin starts getting strange."

"Pimples."

"Not pimples. It hardens, like a thin shell, like it would crunch if you stepped on it. On your arms, your legs, your belly. Like an insect. Like a giant bug. And you're brushing your hair one morning and there's these two antennae. There's these two antennae growing out of your head like wires."

"What kind of bug?"

"It absolutely does not matter. And all at once you have no idea what you are. Like everything that was normal life that you took for granted is turned upside down. You see yourself in the mirror and you understand yourself as the human kid you've been, but now all of a sudden you have no idea if that's true. Am I a kid or am I a bug? The way you've understood yourself, and the way everyone has understood you, has maybe been wrong all along, and that all the things you thought you knew about yourself, your most fundamental self, is shattered, like when that glass fell off the shelf after the earthquake that time. Like you stand in front of the mirror and you ask yourself, Oh my god, what am I? And as you walk down the sidewalk you can see that everyone is staring at you and everyone is wondering the same thing: *What is that?*"

"But that's in your imagination."

"That people are staring?"

"People always think other people notice way more than they do."

"You are a child, and you are turning into a bug. You don't think people notice? You don't think people are like, hang on, what the fuck?"

"You're describing puberty."

"No I'm not."

"Everyone has that moment, sweetie. It's called growing up."

"You do not listen."

"Everyone has that moment, when the hormones kick in and bodies get oily and hairs grow, when they feel like a stranger in themselves."

"Growing pubic hair and getting zits is not the same as going from a human to a bug. It is not the same as going from having shoulder blades to having wings."

"Everyone feels like they're turning into a bug at some point."

"Fuck it."

"No, go on, sweetie. All right, I'm a bug."

"No, listen. So I start growing tits and it feels disgusting. It feels like my body does not belong to me and I have no idea what I am and that a punishment is taking place. I have literally no idea what's happening or who I am and it is a frightening place to be. Like, I'm telling you: it was fucking scary. All the time. I need you to understand that. And there was no one I could talk to about it because no one could understand."

"You could've talked to me."

"It was confusing and shameful and everything about the way I understood myself came into question. Like, hang on, didn't we tell you, you're not a boy, you're a girl! Like, what the fuck?"

"I said you could've talked to me."

"That's not how it felt."

"I remember the day you got your period."

"Me, too."

"I'm not sure I've ever seen anyone cry as hard."

"Well, it was scary and I hated it and I hated that my

body was doing that because in my brain I was something else and I didn't want to be what I was."

"Maybe it's like when I look in the mirror I get shocked when I see how old I am because in my mind I'm much younger."

"Maybe it's like that. I don't know."

"It was hard seeing you so upset."

"It was hard being so upset."

"Did I make you feel better? Did I do an okay job at making you feel better?"

"I feel like this is becoming more about me trying to make you feel okay about something. This is becoming more about reassuring you."

"That's not what I'm doing. I'm here to listen."

"I don't want to talk about getting my period."

"That's fine. I'm just telling you it was really hard seeing you so upset. You seemed so sad and so scared. I remember I wanted to cry but I wouldn't let myself cry in front of you. And it wasn't so much sadness I felt, but angry."

"What the fuck were you angry about? What did you have to feel angry about?"

"Sweetie. I was angry at your dad."

"Oh."

"But also sad. When you got your period and I was doing laundry and washing the jeans you were wearing and I saw the stain—"

"Did you not hear what I just said?"

"It wasn't just a little bit. There was so much blood, sweetie. Do you remember? When I first got my period, it was just a tiny bit on my underpants."

"Fucking ridiculous."

"No, no, wait, where are you going? Okay, please. Sit back down. We don't have to talk about your period. Help me understand."

"You're making this really hard."

"Just go on, please."

"Try this. You're in a bathroom. A public bathroom. There are other women in the bathroom. Three other women. All of you are washing your hands at the sinks. You look up into the mirror that's spread across above the sinks and you have no idea which reflection belongs to you. You have no idea which is you."

"I don't like that."

"That's because it's terrifying. And it was even more confusing when I started having feelings for Ianthe. We were in all the same classes and she had those huge green eyes. And she'd wear these shirts that fell off her shoulder and she wore a bra before most of the other girls and I'd see her bra strap on her shoulder and it was like I had a circus in my stomach. I'd see her come around the corner in the hall at school and my stomach would fall into my hips, just like drop right down, and my whole torso would get warm. I just remember feeling extra alive near her, like this elevated energy anytime we were together. A crackle. And when we weren't together all I would think about was the next time I'd see her."

"I felt that with your father at the start."

"Except that it felt awful. I was a girl. I knew I was a girl. You knew I was a girl. There was this huge sug— secret that I felt like I was being buried under. Like this heap of something on top of me every day, crushing me. Burying me alive. Ianthe thought I was a boy. She liked me because she thought I was a boy. But I wasn't, and I wanted to be more than friends with her. I wanted to see what she looked like without her shirt. I wanted to slow dance with her. I wanted to touch her skin."

"You don't need to tell me this."

"I wanted to kiss her."

"Sweetie."

"I didn't want to want to kiss her. It was horrible feeling that way. I thought I was crazy. I thought there was something so so so so so wrong with me. Like mares don't have crushes on mares and sows don't have crushes on sows. Sheep want rams. Does want stags. Hens—"

"I get it."

"You don't. Because you have no idea what it is to feel like you're going against nature. That you are diseased. Disordered. All wrong. I wanted to lie in bed and listen to songs with her. I wanted to jump off the dock with her at night. I wanted to put my hands up her shirt and it made me feel like I shouldn't be on the earth. I thought I was a monster. Plus I had no idea whether the feelings I had for her were real or whether they had to do with the fact that I was living this secret. Like, did I really like her? Did I really want to jump off the dock with her at night? Did I really want to put my hands up her shirt? Or was it because those were the things a boy was supposed to want?"

"It's not a disorder."

"Oh my god. It *felt* like one. I felt like I was

disordered. Like, there was something deeply wrong with me. I felt insane. Okay?"

"Please don't yell."

"And I knew she liked me, too. But she liked me as a boy and that's not what I was and it was this horrible secret from everyone."

"Well, what was I supposed to do? I couldn't tell your dad."

"I thought about killing myself."

"Sweetie. No."

"I couldn't stop my feelings for Ianthe. And you guys arranged the marriage. And I was going to be found out, and then what? Ianthe wouldn't want to be with me. Maybe Dad would kill me."

"Sometimes I wish I'd never met him."

"I would lie in bed and just be like, you're a girl, you're a girl, you're a girl. Stop feeling this way. Stop thinking about her. I've thought so much about it since then, and the thing with love, I think the main thing with love, the thing that makes it live, is hope. Like hope that you'll get even closer than you are, hope that you'll understand and be understood better all the time, hope that you'll come out of whatever shitty patch you're going through, hope that there's so much more always to explore together. And when there's no hope, that's the death of love."

"Anger, too."

"Anger what?"

"Can kill love."

"Well, I wasn't angry at Ianthe. But I knew there

wasn't any hope. I was a girl. She was a girl. Everyone was glad she and I were together—Dad, you, her,
her parents. To everyone it made sense. But I knew it
couldn't ever happen. And that if it did, my life would
be over."

"I wasn't necessarily glad you were together. It scared
me, too."

"That I was going to get found out?"

"That it meant the end."

"Of my life?"

"Possibly. But I was happy that you were happy. I
could see you loved her."

"I wasn't happy."

"But you loved her."

"I was a monster."

"I wanted to murder him. Sometimes I really did
want to. Sometimes I still do want to. I prayed for you. I
prayed to Isis. I prayed to her that you would know what
to do. That the sugar would just go away. I saw that it
was burying you. But you were never a monster. I prayed
and prayed. Isis, I begged, help us."

"It worked. There was hope. There were options."

"You changed."

"I changed."

"I remember turning around and seeing you walking,
after the change. Your stride was different. It's funny
how certain people's walks are so familiar. And all of
a sudden your stride was altered. It was so subtle. You
never had a swishy girlish walk, not hips like a bell—"

"That's how you walk."

"I have hips, that's why. But then there was something, flatter, more rigid in the movement. Still graceful, still elegant, but heavier of step somehow."

"I held my shoulders differently."

"And your face. Your eyebrows got darker. Even the shape of your jaw changed."

"You can notice that?"

"Oh, definitely!"

"I thought maybe it wasn't noticeable."

"Oh, I love seeing you smile like that. You became what you always were."

"Yeah."

"Things worked out."

"Things worked out."

"You're happy with Ianthe."

"I'm so happy."

"I hate your dad."

"I know."

"I've wanted to kill him."

"That's hard to hear."

"It makes me feel like a monster."

"You're not."

"I'm sorry you had to go through this."

"Me, too."

"It was hard for both of us."

"I know."

"I'm really happy you're happy."

"Me, too."

"My beautiful son."

HECUBA

Good evening. I'd like to welcome you all to the third installment of our speaker series, "Transnational Trauma: Displacement, Migration, and Exile in the Contemporary World." Tonight we're so lucky to have with us the mother of Hector, Paris, Troilus, Polydorus, and Polyxena, among others. Hecuba has witnessed and endured the unimaginable, and I'll let her put those to you in her words. I'll be serving as interpreter for tonight's talk, and, as always, will do my best to create a bridge between her language and ours. Welcome, Hecuba. Thanks for being with us tonight. Let's begin.

"My name is Hecuba," she says. "I am not from here.

"This you know already. You can tell by the color of my skin, and the shape of my eyes, and the launch no the rise of the bones in my cheek, and you can tell by the scarves I windmill or spin sorry wrap, the scarves I wrap around me. You can hear it in the way my mouth shapes the words I speak, in the spread of the vowels, the—the slipperiness of certain consonants. You have an idea of where I belong. The way you—the way you—look at me, you see only a representation of a place, a kind, a certain breed that you aren't sure you want here. I am 'one of them.' If only I could make you know what it is to be rubbed out or no *erased* by people's eyes.

"What do you see when you look at me? Do you see a dog? Is a dog what you see? Some scabby chewed-up mongrel? I see the way you look at me.

"You who belong here, you who were born on this land, you cannot know comprehend this experience of—this experience of exile. Or or exile or—this is me speaking as interpreter now, the more literal translation is is is dislocation. The actual words she used are 'the experience of being pulled out of the socket of your life.' She says, 'This is a state of existing beyond borders.'

"I am not from here and my homeland as I knew it no longer gives up to me offers an embrace. But this is not just a matter of geography, this goes far beyond notions of geography, of the simple act of crossing invisible borderlines that separate here from there. Those boundaries are an irrelevance to me at this time now. The only borders that matter to me are those to be found at the edges of fear and the edges of dreams, the lines to be found at the limits of hate and of love.

"The War took everything. It took my husband. It took my sons. It took my daughter who was torn from my arms and her throat slit in front of me. Do you want me to to to describe the sound her body made when it landed on the floor? Or the sound in her throat as she gulped no swallowed sorry choked choked on her own blood? Or how the light from the window hit the blood on the floor and turned one band of it white like milk? Do you want me to tell you the look of the sight orb no eye of the man machine sorry soldier who did it? The deadness in his eyes? The nothing in his eyes? Do you want to hear how loud I screamed? I did not know I had so much voice inside me. I put my body on top of her body. My hands, my face, jacketed sorry coated no covered covered in her blood.

"And while I wept, a sick sort of relief came over me—there can be no suffering deeper than this. There is a vault or rather basement sorry the literal words *soul basement* sorry bottom. There is a bottom and I have found my way to it.

"But, you see, I had not. There was lower still. There is a place past grief I hope none of you have to see in the complete span of your hours.

"I went down to the shore to collect ocean water in an urn to cleanse the wounds of my dead daughter. If there is a boundary between here and gone, this is when I crossed it. There on the sand, a body. A gray swollen body being rolled by the push and pull of the waves. Limp gray swollen, with wounds that yawned no gaped around the chest and ribs. I did not want to look closer, but something drew me. I was pulled by a physical maternal force that is a mystery. This is where I crossed over. The face. The face. My son. My final child. He was the one who was supposed to be safe.

"I looked up at the sky. In that moment, I was gone. I myself became absence. I had no bones, no brain, no blood. I was lesser than a kite. In that moment, I was the sky. I was spread without end.

"There are no boundaries to an absence.

"Here you see the very interpreter himself has rain of the—cries. He cries. You, you who belong here, you hear this story and some of you cry, too.

"My whole life, my whole self feels like a foreign country I've arrived in. In this place, the streets are made of phantoms no or ghosts. Gray shifts of movement, fogs in human shapes. I move through them as a ghost myself. Moments of memory, familiarity, of some sense of recognition, they happen and dissolve sooner than I know what it is that's appeared. A glimpse of a fruit tree in the yard of my childhood, the smell of char on beef, a shape of a face, my sister? my friend? my husband? my child? These apparitions of what was, there and gone too soon for me to feel anything but their their their inexistence.

"We all of us have scaffolding off of which we hang our understanding of ourselves. I was a woman, a mother, a Trojan, a queen. What happens when every piece of that scaffolding collapses? Where do we find our borderlines? What happens when they dissolve? I tell you.

"I looked at my son on the beach. But I did not see my son. I ate with my eyes his wounds alone, the places on his body where he had been opened. I ate with my

eyes the inside of him. There I saw infinity. I saw infinity the way you see infinity in the eyes of the infant, the
universe that you see when you look into the eyes of the
infant. That is what I saw when I looked into the body
of my son. And it was inside this universe that I made
my decision.

"Perhaps you wonder why I do not cry as I tell you
this. As I said, this is a place past grief I hope none of
you ever one time have to visit.

"I knew who did this to my son and I went to this
man and I appealed to his greed so he would meet with
me and what I did was—"

—

—

—

—

What's she saying? Why'd you stop? What is she saying?
"I'm sorry. Please. I'm sorry. I apologize."
Go on! Don't silence her! Keep going!
"I say it again: I met with this man who murdered
my son and I looked in his eyes. Inside his eyes I saw
nothing. This is not the same as infinity. Not the same as
galaxies. His eyes they held the most dangerous thing,
they held the the top of the sins. Indifference. Indifference. A vacancy where human care should be. I saw that
he saw me for the money I might give him. I was nothing. Sub. A dog. Does this sound familiar? What do you
see when you see me?

"In his eyes, a vacancy of care. And then what I
did—"

—

—

Don't stop! It's not your job to protect us! Hey! Just tell us the words that she's saying!

"I grabbed his face with my hands and I placed my thumbs and my thumbnails into his eyes not placed I pressed my thumbs into his eyes which held all of the cruelty and all the indifference. With my thumbs I pressed and pressed and pressed and pressed. I felt the wet of his eyeballs. For a moment my boundaries were back. In one flash sorry blast detonation of time, all of the borders returned.

"When my thumbs were all the way in, as deep in as they could go, I—

"I popped out his eyeballs. His eyes were not blue, not gray, not brown, not green, not orange, not yellow, not violet. His eyes were the color, oh dear. They were the color of the shit of a baby. And once they were out, each one, the blood drooled from his eyes and women helped me hold him down. And with my hands I reached into the hollows no sorry holes er sockets his sockets those sockets. And I—oh dear, oh god—I plucked oh god I picked out his flesh. I reached into the sockets and I plucked his flesh. It was warm. He screamed. I knew I could scream louder. Here is when—"

—

—

—

Say it!
"I can't."

What does she say? Say it! Go on!

"I can't. It's too much."

Say the words! We came here to know! Say them!

"He screamed. I felt each small bite no morsel sorry bit just bit between my fingers. Here is when I became what you see before you. Here is when I was born a dog. What happens when the boundaries dissolve? Your borders mean nothing. What lives at the limits of loss? Of hate? What terrible place is that? Look at me. I have been. I know. Do not come to this place where everything is fanged and singed and whimpering.

"The border of love. That's a place, too. I have set my feet there. It can be as frightening. Phantoms live there, too. And boundaries dissolve in a different way, a way that joins you with the widening or or sorry the whole, a way that joins you with the whole. That place is there and it is yours to know. And I say to you with these words, you who belong to this place, you who understand what it is to live in this world, go there. Travel to that place. No one deserves the horror that has washed itself over my life. I do not matter. This country does not matter, not to me, not in this hour. Keep indifference out of your eyes, you who belong to this place. You will—"

—

—

Speak!

"You will hear my yowls in the night, I who am a dog. When the darkness hoards the day, you will hear my yowls and you will remember this sadness. This sadness without boundary, born from loss, born from the dissolving of all the borderlines that made a world make sense. My howls, the howls of this dog you see before you, they will penetrate the soft edges of your brain while you sleep, and for a moment, as your dream turns sideways, we will not be separate. We will be as one."

POMONA

How's it that you spend your days? Do you put on shoes that shine and ride an elevator to a desk? Do you pull lobster traps from the seafloor of the harbor with the buoys striped so you know they're yours to pull? Do you watch as your soft child tries to acquire the language that you speak? Do you clean the stalls? Spin yarn? Frame walls, measuring out the sticks of pine sixteen-on-center? Do you lay plates of food upon tables for people who pay? Soften the edges with whiskey? Harden your edges with squats or lifts or long jogs at dusk on elm-lined streets in the town outside the city? Laugh with your brothers? Snap a mask on and dance the whole night? Do you absorb the daily news? Push information through an entrance on a screen? Lose yourself in a trance of prayer? Hang laundry on a line? Give shots to dogs? Teach young others what to know?

Me, I garden. I raise the plants. I've done so for thirty-nine years. Alongside my father and my mother. Alongside my sisters. Alongside the crew of women I hired. What's enough for you? Dirt was enough for me. Ropey roots in soil. Water air and light. Petals spreading. Buds that can't contain themselves and widen into leaves, punchy fists to generous open palms. From seed to sprout to sapling to tree, and then to have an apple, or a peach, or a pear, that you can pull from the branch and eat, and feel the sweet juice of it running down your throat. What a thing! It never got old. Or the firm orange flesh of a sweet potato that you pull from the underground then roast so it's soft as pudding and almost as sweet. The tender layered waves in a head of lettuce. The simple green straws of the scallions. I string a trellis for the beans to climb. I prune and pluck. I graft and snip and trim. I spend a morning pollarding the pear tree that grows against the barn, and it's a day I can feel I did something. That by my hands, I helped something change and grow. There are many ways to make a life. This is mine. I spread fertilizer, deadhead, mow. I tuck bulbs just as deep as they want to be and no deeper than that.

This was all the pleasure I needed. To push a group of bulbs into the dirt in fall, watch snow come and see my breath in cold, and then the thaw, and there in April, a clutch of daffodils rise and spread their yellow selves to the sun. Could there be a greater joy? Call me easily

satisfied, but this was all I wanted. The deep purple velvet of the pansies. The flayed leaves of the gingko biloba.
The name gingko biloba! The bleached bark of the thick
sycamores, white like they've been frightened. Oh gosh,
the staggering variety of life on land. And I think about
how much runs in sync to bring about new growth. The
wind spreads seeds, as do the squirrels and birds, in and
out of them. The sun. The rain. The pollinators buzz
and zoom, chubby bumblebees, iridescent hummingbirds,
the butterflies who fly on petal wings.

Me, I am what you picture when you picture a gardener. Not all my hair is gray. Not yet. Still some chestnut, carrot, wheat. It's long and I wear it in a braid most
days. I wear a wide-brimmed hat made of straw to keep
the sun from my neck and my face. My shoulders are
strong, and so is my back, muscles line my spine from
digging and pulling and carrying sacks of manure from
here to there. My legs are strong. I get freckles in the
sun. The lines at my eyes are deep, deeper than other
people my own age, in part from the power of the sun,
in part from all the smiling. Why wake up if you're not
going to laugh? My hands are strong and the dirt lives in
the cracks and always will. My breasts are smaller than
they were. I miss the heft of them, but this is how it is.
Time is the only one that thrives.

I was so content, growing and tending. I spent time
with men. I spent time with women. The carnal pursuits
didn't pull me. Another way: love, fucking, I thought
they weren't for me. I used to hire men for the crew.
All these Pans and satyrs. Their thick animal dicks on

display. Priapus was the worst of them. He'd whip his dick out any chance he could. The size of it. Thick as a dogwood and long as my arm. Men said, Pomona, I love you. They'd touch me and I'd think, Okay. But maybe it should feel like more? Each time: Is this all? And I'd tell them, You're nice but hit the road. They'd leave and I'd feel relieved to be back to my Siberian squill, Allegheny spurge, pink maiden. Swoon. I rolled with women in the grass, my gardeners. They'd smell like sweat and hay and their skin like mine was warm in the sun. And it was nice, but also, always the sense was something missing. This is fine, to roll and tangle. But I got more from the buds, the petals, the bloom, all the veined and grassy stuff that comes out of the earth.

And now, the peonies have grown five inches in as many days. Fast enough at this stage you can almost see them grow. We're at that point in the season now. No blooms yet, but the buds are starting to swell, and last night they shifted over from the red-brown color of the dregs of wine to the pale green that defines the color spring. "Sexiest flower of them all," one of the gardeners used to say. "Like a woman taking off a dress." That eruption of petals. It's hard not to love.

Spring again and change is all over. There was a man who came and came again. He'd shift his appearance—sometimes a farmer, with dirty overalls and a cow prod; sometimes a gardener, with a wide hat and a spade; sometimes a hunter, with a rifle on his shoulder. He just wanted to spend time. I took him for lonely and we'd chat in the afternoons. Vertumnus was his name, and

I told him I liked it, verdant in there, and autumn, and truth. "And 'us,'" he'd say. And I'd say, You're nice, but no. It's not for me.

One afternoon, an old woman came to the garden. She wore a blue gingham dress and her hair was white like Queen Anne's Lace and though she was old she was still tall and had a force to her. She poured praise upon the fruit and I asked her what I could do for her, what sort of flower or tree or climbing vine she might be looking for. New succulents, I told her, too.

We talked about Japanese maples. We talked about a holly bush. We talked about the spread of lemon thyme and the way it smells like magic when you step on it, when the oils are released into the air and it's like you're walking through a cloud of citrus mist.

"You are amazing," the old woman said. "To bring about this garden. What a fertile place!" She took a deep breath through her nose and closed her eyes. "I can smell all of it, all the trees, all the flowers, all the fruit. You amaze me," she said.

I thanked her, told her I could only take so much credit. She took another deep inhale and took steps toward me and wrapped her arms around me in a strong embrace, exhaling into my neck. And then she kissed my mouth unlike any granny. Okay, I thought. She's lonely, too.

We walked among the plants. She took a rest on a bench I'd made from the trunk of a fallen oak. We sat below a favorite elm of mine, and she admired how the grapevines wound themselves around the boughs. The grapes shone in the sun and the vines helixed around the branches. It was nice that she'd noticed—it was a project I was proud of and I loved the way it looked.

"If the elm was unwed to the vines, it'd be a tree like any other. And without the branches to wind around, the vines would lie limp on the ground. The best of each is brought out in combination," she said.

"You've lived your life as a vine without a branch, a trunk without a vine. Pomona, I am an old woman. I know some things. I'll tell you: all your life you've been pursued, by women, by men. You're irresistible. You've turned down every chance. Reconsider. There is one man in particular who can match you, who could satisfy you in ways that your garden can't. I bet you know who I'm going to say."

I did know. I knew all at once exactly who was talking.

"Vertumnus," she went on. "He loves you like no one's loved you. He'll love you until he dies, you alone. He's gorgeous. And you are kindred in your pursuits— you grow fruit, he loves to eat it! All he wants to do is eat the peach that comes from your garden, let its nectar run down his chin."

I blushed at this, and laughed. "I am almost an old woman."

"You think that matters? You have more youth than you know, and you are never, never too old to be changed by love."

A stirring somewhere in my guts, like the light-dark flickering of the aspen leaves in the breeze. A feeling of ease. Like my whole body was smiling. Then the old woman changed the tenor of her talk.

"People with hard hearts get punished."

My heart was the softest place I knew.

"Have you heard of Iphis and Anaxarete? It's a story you'd do well to know, and I'll tell it as quick as I can. Iphis was poor and he loved Anaxarete, who was rich. He loved her and loved her. He did not push, he tried so hard to be patient, he waited by her door hoping she would see him for who he was, and not just that he was poor. But she shunned him. She put herself on a shelf above him, too proud. She acted as though he didn't exist. Poor Iphis. He tried and tried and loved and loved. But for Ana he did not exist. His heart broke in half. Outside her door, he said, 'Maybe my own death will please you. Probably the only thing that will.' With garlands he strung up on the rafters outside her door, he tied a noose and hanged himself. His neck snapped, he dangled, and his feet knocked against the door. Still she did not answer.

"When his funeral procession moved through the streets, only then did Ana deign to look. She peered from her balcony at the body being carried below. No sooner than she saw him than her eyes began to harden inside her head. Her blood thickened until it stopped running in her veins. She tried to move, but couldn't. Her legs, her bones, her muscles, all became rigid, stripped of life. The rest of her body finally matched her heart and was made of stone."

I listened to the old woman, and I saw through her

disguise, and I was drawn, in a way I'd never known, to the passion with which she told her tale. The words themselves, they dissolved; I barely heard them. An image spread itself across my mind. In it, I was a tree, a huge tree, a giant sequoia with a trunk so thick it would take ten people hand in hand to embrace it all the way around, and tall enough to sometimes touch clouds, with roots reaching deep into the soil, deep, deep into the earth where it's wet and warm. And above, my leaves soaked in the sun and the wind was my dance partner. And my roots twirled themselves around other roots and my branches tapped other branches and my leaves brushed other leaves. What love. And in this image a bear appeared from the woods, a burly creature, coarse-haired and bright-eyed and he rubbed himself against my trunk and pleasure rippled up and down my body. He growled and I shifted to give him more shade. And then he climbed me, clawed himself up into a crotch where one of the thickest branches split from the trunk. He surrendered all of his weight to me, and I held him, and here was new happiness.

And perhaps the old woman could tell my mind had strayed from what she said. She pulled the white wig from her head and became who she was, Vertumnus all along. And he looked hurt, as he had before when I'd told him no, and he looked about to turn away and leave, but the distance in my eyes wasn't for unwant. It was happy disbelief. Here I was coming to know that this person, who I'd seen in so many forms all these years, was someone I loved, someone I wanted to share my life, entwine into my roots, let rest on my branches, help grow like I help my maples, my lilacs, my pears, and let him help me grow. There was still room for me to grow.

I put my arms around him. "Finally," I said.

"Pomona!" he said.

"You can eat my apples. You can eat my peach."

"It's all I wanted."

You think you are a certain way. But then you learn: there's time left for change. Time will change your body, bring you through youth and strength and weaken you in old age. But like the seeds which need so much to grow, you have to tend your mind and heart, and they, too, can crack open, spread, and grow. So I am old. I am different from what I was, different is growth. I changed my mind. Time changed my mind. We walk the vineyards, pull grapes from the vine, explode their skins with our teeth and feel their sweet juice in our throats. What more could there be? What more? I braid my hair. I kneel in dirt. I take his hand. We leave space for change. We make things grow.

SIRENS

Put your eyes in the eyes of the seagull. See the waves from above, the shifting contours moving below you as the water rises and retreats into itself. Twenty feet above. Two hundred. Half a mile in the sky. Look! Wide blue view below you, everything is movement, a-swish, awash, splashing, spindrift racing the wind toward some unseen finish. Sister, brother, breathe the sea.

Everything is movement. Everything is song.

We're golden-feathered bird girls and we sing by the sea. Bird bodied, gold winged, bird legged, bird clawed, girl shouldered, girl faced, girl voiced. Our harmonies are wind through trees, ice freezing across water, the moans of ecstasy and lamentation, all the birds, all the fish, all the creatures of the sky and sea waking up at once. We are the sound beyond the weather, the sound on the other side of the sky. Our song will bring you voidward. Our song will bring you home.

Before, on land, when we were girls, we were in the grove with our friend Proserpina. The day she disappeared, that morning in the meadow, we sang together as we collected violets and white lilies. We filled our skirts with petals and our voices carried over the field.

We sang and we picked flowers and then our friend was gone. We didn't know then where she went. We cried her name to the stars. No one knew what happened. No one knew where she'd gone. All at once, an absence.

A mother's nightmare. Ceres's mind cracked open. Some would say: the earth grieved with the goddess. More true: a mother's grief is powerful enough to change the world. Color slunk away as though it had been shamed. Our long summer ended. Ceres wanted to find her daughter. We wanted to find our friend.

So we three girls set out in search. We looked all over the land. On our feet, we looked high and low. On craggy peaks, in darkened caves, in wooded hollows, behind the waterfalls, between the trees. At the edges of the farms, in the cellars of the temples, in ditches and gardens and bogs. The rain soaked us. The snow made us cold. We looked and looked. We sang as we went. Maybe she would hear us. Maybe she would hear us and call out.

On feet, we could look only so far. "Help us look wider," we said to Ceres. "We haven't explored the seas. Let us look there." Ceres agreed, and that's when we were turned into bird girls. On our golden wings we soared above the waves. We sounded shores with song. We tried to find our friend.

O void, O void, O swallowing abyss, O void who holds the whole vast shadow cast by time, sing in us, O void, deliver us our friend.

We never found her. We flew above the sea not knowing that we should've dived into the underground, lower and lower, into Pluto's realm of gloom and dim. That morning in the meadow, he fractured the earth, put his arm around the waist of Proserpina, and took her down below. Below, she sat on a throne of black marble, cool against the skin of her arms, kidnapped, captive, a hostage to the wants of Underworld's tall and too-thin king. She was torn from the aboveground life she knew and loved, and torn another way as well. Our stolen friend. When she made her annual return, we were happy to see her back, but she was not the same, oh no, she was not the same at all.

We turned to bird girls to find our friend. We soar and perch on rocks and sing. We sing for our lost friend. We sing for ourselves. We sing because we love the song. But our simple song got twisted. The men in ships they heard us sing and they could not resist the sound. And so they called us dangerous. When it's they who lack control. And so we're known as monsters. When what we are is bird girls, our voices like the sounds you hear from the womb.

O void, O void, O swallowing abyss, O void who holds the whole vast shadow cast by time. Sing in us and deliver us new notes to sing this song.

We're golden-feathered bird girls. We sing because we always sing. And O sister, do the men get lost? Do the sailors, in a frenzy, in a trance, sometimes aim their ships at rocks? Do our harmonies haunt and vise the mind, pressing out all sense? Do the men sometimes leap from their boats and try to swim to where our voices are? O sister, yes they do. Is it our fault, or our intention? O sister, it is not. We sing a song of consequence. We sing a song of cost. They know it's so and call us monstrous. Sing. Put your eyes in the eyes of a seagull. See the ships at sway. Listen for our voices. Soar above the waves. Sing. Watch those men lose themselves. Watch them rot. Everything is movement. Everything is song.

Now sing. O sister, sing and sing and sing. Let the sound fly from your mouth. Let it land and light the dark. We three bird girls, we'll sing out with you, we'll join our voices in the chorus, and the sound will rise like bells, like wind, like strings, like prayer, the song that's yours to sing. Louder, louder. You'll see. And if the song doesn't land and light the dark, sister, keep singing. Your song! Holy! Consequential! True!

EURYDICE

I went through phases. I started, like most kids I guess, with my parents' records. The music they liked. Banana Rabbit. The Volcanoes. Death on Mars. Lulu Allellel. Psychedelic folk rock from when they were young. I hated the stupid pop my friends listened to. It was like sucking on a stalk of celery versus digging into a steaming bowl of ramen, pork bone broth, scallions, egg, noodles, the whole deal. I'd tell them, "The shit you're listening to is garbage," but they hated the shit I was into, so it was fine.

My first concert, I was probably eight or nine years old. My parents took me to a festival and we slept in a tent. I was scared at first. Definitely the most people I'd seen in one place. And they were adults to me, but they weren't acting like I understood adults to act. Flailing, dancing, arms out spinning, staring up at the stars. Lots of colors. Bonfires. Drums all night. But people were friendly, and amazed to see a kid around, so I got a lot of good attention. My dad was a musician. A famous one. Like one of the most famous ones. Like people used the words *rock god*. People would say, You're the child of rock royalty. If I told you his name, you'd be like, holy shit, that's your *dad*? And then you'd look at me and say, Oh yeah, I can see it. You guys have the same mouth. But when you're growing up, you have no idea what normal is, so it was just normal life to have a dad who was gone for months in a row on tour, whose face I'd see on posters wheat-pasted on walls along the sidewalk, sneering that sneer, all those necklaces. That was my life. I didn't know that most kids didn't have rock god dads, that most parents were things like mechanics or librarians or biology teachers.

It wasn't that first concert that convinced me. Maybe I was a little too young. It was the first concert I went to alone. My dad was away, as usual, and I pretended to go to bed, and then snuck out to G.G. the Hare's, which was this tiny little rock club in the good part of the city, to see Womb play. Don't know it? It was a band fronted by this woman who was six-two, and she had a voice like no one had a voice. Like it was coming out of some ancient fountain. Like it held in it every story, every folktale, every epic poem, the entire oral tradition, all the whole history of song. She sang with her eyes closed the whole time, sort of disappeared into herself, wearing this long black robe. And I stood there, I was probably fourteen, and I was just like, This is what I want my life to be. It was like her voice was a living creature that crawled inside me and made its home in my body, moving all around it. It felt like she was singing for me, and at the same time, I could feel the whole room against me, all the other bodies there to listen, and I knew that everyone's body was feeling the music like mine, like it was vibrating in their lungs and intestines and hips and shoulders like it was in mine, like all of us were swept up and united in this one moment. The next morning I told my mom I wanted a guitar. She let out a long sigh. Like she knew this day would come.

After the sort of hippie folk phase, I got into heavier stuff. Louder. November's Lament, Toad Migration, Jenny's Back, Lunch. Stuff like that. I'd go to shows and it'd be walls of sound. Sound so thick it felt like you could lie down on it. My hair was already dark, and I copied what I saw, lining my eyes in black. My friends were still listening to their stupid pop, and I derived maybe more pride than I should've from knowing and loving bands that not that many people knew or loved. I went to school and I practiced guitar and my dad was mostly gone and when he was home my mom and him would just shout at each other all night and in the morning there'd be tumblers and bottles around and sometimes spills that no one had cleaned up. I heard him say things like "You're a worthless cunt. Everything that came out of your mother's stretched-out pussy was ugly and worthless." I don't even like repeating that and I wish I'd never heard it. She was pissed in her quiet way because he was either gone or drunk and "humped a hell of a lot of twenty-year-olds," as she put it. He was pissed because she was doing just fine without him. He hated that. But instead of saying, "I need you and I want you to need me," he'd tell her she was unfuckable and that she looked like a heap of rags.

Creative people have different sorts of temperaments and different sorts of tempers. If you're worshipped by a stadium full of screaming people and come home and the mother of your child can take you or leave you, it's jarring for the ego. I wasn't sure why my mom put up with it. I'm not sure how anyone really learns what normal is supposed to be.

I practiced guitar. I sang. I was in a band. I wasn't a great singer but I was earnest and committed and sometimes that's better than having a quote-unquote good voice. Most of my favorite singers couldn't sing either so I felt like I was doing something right. I practiced and practiced. And played shows to four people and got hit on by bartenders and sweaty club owners who looked like ogres. I kept practicing and kept playing and played shows for thirty people and kept practicing and kept playing and played shows for two hundred people and got recognized once on the sidewalk. Quick eye contact with a dude and he says "Oaken?" as we passed each other. That was the name of my band. I turned. "You're the singer in Oaken, yeah?" "That's me," I said. "My girlfriend and me were listening to 'Shadowland' last night. I love that song." "That's really nice to hear. Thank you." "Thank you!" he said. "We love your music."

And I smiled for the rest of the day and maybe into the next day, and kept it in a pocket in my brain to take out when I felt low.

I never talked about my dad. I didn't admit he was my dad. Because I didn't want any attention or shows or deals just because I was his daughter. I had practiced until my fingers bled and rehearsed until I had claws in my throat. I didn't want to worry that none of that mattered, that my success might have nothing to do with how good I was or wasn't and only because I had a mouth that looked like his mouth. And every time someone found out who he was, the fear came, a two-fold bad fluttery feeling that the person was only hanging out with me because of that, to brush up against fame, like I was a one-way ticket into people's dreams come true. And that what meager success I had I hadn't earned myself. I had a hard time keeping people close. What I had was the music. Whenever I was lonely or alone, there was always the music to be my company. So I practiced and I played and the crowds got bigger and the tours got longer. The songs I wrote were getting better and stranger and I felt braver, like I could really tilt for the cliff. No one to talk to on a Friday night: there was always a song to work out, the guitar to pick up and translate the sound in my head through my fingers into the instrument and out into the room. I got good because I was bad at other things, namely being with other people.

I was bad at picking boyfriends. I think it was hard for boys to see me be good onstage. To get the kind of attention I did. To see me doing well at the one thing I wanted to do. I dated a writer who hadn't published anything who compared his novel-eleven-years-in-progress to "modern-day James Joyce." When he'd said that on our first date, I'd laughed because I thought he was joking, because who can, with full-body seriousness, compare an unpublished work to one of the best writers of the twentieth century? A young man writer who had not published a single word. That's who. I laughed, thinking, *Oh, maybe he's funny, that would be nice.* And he got this look like he'd just swallowed a bee and said, "Must be sweet having a dad get you a record deal." And I realized he was not trying to be funny at all, that he was quite serious about writing the next *Portrait of the Artist as a Young Asshole.* I didn't tell him that I hadn't spoken to my dad in three years at that point and that as far as I knew he had no idea I was even in a band. "It *is* sweet," I said. "I don't have to do anything! I don't even know how to play guitar!" I said. "Art is really about putting in the hours," he said. "I guess I should try that," I said. I dated him for over a year. Spent nights on his mattress on the floor. Gave him sensitive feedback when he'd send me his shitty poems. Why? No idea.

I dated a painter who liked me because I wouldn't let him paint me. His day job was at the art supply store and he'd ask the hot art students who came in there buying mat board and Ilford paper if they'd be willing to model for him. "I don't really like painting," he told me. "But I love looking at naked girls." Another time he said, "Can you believe this is my life? These chicks come to my house and they take off their clothes and they let me stare at their tits for an hour." He was one of those people who was obsessed with being clean and would shower twice or three times a day and wash his hands every fifteen minutes it seemed like. One time after we fucked, in the thirty seconds he'd let himself lie there before he showered the sex off him, he told me that he sometimes pictured my face on the bodies of the girls he painted. "It makes me hard. Then I tell them I'm hard." "Then they walk over to you and give you a beej and let you fuck them?" I joked. "Basically," he did not joke back.

In his paintings, none of the girls had faces, and the canvases were dark reds and black and slashy and an energy of violence and anger came off of them like loud radio static. "It seems like what you're painting is hate," I said. "You're the only person who's been able to see that," he said, and it was the only moment he ever looked like he actually loved me. Two years with him. And I can't remember him asking me a single question about myself.

I met O. at a show. We'd just finished playing and I was taking my guitar off my shoulder when I saw him in the crowd. I recognized him right away and my hands went cold and I remember thinking thank god I hadn't seen him before. It was a good show, and I was buzzing the way I always buzzed right afterward, thrilled and spent and wanting a beer. He was four rows back, looking at me. And my body reacted; seeing him reversed the direction of my blood. I went backstage, hugged the rest of the band like always and we had a beer together like always and we agreed that the show was really, really good, not like always, and we beamed with it. "Did you guys see O. in the audience?" "Holy shit, really?" "I think it was him." "I thought he was on tour in Sweden." "That tour wrapped up a month ago, I think."

The crowd had mostly drifted out of the club when we came out to load our instruments into the van. But there was O., undeniably him, beautiful man, and famous by then. My height, not tall, not dumbly thin like so many musicians. He had heft. He looked like someone who could give a good hug. His curly hair was long then, tied back into a plum-size knot at the base of his skull, a few loose strands fell around his cheekbones, and the strange thing was that when I saw that, it was as though I could feel the strands on my own cheeks. He wore a leather bracelet around his left wrist. His beard wasn't the big bread loaf made of hair like so many dudes who sang those sorts of songs had. A regular-length beard. Dark sad eyes. He stood by the merch table, seeming weirdly nervous, like someone who's looking at something without seeing it because they need something to do with their eyes and need to seem like they're not looking at or waiting for the one thing they really are.

I got another beer and walked over toward him. We stood next to each other facing the splay of Oaken records, the T-shirts with the snake hatching out of the acorn that one of my artist ex-boyfriend's friends had designed.

A slim nerd came up to him. "Hey man, sorry to bug

you, you must get this all the time, but could you sign this for me?"

"Happy to."

"Your music means a lot to me," he said.

"Really pleased to hear that. Thanks, man. You know, hers is the autograph you oughta get. Pretty amazing show tonight, right?"

"It was a really good show," the slim nerd said to me.

"Thanks for coming," I said.

"Have you listened to the new record?" O. asked him. "You should definitely get it if you haven't."

The kid picked up the album and pulled some bills from his pocket and paid for it and thanked us and joined up with his friends.

"I'm glad you came," I said to O. We had never spoken before. We had never met.

"The pleasure was mine," he said, extending his hand.

As we'd stood there, before saying a word to each other, I'd noticed, the way I'd noticed only a few other times in my life, that it felt different standing near him. That the air was charged in a different way. The way I picture it is that whatever little particles we blast out of ourselves, that come flying off us at all times without us really knowing or seeing, whatever bits of light or energy or pheromonally charged sparks of mystery matter, with most people, these currents just sort of swim around each other, or repel each other like magnets. But sometimes, with some people, the currents collide, they heat up and speed up and the feel in the air changes, and you're aware of your charge, and theirs, and the chemical blending of both. With O., it was immediate. Before we even shook hands, I knew.

We walked out of the club and walked around the city for four hours under streetlights, past dark apartment buildings, past sudsy drunks spilling from bars. We did not stop talking. Finally I said I had to go to bed, though I felt as far away from sleep as I'd ever felt in my life.

"It was a really good show," he said.

"You're kind to say it."

"There was that one fuck-up during the third song when you lost the chords, but you recovered quickly, and I bet no one really noticed."

I laughed because I didn't know what else to do. "I was hoping no one noticed."

I should've known right then. He was someone who needed to make other people feel small for himself to feel okay. I didn't realize it then. I didn't realize it for a while. I went home and lay in bed awake as I knew I would, but I wasn't thinking about him, or about the thrill of the conversation, the immediate connection, the way our particles collided. I was thinking about that one fuck-up. My fingers landing wrong. I'd forgotten it, it was lost in the success of the rest of the night, the gelling and good energy in the room. But then that's all it was. Two wrong notes.

It was already too late.

We spent time. We played music together. We moved in together. We were inseparable. When we fucked it felt like we were an entire decade, not two people but an era in time. We laughed. We showed each other all of ourselves. Our fights were horrors. Days-long tornadoes of tears, silence, swearing, smashing. Two big personalities, I thought. I'm tough. I'm strong. Two passionate, stubborn people. This is how it is.

"You don't deserve to be loved," he'd tell me. "You know your parents don't love you, right?"

Jealousy isn't quite the word for what he felt, though there was that. He was afraid that if I was too talented, or had too much success, or realized my potential, or felt good about myself, I would disappear from him, I would leave him. So he did his best to undercut me in a perverse variety of ways.

I'd slink inward, disappear behind my eyes, go *cold*. He couldn't stand it. I threw mugs, ground my fingernails into my flesh, and one time drove a knife into the wood of the kitchen island, over and over, stabbing it so it scarred, and I was scared because it wasn't the wood I wanted to stab. But my power was silence. While he roared, I absented myself, took the heat of myself away, emptied myself out of my eyes. I became a statue. Made of cool, smooth marble, with robes draped like liquid over my body, with a smile that telegraphed pride and disdain, satisfaction and ridicule. A stillness saturated me, and my eyes were blank like eyes on the busts on the pedestals in the palatial, skylit rooms in hushed museums where footfalls echo and crowds of statues stand fixed across millennia. In those statues, humanity is sculpted into every muscle, every swollen vein, every tendon stretched and showing weight and movement, but not into the eyes, no humanity in the eyes. Not a deadness, just a lack, an absence, blind and vacant, a milky depthlessness. Elsewhere, the eyes say. Body there, in every curve and swell of flesh and fingertip, body very much *there*, but to look at the face, something living gone from it. And like that, my eyes were a whiteness, unseeing, and deadly cold. And with my small smile, I could humiliate. I learned it young, and wielded it irresponsibly, that cruel and wicked smile, those lightless eyes. That smile brought blood to his face, a guaranteed right-hand turn on his volume knob. He couldn't stand me not being present for him every second. "You have no idea how ugly you look when you're like this," he'd say. "Thank you for letting me know," I'd say.

The first time he shoved me, we'd been drinking. He wept for three hours, begging forgiveness. I should've known then, too.

The storms would pass. The ice casing around the heart would melt and we'd go back to remembering we loved each other. What bliss that was, to come out of a fight. The first time we'd play music together after a battle, when warmth and closeness were returning. Entering into infinity together again. Tension and the release. Fear and the cessation of fear. Anger and the relief of anger. This was my drug. This was my ultimate intoxicant. I can handle anything, I thought. I was so in love.

We were playing one afternoon, just fucking around singing and playing. You've heard O.'s voice, you've heard the way he plays. He got a lot of attention. I liked the slow songs best, the sad ones. Sometimes I wondered why he got so much more attention than anyone else. He was good. He was so good. But I wondered, privately and never out loud, if he was as good as everyone thought he was.

"You could be really good," he said.

Didn't he know that I already was? That I was maybe actually better than him?

"If what?" I said.

"If you gave it the time, if you really committed yourself to it."

He knew how much I practiced. He knew the hours I put in.

We were nearing a fight, we both knew it. It came, cinched us like a too tight belt.

"You know that when people say they like your music, they're lying, right?" he said. "You know that when people say nice things to you, they're not telling the truth, right?"

Oaken had just put out an album. It was good. We, the band, were proud. I was proud. I was getting compared in the press to my favorite singers. Critics were writing that I was bringing to mind Lila and the Night Forests, and the early work of B.D. Char. My own and actual heroes. My name and their names in the same sentence. People were saying they liked my music. A lot of people. I'm not bragging. These were facts.

"They're lying. You know that, right?"

Every compliment I got, every kind thing someone said, that's what I heard.

"I fucking loved 'Alligator Tooth.'" "I listened to that first Oaken album on repeat for two years straight." "Your music saved me. I honestly would not be alive." I'd thank them all, feel grateful, and from the back of my brain, in a stage whisper, in his voice: *they're lying.*

When I think of this now, how he ruined that sort of kindness for me, how I could never believe one good thing someone said, how I heard his voice like a jittery little demon hopping up and down on my shoulder reminding me that every nice thing anyone said was a lie, how I let him ruin it—I feel something I don't have the words for.

He smashed a lamp my grandmother had given me. He melted my favorite pick. He snapped in half the pen I'd been given at my first record release party to sign records with. He grabbed my shoulders and slammed me into the refrigerator. When I was trying to leave and he didn't want me to, he swished my legs out from under me and broke my tailbone. When he asked me to marry him I said yes. How do I explain it? I was in love. I had a distorted sense of love. I liked to consider that I was the rare human who could handle more than most, that I was uniquely suited to handle the rages of a creative temperament, that I was meant for storms. I had anger of my own, after all. That I was able to withstand so much proved to me, wrongly, so wrongly, that I was strong. Coming out the other side of every fight, bruised sometimes, crushed, wounded in the tenderest parts, reinforced how strong I was. I liked to understand myself as strong.

The day of the wedding I had to go to the pharmacy to try to find concealer for my arm because he'd pinched me so hard during an argument the week before and the bruise was as dark as a plum with green at the edges, like a little purple planet glowing green around the rim. I'd wanted to scream out in his face with pain when he did it. I pressed my molars together instead and stared at him as he pinched my flesh tighter and tighter between his fingers. *I am buying makeup to conceal a bruise on my wedding day*, I thought, standing in line under the fluorescent lights of the pharmacy, bins of discounted Cadbury Creme Eggs beside me.

He came into the room as I was getting dressed. I was standing in front of the mirror in my bra and my jeans, putting moisturizer on my face.

He came over to me, put his fingers tenderly on the bruise.

"That looks bad," he said, and for a second I thought I heard regret in his voice. "You bruise so easily."

I started to feel cold. He kissed my cheek and pressed his hand over my heart.

"I love you," he said. "And I know you'll never love anyone like you love me." He tried to make it sound affectionate, loving. It didn't sound like that. It sounded like a threat.

I stood in front of the mirror and I couldn't look at myself. And I couldn't look at him.

"Does it still hurt?" he asked and pressed on the bruise. It did and I snatched my arm away. "Sorry. Sorry." He took a step back. I was so far inside myself I barely existed. "I wrote you a song," he said. "I'm going to sing it to you tonight."

I knew in that moment that I would not hear him sing it. That there would be no aisle, no wedding, no ring slipped on my finger. When he left the room, I slipped my dress over my head, over my jeans. I did not conceal the bruise on my arm. I did not put on lipstick, and I walked away. A wedding dress, my jeans, white sneakers. My hair was brushed and clean.

I knew where to go. I knew exactly where I was going. My friend Simon and I had a way we used to say it when we felt the urge to go to the Cobra Club. "Got bit by the viper," we'd say when we wanted to head down there. I got bit by the viper. I crossed the river to the other side of the city, and down I went.

The Cobra Club didn't have a sign. On a small side street near the mural, near the liquor store, around the corner from Mary Chang's Szechuan and More, a black door with a dark red snake, not coiled, straight up and down bisecting the door like a spine.

It's a heavy door and it's dark inside and cooler. The door closed behind me and I stood at the top of the stairs as I had many times before and looked down. Shadows slinked across the floor. I've always loved the smell of clubs. That yeasty tang, that sour under-bridge smell, a little like piss, a little oniony, like a man who's danced for two hours, who's had music fill his body and is releasing it through his pores. At the edges, tires, wet wool, the curdled bleach of semen. It was comforting and thrilling at once. A smell of potential. Unchanging, altering. You knew: This is not fresh air. This is not the outside world. And down we go.

I descended those stairs slowly. I let my eyes adjust to the dim. Down, down, down. Every time I was surprised by how deep underground you had to go, how many stairs there were. The smell intensified as you went lower. The shadows slinked on the walls. The stairs were damp, were always damp. Stalactites came to mind, stalagmites. Permanent drips. The walls were thick as though after night after night of sound, the noise had been absorbed into them. The walls held ten thousand different wails. Ten million.

I passed Sissy on the stairs. He climbed up holding a case of empty bottles. He'd climb down again with a full one. All day, all night, up and down, the bottles tingling together like wind chimes, Sissy's shoulders hunched forever.

"Hey, Siss," I said.

"Cool dress," he said.

There was HayDaze, who owned the club, standing by the stage, most hospitable human you'd ever met. Always room for one more. He had a winter smile. Storm cloud eyes, pale gray skin. The mustard-colored curtains sashed at the side of the stage gave him a jaundiced look. Long legs and a narrow chest. I'd see him around at shows. He looked gloomy, but I haven't met many people as charming. He waved when he saw me. His wife, Penny, sat to the side on a throne by the bar looking wan in the gloom. She was much younger than him and the rumor was she wanted out. She'd tour for a couple months each summer, but was always back down here come fall. I'd see her out in July and August—she'd be tan, wearing tiny shorts, had a laugh that would make the flowers grow. Here, she was limp, and sullener every season. Moody, I guess you could say. Seasonally depressed maybe. Or maybe sick of being married to a club owner whose breath always smelled like burnt hair.

I didn't tell anyone about O. or the wedding or the leaving of the wedding. A few people eyed the bruise. I was glad to lose myself down here, to be dissolved into this world where the stars didn't exist, where the planets didn't spin, where there was always room for anyone.

"Who's playing?" I asked.

"You know Standard Pantry?" HayDaze said. "From the west."

"Heard of them, I think."

"Nice dress. You getting married?"

"Not today I'm not."

"Good choice."

"I'm not deaf," Penny said from her throne.

"Most people can't handle it, Pen love. You know." HD put a warm hand on my shoulder. He saw the bruise. "You're always welcome here, you know. You stay as long as you want." My throat got tight like a towel being wrung out which was my first step of tears which I did not want to come. It felt good to be welcome.

The band started to set up. Four dudes who looked like they were bused in from a commune or a cult from the other side of the country. Something in the face bones. Something in the clothes, how loose they were, and so much fringe. They all wore sandals. All the boys had long hair and I remembered how much I love a boy with long hair. My mother never said to me, Now don't let yourself be with a mean man. She never said, You deserve to be loved. She never said, You deserve to be treated with respect. Maybe those things are supposed to go without saying? Learn through suffering, she did say. *Vita dura est.*

I liked watching bands set up. The focus, the fear, the feeling, each time, this is actually happening; in an hour or two, we will stand here in front of a room of people and give ourselves to them. It's good to watch people who know what they're doing. The precision of their movements, where they place the guitar stands, how high they raise the mics, where they tape the set list.

Some people choose the wrong kind of love. Some people cannot help it. For some people, a mind-map is made, and what feels familiar about love is getting hurt, is getting reminded that you're worthless, is the powerful feeling of someone else giving voice to a voice that lives in you that tells you that you are pathetic and stupid and bad. What a thing, to find the one person who tells you the same things your own brain tells you. It feels like you've found someone who connects with you deeply. Some people know that this is the sort of love they're drawn to and they teach themselves new ways of feeling; they try to draw new lines on the mind-map. They learn about what it means to feel respect. Other people surrender to the way they understand love to be, and resign themselves to thinking, *This is what I want, this is what feels right to me*. Maybe they were spit on by their mothers when they were small, or ignored. Maybe their fathers threw them into a bureau when they were mad. And so when they're thrown into bureaus again, it isn't—*What is this horror happening to me*, it's—*Oh, this is familiar, this is love*. It's hard to learn what normal is. How are you ever supposed to know? Some people recognize that the love they're drawn to isn't love at all, and so they opt out of it. Some people who are alone are alone because they know it's safer for them to be alone, they know they choose the wrong loves over and over.

Standard Pantry had started sound check when we heard it. From the stairs, a voice, a guitar. The club quieted. The shadows stopped slinking along the wall. Legs appeared coming down the stairs, and there was O. with his guitar, singing through tears. Everyone stopped.

Sissy stopped with a case of beer bottles on the stairs. The three door guys who moved as one paused. They didn't speak; they growled. Studded belts, leather pants, spiked collars around their necks. They decided who was in and who was out and they were stilled, one holding on to someone's ID as the person waited to have a hand stamped. The light guy stood reaching for the spotlight at the back of the club; he was too short, and paused, arm raised, it seemed like it would always be out of reach. The crazy dude who went to every show and spent the whole time spinning—spinning and spinning like he was on fire, that insane-oh—even he stopped to listen, looking worn and dizzy. The grizzled drunk slouched at the bar with a liver that must've looked like vultures had beaked it and made it their meal, he stopped taking sips of his whiskey. I looked around, all the shadows crying.

O. kept singing and kept playing. And no one moved and no one spoke and if you can imagine the most beautiful song, the saddest and most beautiful song, in the purest voice, and the vibrations of the guitar strings seeming to come not from the instrument but dropping down into the club from the night sky, and not from one instrument but from a thousand, that is what it sounded like. Beautiful enough to stop the planets from their orbits. To change nature. All other senses fell away. We were all only ears.

He played the song, the one he wrote for our wedding day, and I did not want to be moved. But I was. The pocket behind my eyes that held my tears warmed and filled and one spilled and another. His voice. The hard part in my heart softened. A slideshow of all the times we'd laughed. All the times he'd made me plates of food. The swims and easy mornings and the music. My heart softened as it always did. I moved across the club toward him.

"Please," he said. "Please."

I couldn't help it. "Okay," I said. Tension and relief.

He took my hand and started walking toward the stairs, pulling me after. I looked around at the club, at Penny on her throne, her hand over her heart, at HD by the curtains nodding, at the light guy still reaching for the spotlight with a smile on his face, at the boys in the band with their long hair whispering to each other

"Was that O.?" one said. "Of course it fucking was, who else could it be?" said another. The grizzled drunk lowered his head onto his arm, the spinning man seemed about to start his spin again. The door guys grunted and moved out of our way. Sissy said, "Don't go."

But O. was pulling too hard. He was holding my hand too tight. I heard him muttering. And the muttering meant he was furious. A quiet stream of poison came from his mouth, quiet enough that only I could hear. "You proud walking away like that? Useless, worthless cunt. Talentless cunt. Got Daddy's big mouth and think you can sing. Joke. Your life's a joke. You've turned my life into a hell."

We neared the top of the stairs. I saw the door, the snake painted on the inside, too, upside down on this side, head at the bottom, tail at the top. I stopped on the stair. He did not turn. "What are you waiting for?"

Run, I thought.

"You haven't delayed this enough?" He tugged at my arm.

Run, I thought. I stood near the top of the stairs.

He started to sing one of my songs. Except he twisted the words and mocked my voice. "That's how you sound," he said.

And then he turned. And there in his eyes was the brutal thing that meant he was scared. I knew in my blood that scared made him dangerous.

This is the way we burn from our mistakes. I pulled my hand away. I imagined I was made of a cloud and just let it slip from his grip. I turned around and I floated down the stairs, down down down, back into the embrace of the Cobra Club, where there was always room for one more. Even the sold-out shows. There's always room. Everyone finds their way here eventually.

I heard him shouting behind me, "You're never going to love anyone the way you love me."

I laughed. I laughed and laughed. I laughed so hard the room shook, the plates of the Earth shifted, the tides changed. I laughed and laughed and laughed and then I bent over and I screamed.

AFTER OVID

We sit. You and I, my brother, my sister, my friend, my love. The food on the plates on the table is warm in front of us. The warmth of it rises. We are hungry. We sit across from each other and we glow at each other, my brother, my sister, my friend, my love. We glow at each other and we talk at the table.

The table is made of wood from the house of my grandmother, from a tree whose width speaks hundreds of years. It was felled and milled after decades and decades of rising from the earth, sinking into the earth, moving toward the sky, at sway in the wind, soaking in sun and rain, for decades it did, and before that, it was thinner and shorter, and before that, thinner and shorter still, so thin you could bend it with your hand, and before that, so small, you could, with a gentle grab and tug, pull it from the earth, its little earth hairs dangling, and toss it to the side, and before that, a seed smaller than the nail on your smallest finger, that sunk into the earth, spread by wind or bird or animal, and cracked and opened and reached down and took what it needed from the soil and took what it needed from the sky. We rest our elbows on the wood that came from that seed that grew and lived and lived again in the house and lives again holding our weight, holding the weight of the food that's warm in front of us. And when we place our palms on it, we feel the distant hum of its aliveness.

Over the table our words pass back and forth and we eat. There is meat and bread, an orange we're saving for later to share with some cheese. There's water in glasses and wine in glasses. We savor the food and savor the talk. The words change, but always we say the same thing to each other, my brother, my sister, my friend, my love. We tell the same story again and again. The one story we tell, the one story that takes a thousand shapes, tries to answer the same questions. In whatever form we give it, in whatever words we use. How can we make sense of change? What to do about the ends?

And we ask, Are you with me?

I knew you when you were a child. I knew you when you were young and soft. You knew me then, too. Even if we met much later. There is a knowing beyond knowing and I see the child in your eyes, my brother, my sister, my friend, my love.

We made the food together. We stood in the kitchen with knives and spoons and heat and we were happy to be there together in the warmth of the kitchen, in the smells and sounds of the kitchen, the onion in oil, the sizzling fats. We are alive together, my brother, my sister, my friend, my love. And I see the lines around your eyes and the strand of gray or white in your hair. And you can see it in mine. None of us are children now.

Our poet says, "For all things change, but no thing dies . . . In this world—you can believe me—no thing ever dies. By birth we mean beginning to re-form, a thing's becoming other than it was."

"You can believe me," the poet says. I want to. I want to trust the poet.

"No thing ever dies." But how do we go on?

We sit at the table. We talk at the table. We take warm bites of food into our mouths.

"When you die," I say, "I would like to eat a bite of you. A small medallion of flesh from your flank or your thigh, cooked over flame. A bite of you to live inside me, to have you move all through my body, and then to release you from me. But not all the way, because some particles of you would get absorbed in my blood, and you would swim inside me and thud through me as my heart thuds. I want you to live on in me."

And I say, "When I die, I would like you to have a bite of me, to take me into your body, to live in your blood. I would like to live on in you."

"Yes, I want that."

And if I have you in me, when I die, I will be put into the earth as body or ash and a seed will sink and split above me and its roots will sink into me, into us, because you are with me, and the roots will take what they need, and we will be in the tree, and the tree will grow and be felled and a house will be built, and the house will be felled, but a board is saved and a table is made and two people sit at the table and take the food inside them and live. And we are in the table, you and I, my brother, my sister, my friend, my love. We are in the tree and the light and the water, in the meat and the bread, in the stones and the eyes of the birds, in the hooves of the creature who gave the milk to make cheese, we are there, in the galactic spiraling grain of the wood, we are there in these things from the beginning of time before things had names. We are there, and continue to be. The ghosts of ourselves, the ghosts of the children we were, we're there, compressed in the tight grain of the wood.

And now, tonight, as we sit at the table, it is not just you and me, we are never alone. Time sits with us, too. Time is our host and we are its guests, and it is our constant companion. We inhabit it. We thud through it. We ride the milk river of its flow.

Time is not a generous host. It is greedy, insatiable, inconstant. Time, our greedy, hungry host. It will eat us, eat all of us. It will swallow us whole and take us in and we will move through it, forward and back, everywhere, all directions. No thing dies. We will move all through it. Milk river time, ocean time, shadow time, nameless time, placed time and placeless time, human time, star time, spider time, bird-wing time, boulder time, wrist time, penis and vagina time, wind time, thread time, flame and flower time, house time, sky time, swan and thunder time, breast time, black time, abyss time, when time, gaping endless all Time.

It will take us in, you and me, my brother, my sister, my friend, my love, and we will move all through it and we will emerge to become Time itself.

Eat, talk, laugh in the meantime, tell, kiss, help in the meantime. The place is now, you are here. Time makes space for change. The place is now, you and I are here. An embrace before it's over. A slice of orange while we're here. A piece of bread. Chew and chew. Nothing stays the same. We are swallowed up each moment into the whole history of new.

AUTHOR'S NOTE

This book started on a morning in late February 2018. I'd just finished a season of carpentry, and I hadn't been writing much. I wanted to get my writing muscles back. I'd been dipping into *The Metamorphoses*, as I do from time to time. I was reading the Callisto story, and thought it might be a good exercise, a good way to flex those writing muscles, to rewrite the story in her voice. "I am a bear," I started. "I live in the sky." I wrote her story and I liked the way it felt. I liked hearing her voice in my ear. The next day, I wrote another—Daphne. After three, it took hold and took off. I read a story, reread it, then spent the day listening to the voice in my mind, trying to hear what this woman sounded like, what story she wanted to tell and how. I moved through Allen Mandelbaum's elegant, sensual translation (Harcourt, 1993), and told the stories of almost every female figure in Ovid's nearly twelve-thousand-line poem.

The Metamorphoses, translated into English for the first time by William Caxton in 1480, and dozens of times since, recounts over two hundred myths of transformation; it is a history of the world from its creation out of chaos through Julius Caesar. It is a book about time, which means it is a book about change. It is beautiful and brutal. It is earthy, aetiological, ethereal, of our world and otherworldly. I read through the poem and listened to the voices of these women as I moved about my day and went for long runs and it was a time unlike any other in my life. In three months, there was a book.

Some stories rose out of only a few lines of poetry; others emerged as condensed bursts from episodes that unfolded over hundreds of lines. Some hew to Ovid; others veer away from him. (Certain lines are lifted directly from Mandelbaum's translation, too good not to include: "My shaft is sure in flight," from Daphne's story; when Phoebus says "I am the world's eye" to Leucothoe; and "the gods help those who dare" in the story of Atalanta.) Some of the figures called out with voices that seemed lodged in a time of gods, goddesses, nymphs, and satyrs; others seemed to speak in a language closer to our own time. As in Ovid, these women vary in age, in background, in experience.

There are a few stories I did not include, about a dozen, because their plots or themes rang too similar to other stories, or because I wasn't able to hear the voice as well when I tried to listen. I left out the ones whose stories eluded me, to whom I couldn't do—or bring—justice. I wish I'd listened harder to some of them. All of them have something to say, if I'd listened closely enough. I reworked the order of the stories, too, mostly in an attempt to let the women's voices be in better conversation with one another—so that we could not only hear them speak their own stories, but maybe hear what might happen if they could hear each other, too.

Connors for his friendship and support. To Professor Sheila Murnaghan and her class *The Odyssey* and Its Afterlife, which changed everything. To Leona Cottrell. To Gini Jonas. To Paul Makishima. To Lisa Gozashti. To Rob in the period of revision. To Matt Weiland for helping me learn how to tell a story. To Allen Mandelbaum (1926–2011), whose translation of *The Metamorphoses* has had a lasting impact on my life.

Thank you to Ledig House/Art Omi, where this book was finished, for one of the most magic months of all, and the wild-minded heroes I encountered there: Justin Go, Tishani Doshi, Hanna Bervoets, Martí Domínguez, Ida Hegazi Høyer, Abubakar Adam Ibrahim, Liliana Colanzi, Carol Frederick, Gisela Leal, Amy Sohn, Rich Benjamin, Edie Meidav, and Manuel Becerra. How lucky we all were.

I have gratitude also for the Harvard Book Store, Porter Square Books, the Brookline Booksmith, the Charles River, and Shays.

Profound thanks to Jenny White for over three decades of friendship.

And thank you, John, for the exchange.

ACKNOWLEDGMENTS

It is a deep and distinct pleasure, an actual thrill, being both understood and pushed, and Jenna Johnson, as editor of this book, did both. For her intelligence, intuition, and humor, I am hugely grateful and feel so, so lucky. Thanks, too, to Lydia Zoells for her wise and sensitive feedback, as well as the close attention of Nancy Elgin and Frieda Duggan. Boundless thanks to my spirited agent Gillian MacKenzie, and all of MacKenzie Wolf, for helping this get to exactly where I wanted it to be. To Matt Buck for the electric cover. To Lauren Roberts. To all of FSG. Thank you.

Deep thanks go to my family. To my parents and Pam; especially to my brothers, Will and Sam, without whom I would be lost; and to Molly and Miranda. I am grateful to Alicia Simoni for her understanding and insight, and to DeFo for so many years of hugs. Thank you to soul friend Sharon Steel; to the curious, engaged, engaging, and singular Éireann Lorsung; to comrade and correspondent Phil